GW01486314

MODEL

FOR

MURDER

D S NELSON

Black Hat Books

MODEL FOR MURDER

First published 2014 by Black Hat Books

ISBN: 978-0-9928480-1-9

Copyright © D S Nelson 2014

The moral right of D S Nelson to be identified as the author of this work has been asserted by her in accordance with the Copyright, Designs and Patents Act 1988.

All rights reserved in all media. Without limiting the rights under copyright reserved above, no part of this publication may be reproduced, transmitted, downloaded, decompiled, reverse engineered, or stored in or introduced into information storage and retrieval systems, in any form or by any means whether electronic or mechanical, now known or hereinafter invented, without express permission of the author.

This book is sold subject to the condition that it shall not, by way of trade or otherwise, be lent, resold, hired out, or otherwise, circulated without the author's prior consent in any form of binding or cover, other than that in which it is published and without a similar condition including this condition being imposed on the subsequent purchaser.

All characters and events in this publication are fictitious and any resemblance to real persons, organisation, place, event or thing living or dead, is purely coincidental and completely unintentional.

www.dsnelson.co.uk

info@dsnelson.co.uk

Cover art by Kathryn Ellis-Blandford
krizena@hotmail.co.uk.

1.

Ghede Nibo

The Voodoo spirit Ghede Nibo is revered as the leader of the dead. This cross-dressing loa is thought to be transsexual, gay or pansexual depending on the situation in which he is portrayed.

Harold Salter was the first to die.

The headline read:

'NEWSAGENT MURDERED!'

A simple statement of truth. Cold hard fact. Murder.

The village was disturbed. Hushed coffee-shop conversations with shaking heads and slabs of consoling chocolate brownie. Children kept close to their parents, their instructions to *stay here* added with a little more urgency. New alarms fitted, new dogs acquired; no one was taking a chance.

Tuesbury, by today's standards, is a close-knit community; we all know each other, whether we want to or not. It's part of village life, the gossip that is. Malicious or well meaning, it's a fact that we all think we know each other's business. The event itself is obvious but in a community such as this, the aftermath of murder is insidious. Like a red wine stain on a carpet, it takes seconds to tip the glass, but much longer to rid yourself of the ugly mark.

Speculation was inevitable. Was it Mr Trent at number ten? Normally a regular in The Badger's Holt, he hadn't been seen in the local for a while. Last night, Miss Derby had seen him putting large black bags in someone else's wheelie bin. Or what about Harold's partner? There'd never been a cross word between the two of them but wasn't it the quiet ones you had to watch? Were there clandestine dealings going on in the back office of the newsagent Harold owned? Rumour was rife. I dislike rumour.

So who am I and why am I interested?

I am Blake Hetherington and I have been involved in the solving of four murders to date.

Am I a police officer?

No.

A newly qualified pathologist perhaps?

No. I prefer people alive.

A serial killer then?

Not yet.

I am not any of these things. In fact I am a fifth generation milliner: a hat maker. Retired to be precise. I now spend my days completing bespoke hat orders in a shed on my allotment in the quixotic village of Tuesbury. Hats? Yes, hats. You could say people-watching is a hobby of mine. Observing their behaviour fascinates me. A choice of hat, in particular, will tell you everything you need to know about a person.

I, of course, have a partner in crime. Don't all the best detectives? Poirot has his Hastings, Miss Marple has her

Luke and Sherlock his Watson. I have Miss Delilah Delibes.

We met as a result of my attention to the little things in life. My observation of people was noted by an old customer and eventually led to Delilah, two years ago, asking for my help. Together we have solved four cases of murder although, I am afraid to say, the police have not always been successful in convicting the perpetrators. I enjoy an avuncular relationship with Delilah, which suits us very well. She has found an audience for her creative and agile mind, whereas I find the company of someone younger than myself keeps me on my toes in my retirement.

Miss Delibes is an archaeologist with a Masters from Cambridge, which, in my opinion fosters her unhealthy interest in death. This interest seems to be further fuelled by the gruesome spectre of murder that appears to have followed us since we met.

Delilah grows flowers on my allotment and some herbs. It's nice to share the duties of owning a plot and she often cuts some of the flowers for a small vase I have on the windowsill in the shed. She insists I keep the place inviting for the customers, but customers rarely visit me here. I prefer instead to visit them in their own surroundings. You can tell so much more about a person that way. Their home, like their hat, is a reflection of their personality. Delilah often stops for a cup of tea and she and Bertie keep me company in the shed as I work.

The allotment society has, at various points, raised protests with regard to my running a business from my shed. I suspect Olea Faba, queen of the plots and general all round busybody, is the ringleader. Delilah aids me in my subterfuge by gaining information from a friend she has on the council and I am always warned of an inspection. The council have yet to find evidence of my business and when I am not there, the curtains remain closed.

Lately Detective Sergeant Claringdon has joined us. His ulterior motive? There must be one. Why else would any self-respecting police officer associate himself with such amateur sleuths, unless he is conducting a covert investigation. The real reason of course is that he is in love with Delilah. Her bobbed brown hair, blue eyes and fresh complexion are difficult for any man to resist. The sergeant is a tall, dark, mysterious type with a love of squash and cricket, and his amore is reciprocated by Delilah. In my opinion Claringdon is a very suitable beau for a young lady. With Delilah's penchant for a murder mystery, I only hope it does not end in disaster. Claringdon sees me as a father figure for Delilah, as her parents are both conspicuous by their absence. I prefer to see myself as the slightly eccentric uncle.

So this is the company I keep.

It wasn't long after the murder that my daughter rang. She lives with her family in Devon. Her visits are rare; occupied with her own family, as is only natural, a four-hour drive would not be a relished by a one, two and four year old. She had seen the latest news from Tuesbury while googling my website. No doubt checking up on me. As a result I had just suffered a one-way conversation with her on the phone:

'You won't get involved again, will you Dad?' she had stated curtly before I'd even had a chance to ask how she and the children were.

'In what, dear?' I'd said, knowing full well to what she referred

'Another murder, Dad. It's not your problem, just stay out of it. I don't care what that Delilah says. This is not your job. Leave it to the police.'

I hung up, depressed at the knowledge that my daughter knew me too well. I had stared at the newspaper still lying on the coffee table. Curiosity got the better of me and I could not help but pick up the paper and read the article describing the departure of Harold Salter once more.

The promising headline was let down by a page full of hypotheses. Could it have been a dog snatcher who had decided Prince, Harold Salter's spaniel, was his prize? But Prince had escaped and the idea of dog-snatchers committing murder; is that really plausible? A further theory inferred that a crazed murderer with druidic tendencies was running around the aptly named Druid Wood.

Pride of place in the article was a photo of Prince, sitting outside the newsagent's. It was a grainy picture, probably taken on a camera phone. The sort people take when they feel they must do something to be a part of the latest events: something that proves they were there, as if memory will not suffice, or else their word is worth nothing. In the absence of solid fact, I sat back in my armchair to conjure my own hypotheses. This is what I think happened:

Imagine the scene: a bitter day, in late winter. The grey clouds threaten rain and the wind is far from lazy, chilling you to your bones. Harold Salter sets out for his early morning walk with his cocker spaniel, Prince. Nearing the end of their walk, Harold stops momentarily to pick up a stick for his dog. He is hit from behind. He doesn't hear the footfall, heralding his approaching demise: the snap of a twig, a cloud of moist breath gathering in the cold morning air, the crunching of dead leaves underfoot, the soft spring of undergrowth returning to its original position. The blow has fractured his skull. The fall forward onto a tree stump has sealed the deal. Despite the little spaniel's best efforts to raise the alarm, there Salter remains, for another hour.

My memories of that day are few. I rose early, as usual, to complete some commissions in the shed on my allotment. I was at work by eight that morning. Delilah had travelled into London to finalise some paperwork for her trip to Haiti. I was looking after Bertie, her Jack Russell, who sat beneath my workbench, a handy foot warmer. From the safety of the shed I could see old Druid Wood bending under the strain. The rooks shouted at the wind as it shook their nests. The distant chew to a year's newspaper subscription: they were all customers and friends to him. Even the local school children could not vex him.

Steve, his partner, seemed a pleasant man; referred to more often than seen. The spaniel, Prince, as previously mentioned, spent his days in the corner of the shop sleeping and being fussed over by the locals.

Harold was a wholly decent man who appeared to think the best of everyone. It would not have been difficult to catch him unawares. It could even have been someone he knew. I doubt that he would have seen any evil in them. One wonders if he even cried out, or simply smiled as he fell to the ground. If he did shout, then no one but his attacker heard Salter's final cry. Certainly no one has come forward to claim the knowledge. Harold Salter died and no one heard.

Looking back on the events of that spring, I do not need to rely entirely on my memory to tell the story. I have kept the original article, subsequent reports in the Tuesbury Herald and even the nationals, for events, when they reach a certain magnitude, rarely escape the public at large.

Although some may say I am sentimental, I am not one to keep grim souvenirs of events such as these. Initially it was the total lack of a motive for murder that caused me to hang on to the article. The vain hope that like a Rorschach test, if I stared at it long enough a picture would reveal itself and my mind would be at cause to go and look for Harold, who was rarely ever seen without Prince, and our newsagent would still be closed.

So we know now about the circumstances of Harold Salter's death, but what can we learn from observing the man himself? That fact that Harold Salter never wore a hat spoke volumes. If you want to hide from an unwelcome gaze, a hat will provide you with the means to do so. A wide brimmed sun hat, a fedora tilted forward, a baseball cap pulled down tight: the options are endless. But Harold never wore a hat. Even in the winter, despite his bald and shaven pate. Not even to go to church. The only mitigating fact was that he was a man in his forties. I have observed, that men of that generation consider hats that are not designed to keep out the cold or represent their football team, a pretension. Harold was not pretentious. Either way you look at it, Harold had nothing to hide. He was a *'take-me-as-you-find-me'* man. I too rarely wear a hat.

However, even with the lack of a hat we can tell a lot about Harold Salter's personality, which ultimately played a part in the way he met his end. He was a practical and amiable businessman. He'd lost his hair young and his burgeoning waistline reflected his love of beer and Rawlinson's, the local butcher's, pork pies. His cheery paisley shirts and jeans only just kept his stomach in check. Bright blue eyes underneath carefully manicured eyebrows sparkled with mirth. He always had a smile for his customers; no matter what their needs. From a penny under the desk where I worked. He'd raised his head, sneezed and settled back to his dreams. Was that the moment it happened, while I was merrily working on my latest commission? But this is all just supposition and proves nothing. It could have been any dog I heard that day.

It was Mrs Dellaware, a long-standing member of the Tuesbury community, who first raised the alarm; not Mr Salter's partner, as you might expect. Steve was visiting his ailing mother and oblivious to Harold's fate until much later that morning. Outraged, at being unable to collect her *Knitting Weekly*, Mrs Dellaware banged on the door of the dark newsagents, raising merry hell and ultimately Detective Constable Alston from his post-night-shift sleep. One of the quirks of small villages is, that there's never a policeman far away. They often live on the rural outskirts of their patch, perhaps in the hope of avoiding crime on their days off. How wrong they are.

Anyone who's turned on the television in the last month to watch a drama or listen to the news, knows that a search would not normally be conducted so early on, for a forty-one year old missing newsagent; even if you are missing your weekly magazine as a result of his disappearance. Therefore, it is not surprising that Mrs Dellaware was sent home with an unofficial caution from a disgruntled police officer, leaning from the window of the flat above the butcher. If Prince had not returned ownerless to sit outside the shop and howl, waking DC Alston for a second time. Alston would not have had

As she described the scene, I could feel the cold of that day on my face; the bitter touch of Old Man Winter holding back the coming spring. I could almost smell the decaying leaf matter, the mud beneath and the fresh scent of pine needles, possibly the last thing Harold knew before he left this mortal coil.

'Blood all over the tree trunk, I'm surprised they haven't cleaned it up or at least made an attempt to disguise it. Gruesome!' Delilah had said.

Her morbid details of a blood spattered tree trunk brought me again to the conclusion that Harold Salter had turned from the path and had his back to his assailant. She described an old tree trunk that had been moved to the side of the path. To fall forward onto the tree would mean he stopped and turned away from the path.

So what about Prince? Did he defend his master? He sleeps in the corner of the newsagent's without a care in the world, revelling in the attention of customers, new and old. Would he have met the murderer with similar joy or would canine instinct have kicked in? Could the attacker have teeth marks somewhere about their person that would identify them? I remember, on the morning in question, hearing barking from the woods at about quarter past eight. I hadn't been working long so my ears were still tuned to the outside world, as opposed to switched off as they are when I am deep in concentration. Barking is not an unusual sound. There are many dog walkers in Tuesbury. Bertie had shuffled onto a fallen tree or is it just the drama of my imagination? Well, not if we take into account Delilah's comments on the event.

As previously mentioned, she had been in London on the day of the murder, and on her return, I imparted the news. Annoyed at missing the action, it was no surprise that Delilah was keen to visit the scene of the crime. She went on the pretext of walking Bertie. I declined to go with her, conscious of my daughter's views when it came to me becoming involved in any more cases of murder. Jane was fond of pointing out that the shotgun injury to my foot, and the broken collarbone at Christmas were all due to *'Delilah dragging you into goodness knows what'*, as she put it. On a cold day the throbbing of my foot and the ache of my shoulder are reminders enough without my daughter's chastisement.

Delilah would not be dissuaded from investigating the scene. She can be incredibly ghoulish at times. She was gone for two hours before she called round for tea. She insisted on describing the little clearing in the woods with alarming detail, including the blood on the horizontal trunk of a fallen beech tree. I didn't stop her. There was no harm in listening.

'It was incredibly easy to find', she had announced. 'The police tape's still there. It's a bitter in the woods at this time of year. That wind whips between the trees and straight through you. Bertie didn't like it. There's a dark aura there.'

sound of a shotgun told me that someone was culling rabbits on Lord Blackwood's estate. Above the wind these were the only sounds to be heard. The rooks, the trees and the frosty shot all masked a murder.

So how is my version of the tale any different from a newspaper hack's, you may ask? Well, I like to think, my tale is based on knowledge and logical deduction. It is also based on bitter experience.

First we need to look at the facts. The paper reported that he died of head injuries. Gruesome detail is a fondness of the press that dates back to the penny dreadfuls of Dickensian England. *'Injuries'* suggests plural. He was not battered to death. I feel sure it would have been reported if he had.

Here I make an assumption, that in order to kill Harold Salter a serious head injury such as a fracture or trauma to the brain is necessary. I imagine the scene. The killer approaches from the front in full view of the victim. The victim puts his hands up to defend himself. It must be very difficult to fracture the front of someone's skull with a weapon without them deflecting the blow, at least in part, with outstretched hands. From this I conclude he must have been hit from behind. To surprise a victim, by approaching this way, is easy enough to do on a day when the wind is high enough to mask the sound of footfall. A stationary target is much easier to hit than one that's moving, so I assume Harold had stopped. So why in my story do I suggest that he also hit the front of his head? In my minds eye I see him falling forward peace once more. Now, it is the truth and the part I played in uncovering it that keeps me holding on to it.

Looking back, it's easy to link the various circumstances together. Even before the defining murder, events began with a benign occurrence, as they always do. The bizarre goings-on at the allotment last year coincided with the temporary desertion of the rookery. The time before that it had been a floating bowler hat that piqued my curiosity.

This time something had lodged itself in the grey matter and refused to be teased out. I'd seen or heard something over the last few weeks that had a connection. It might give a clue to the motive, but whatever it was, my failing memory would not reveal it. Something was missing and I would have to wait for almost a week for the first clue to reveal itself.

2.

Ramasser

Ramasser means to collect or pick up and in the Voodoun religion it signifies the gathering of unclaimed spirits abandoned by others.

The week went by and Saturday came. The sun shone through the window of Café Barista and Delilah and I considered our choices. We were at a table in the window. People watching is a hobby of mine and a window seat facilitates this; preferably side on to the window so you can look out and still observe your fellow customers within.

Since the events of last year we had been forced to move our morning coffee to Café Barista. Not my first choice but according to Delilah they do *'a fabby fried breakfast'*. For myself, I supposed, they provided a passable almond croissant. Nowhere near the standard of Pane's Bakery on the High Street, which has a conveniently integral teashop but no fried breakfast to satisfy Delilah.

Café Barista is on the London road and a two-mile walk out of the village. I do not possess a car, preferring to travel by train, and if I can walk somewhere I will, despite the occasional necessity for a cane to aid my aching foot. The day I do not walk anywhere is the day I have given in to the ravages of time.

Having spent the last forty years commuting outside the village to the family hat shop in London, my visits to this end of the village were infrequent. The High Street, just ten minutes from my house, provides me with most amenities. The shops on the Huckspeth Road cover anything I can't get on the High Street. Delilah's thirst for fried comestibles means that Café Barista has joined the list of Tuesbury establishments I frequent.

The only other businesses on the London road are a very functional industrial estate with a brilliant haberdashery, the golf course, the Martins' farm and a model village. Now I am no longer in the heart of London, I am lucky to have a haberdashery, so close, for supplies, and when they do visit, the grandchildren love to go to the model village.

As we drink our coffee, Delilah is chattering away about what she has dubbed, 'The Salter Case'. Given my daughter's request, I am trying my best not to engage with it, but this is hard when faced with such a verbose and enthusiastic comrade.

'Rob reckons it's a hate crime, pure and simple, but I don't know, surely we're past all of that? We have a lesbian vicar for goodness sake!'

I gave her a half smile and stirred more sugar into my espresso. This was true. Persephone Lambert had arrived in the village three years ago to minister at the church. The congregation had depleted initially but with Reverend Lambert's more upbeat sermons and the installation of a play area in the church, word soon got round of family friendly services, the subtext inferring free childcare: the church was burgeoning once more. However, there were still some in the village who considered a gay vicar blasphemous, unwilling to believe their own Almighty God really does love all his children.

'I hadn't even realised Harold was gay!' Delilah said.

I laughed. I couldn't help it.

'But he wasn't!' She insisted.

Sometimes her total lack of observation surprised me.

Harold Salter was gay. Not in a stereotypical way. There were no limp wrists, no flamboyant shirts; not even a lilt to his voice. No, he was a man's man. What gave him away was the kindness he had about him that only comes from years of discrimination. Harold was sinned against rather than the sinner. It was no surprise to me that Steve was more than his business partner. Given the contempt some still held for our vicar, Rob, or Sergeant Claringdon, as I prefer call him, might have been onto something. It did appear to be the only motive. However, I, like Delilah, didn't believe it.

Harold Salter had been in the village for twenty years; his partner eight. Had it honestly taken someone twenty years to decide they didn't like the man because he was gay? At this point a thought occurred to me. Just because Harold Salter had lived in the village for two decades didn't mean his killer had. I started to think about the newcomers to the village as Delilah rattled on.

'Anyway, he says hate crime's on the up. In two thousand and twelve there were over forty-three thousand hate crimes in the UK. Over four thousand were to do with a person's sexuality. Rob says that…'

Delilah's voice became white noise as I went through a list of possible suspects in my head. If we eliminate anyone who's been here for more than a year, that leaves us with five people. Miss Derby moved here in September, that's six months ago. As she's the new infant school teacher I'm tempted to rule her out. To my knowledge, primary school teachers aren't high on the list of professions with psychopathic tendencies. Not according to Hare's Psychopathy Checklist anyway, although I'm sure that working with thirty children under the age of seven everyday would drive you to some sort of personality disorder. Then there's Mr White. He moved here to be closer to his son and his family. Mr White is an ex-banker from the city, some of the only people who can afford the thatched houses on the High Street in Tuesbury these days. Now *there's* a profession that's high on the checklist. However, at seventy-five years old with a *'dodgy ticker'*, as described by the long-suffering Mrs White, he's not top of my list. Gambolling about in the forest isn't completely out of the realms of possibility but discreetly ambushing someone when you are short of breath is no mean feat.

'…there's been some strange goings on in the model village.'

Delilah interrupted my thoughts with this last statement. There was always something going on in the model village but I'd rarely heard them called strange; eccentric yes but not strange.

'Mm?' I managed, too late to cover the fact that I had not been listening. Delilah frowned and tutted at me.

'Delilah, it's very rude to *tut* at one's elders.'

'And it's very rude to ignore a lady when she's talking, Blake.'

Bertie stuck his head out from under the table in response to Delilah's tone. He peered at me accusingly.

'Touché! Now, strange you say?' I lent down to scratch Bertie behind the ears to indicate there were no hard feelings.

'Very strange; criminal damage in fact. According to Rob, the desk sergeant almost laughed Mrs Tudbury out of the station. It wasn't until she told him where it was that he paid any attention.'

'And where was what?'

'On the model of the newsagent.'

'And *what* was it?' I raised an eyebrow.

'They thought it was paint at first but Rob had it analysed and it's nail varnish! I suppose it's gone now, but they'd need remover for that and goodness knows what it's done to the little door. Near annihilated it I should think.'

'Delilah, what was it?' I said again. Delilah's insistence on starting at the end, finishing at the beginning and plain missing out the middle of any story was a highly irritating and female trait.

'A little tiny red cross; right across the bottom of the door. If they'd painted it on the window they could have just removed it. I think they make them out of acetate. Mrs Tudbury was most upset.'

With this last sentence Delilah sat up in her seat as if she'd just remembered something. She leant forward conspiratorially. Pushing a few stray waves of her brown wavy hair behind her ear, with a glint in her dark eyes, she delivered her finale.

'Oo, some of the model people are missing too!'

'That's it!' I said.

'Six! ...Wait a minute, what do you mean that's it?'

'That's what's been bothering me about Salter's death. Those models went missing two weeks ago didn't they?'

'I don't know.' Delilah looked puzzled.

'Yes they did. I remember a little paragraph in the lost and found column of the paper'.

'You really do read that paper from cover to cover, don't you?' Delilah said.

'I think we should go and have a look.' A piece of the jigsaw had revealed itself at last. My intrigue banished my daughter's words from my head. I got up and started to pull my coat on. The waxy smell of the old Barbour jacket enveloped me as I pulled my arms through the sleeves. It was a comforting aroma.

Delilah didn't need asking twice. Wrestling with her body warmer with more speed than haste, she had one arm in and one out as she attached Bertie's lead and marched towards the door of the café.

Throwing some loose change as a tip in the espresso cup's saucer I hurried after her. With two miles to walk for coffee, today I had my stick, so I moved a little quicker.

Squeezing my way between the tables I followed in the wake of Delilah as she tried to get the other arm into her gilet and control an excited Bertie. Finally we made it to the door.

The model village was only a minute's walk back in the direction of Tuesbury centre. The fee for entry was six pounds normally but Tuesbury residents could enter at the greatly reduced price of three pounds and for OAP's, one pound fifty. Life experience and discounts are some of the only benefits of my age. We paid the surly teenager in the booth, clearly annoyed he had to work on a Saturday, and clicked through the turnstile.

Our model village has a reputation with both young and old. Several volunteers help Mr and Mrs Tudbury run the tiny village. Their hook is authenticity. Every resident in Tuesbury village has a model counterpart. On a Sunday the miniature church on the green plays bells and choir music at the same time as the real church. Every wedding, christening and, rather more grimly, every funeral takes place as a mirror image of reality. The Martins' farm stretches across the northeast quarter and Lord Blackwood's estate is represented to the south. The riding stables are complete with tiny versions of the livery and its residents. Lord Blackwood's favourite hunter, Nelson, stands in his own field. The Tudburys even installed a tiny version of the controversial solar panels, when Lord Blackwood installed them, next to Druid Wood. The golf club members tee up; the children and their parents gather at the school gate; on May Day the maypole is deployed - you get the idea. It's an ever-changing organic and evolving work of art.

The sun sat low in the sky and I squinted against the bright light. The little houses on the High Street greeted us. Their serene and peaceful façades hid the truth behind chintz and lace curtains. Anyone visiting this miniature haven would consider Tuesbury bucolic, the epitome of English village life and move here immediately. If they'd read the papers over the last few years they might think twice. Despite the Tudburys' reputation for authenticity, the allotment murders of last year had not been re-enacted and instead had been neatly swept under the AstroTurf. The only nod to the events of last autumn was a tiny plaque that had appeared on the gate to the allotments. You couldn't read it, but everyone knew what it stood for. The day one of the most annoying men in our village, Derek Nyeman, found himself a help rather than a hindrance to his community.

Delilah stomped down the High Street and stopped at the far end opposite the replica newsagents. Bertie sat beside her patiently waiting for something interesting to happen. Up until this point, to him her body language must have promised so much. She bent down slowly cocking her head, her backside in the air, a most unladylike pose. I walked up the street to join her. Sure enough there on the door was an ugly scar in the paintwork where the cross had been removed.

'We'll be repaintin' that in the spring', a soft Devon accent announced followed by the face of Bernard Langsteen, one of the volunteers. His flat cap was pulled down tight against the sun and he indicated the door of the newsagent's with a trowel he was using to titivate a flowerbed.

Bernard's face was level with Delilah's nether regions and she straightened up abruptly as Bernard made his presence known.

'Hiya Bernard,' she smiled. 'Couldn't get it off without damaging the paintwork then?'

'Nahh, that's a rum do that is.' He said, standing up. 'Fancy someone disrespectin' the dead like that. Poor Harold, God rest his soul.' He turned to look at me. 'Mr 'everington…' He tapped the peek of his cap in greeting. Bernard's choice of hat and use of arcane phrases contrasted with his young face. Cousin to the Martins' children, he'd moved to the village when he was ten. Bernard's mother came to help her brother run the farm, when his wife died young. It seemed only yesterday he'd returned from university all set to rule the world with his degree in Business Management. He quickly fell into the routine of the family business and worked at the farm most days. I never knew why, but he volunteered at the model village when he could have been gallivanting about the countryside with the other young farmers.

'I read some of the models have gone missing too.'

'They 'ave that, Mr 'everington, six of them. We'll 'ave to start making replacements if they don't appear again soon.'

'Can I ask which ones?'

'Don't suppose it ma'ers much.' He shrugged and started to list them with his fingers. 'Mr Sal'er, Mr Rawlinson, Mr Pane, Mr Dockerty, Mr Davies and Mr Kinney. We got so many models 'ere, we're not sure 'ow long they've been missing. It's a bid odd one of them being Mr Sal'er though, what with that cross as well. Someone playing a prank I reckon, bit sick though', he finished.

'So that's the newsagent, the butcher, the baker, the bookie, the greengrocer, and the fish and chip shop owner.' Delilah listed back.

'All on the 'igh Street too, well 'cept the greengrocer's, that's on 'uckspeth Road,' Bernard nodded. 'Oh and the bookie's, that's Kent Road.'

I too had begun to try and make connections in my own mind as Bernard talked. Basic at first, they were all male, all business owners and the majority were indeed on the High Street.

'Do you have CCTV here?' I asked.

'Yup, the police have already looked but they can't see anything. We often get kids in 'ere drinkin' on a Friday night - we lock the gates, but they get in somehow. Where there's a will there's a way. Someone behaving suspiciously did come into the village a week ago last Thursday, but they can't see who it were and we're sure the cross wa'n't there last week. That only appeared yesterday morning.'

'A week ago last Thursday? And Mr Salter was murdered the next day!'

'Yup, the police said that too, Mr 'everington, but it makes no difference. It was a dark night and the person on the camera was wearing a black duffel coat. Pulled their hood up tight around their face. It could 'ave been anyone. You couldn't see a thing.'

This had obviously been the intention of the intruder. Who wanders around a model village at night without some sort of mischievous intent? Could the models and the murder possibly be linked or was this, as Bernard had suggested, simply a prank in bad taste? This case was certainly getting more interesting and my daughter's words of warning were fading fast in my memory.

3.

The Corn Dolly

"Tis but a thing of straw" they say,
Yet even straw can sturdy be
Plaited into doll like me.

Minnie Lambeth 1957

On Tuesday, I found myself drawn to the baker's. I'd been working in the shed since six-thirty that morning. I was working on a commission for Lord Blackwood. He wanted a new hat in time for the Cheltenham Festival, where his new thoroughbred, 'Tipingee', would be debuting.

Rufus Blackwood is my oldest friend, living in Tuesbury that is; and yet I know very little of him these days. We grew up together, adventured together and grazed knees together and yet as is so often the case, adulthood came and we went our separate ways. He followed his father into the diplomatic service and I followed mine into millinery. We found ourselves in different countries, miles apart and with new friends to make. Since his return to the village in his early retirement ten years ago, we had still failed to reacquaint ourselves with each other. This is until he discovered I had not entirely retired and commissioned me to make him a hat. Perhaps out of guilt at a friendship neglected or a genuine interest in my trade, I wasn't yet sure. What I did know was, this was the first hat Hetherington milliners had made for the Blackwoods since my father passed away.

I was making him a splendid fedora with a fan of silk fabric in the headband that matched the colours of Lord Blackwood's jockey. Two tiny buttons covered in matching fabric accompanied it. I was taking the greatest of care with this one. Only perfection would do: the tiniest of stitches, the finest silk and of course the deepest and softest of blue felts.

In the course of discussions regarding the commission I had heard much about his new horse, although I was yet to see it for myself. Blackwood insisted that I should come with them to Cheltenham where I would see the horse in all its glory. Well, how could I refuse? I was now working frantically to produce a hat worthy of a thoroughbred's debut and one that I wouldn't cringe at when standing next to it. It's fair to say that an artist is always their own worst critic and if I had to stand next to a hat that had a stitch one millimetre out of place I would not be able to bear it.

Now, five hours later, my fingers were cold and sore and my stomach complained of neglect as I was beset by olfactory hallucinations of almond croissant. We were still in the last days of February, the cold wind clung on to the vestiges of winter as spring bulbs peeped the tips of their leaves out of the half barrel planters on the High Street. Thankfully the baker's was always warm and now standing in the queue I rubbed my hands together to get the feeling back. The scars from my old carpal tunnel operation itched under my leather gloves as the blood rushed back to my fingers.

It was a busy morning, and the small tin loaves were going fast. The all-pervading smell of fresh bread hung in the warm air. The soft scent of dough tugged at memories of rainy afternoons spent at home, while my mother cooked bread. The bread-slicing machine hummed with its work, as the baker's daughter, Verity, sliced the loaves for waiting customers. At the back of the shop, customers chatted over coffee and pastries adding to the general hubbub that brought the bakery alive that morning.

I was there for my usual almond croissant. I wasn't meeting Delilah today so I had two all to myself. I planned to take them back to the shed and make a pot of my favourite, Monsoon Malabar coffee. I could smell it already.

Waiting for my turn, I observed the new display in the window. Albert Pane was an enthusiast when it came to tradition and part of this involved corn dollies. Over the year they would fade and from August onwards he would set about creating more until he had enough to revamp the shop window for the New Year. This year was a magnificent display and I had not yet had the time to look at it properly. Little labels were provided next to each one to say what they were and where they had originated. I made a mental note to stand outside and read a few once my croissants were in hand.

Albert Pane himself was a thin man with swarthy skin. Crows' feet bracketed his piercing blue eyes, indicating a love of laughter; the creases around the mouth: a love of nicotine. His white apron was crisp and neat, I have long suspected, a show for the customers. His working apron could not possibly have been this clean. His hands were always cold, the sign of a good baker some say. The knuckles on his thin fingers had become exaggerated with age and one assumes arthritis although I have never been so crass as to ask.

'Mr Hetherington,' Albert Pane addressed me formally as he always does: one businessman to another. 'Still a nip in the air out there today!'

'There sure is Mr Pane, but the bulbs are venturing forth, I think spring may be around the corner.' I was distracted by the disappearance of one of the two almond croissants I had my eye on.

'Don't worry; I have a fresh batch out the back. Two, is it?'

I nodded and my stomach murmured its appreciation, thankfully muffled by my Guernsey sweater, scarf and wax jacket.

I paid and thanked Pane for his efforts and made my way out of the shop to inspect the corn dolly display.

A Durham Chandelier took pride of place this year. A beautiful piece created with real skill. Three tiers were attached to a strong centre and on each corner of the three tiers hung tasselled plaits of straw. The information provided with it said *'Durham Chandelier, inspired by my ancestors who hail from the North East. Made with a traditional dolly centre, this technique was taught to me by my uncle.'*

Below the chandelier, lined up in the front of the window, were a variety of creations with a doll shaped figure entitled *'Mother Earth'*. I was about to read more when a voice beside me made me jump.

'Good morning, Mr Hetherington, cold one today.' Mrs Dellaware smiled as she hovered by the door of the baker's waiting for a response. Her perfume mingled with the aroma of the bakery, adding a floral note to the smell of wholemeal flour.

'Yes, yes,' I indicated my agreement by thrusting my hands into my pockets and raising my shoulders to my ears.

Mrs Dellaware, as I have mentioned before, is a long-standing member of the community. She has lived here almost as long as I have, moving to Tuesbury when she married her husband. Now a widow, she has become somewhat of an eccentric in the village. I have heard people refer to her as *'having birds in her attic';* an affliction I initially thought could be rectified by the employment of pest control until I grasped their analogy. I have never found Mrs Dellaware to be anything other than sane. I've noticed she has the odd nervous tic and at times I have seen her sitting on a bench on the Village Green staring into space but eccentricity does not qualify one for insanity. Constance Dellaware may appear weak-minded but she was as strong as an ox when it came to ignoring the whisperings of the villagers.

'I suppose you've heard about poor Mr Salter?'

Despite being a victim of it herself, Mrs Dellaware was not averse to gossip, as are most in such a small community. As previously stated; I do not like gossip!

'I have.'

'I told that constable there was something wrong but would he listen?'

'Mm.'

'My nerves have been on edge ever since! Donald says I shouldn't worry so much but it makes you feel peculiar knowing you knocked on someone's door when they were lying dead in a wood.'

'Indeed'.

'Still I mustn't complain, it's poor old Harold we should feel sorry for. Anyway I shan't keep you, Mr Hetherington, I need a small granary for Donald's sandwiches.'

In hindsight, it may have been polite to enquire after the health of Donald, the newest member of our village. Donald Yveny was Mrs Dellaware's nephew; a very exotic character. I'd noticed him frequenting The Badger's Holt pub and Dockerty's Turf Accountants on more than one occasion. He had a strong accent, although I had not yet identified what it was, and he spoke English impeccably well. I did not wish to provoke further conversation in regard to the unfortunate Mr Salter and so instead I nodded goodbye.

I was now completely distracted from the bakery window and, with the mention of Harold Salter's death, it got me thinking about murder again. Something I had not done since Delilah and I had visited Little Tuesbury. For the last week, I had been consumed only by Lord Blackwood's commission. I had, of course, made a mental note of the missing models mentioned by Bernard but with only two weeks left to finish the commission, I was forcing my brain to concentrate on one thing. Not something I'm good at.

As I walked back down the High Street toward the allotments and the sanctuary of my shed once more, I pondered the significance of the missing models. Given that one of the counterparts was now dead and had a cross on the door of their shop to boot, I was making the assumption there would be more to come. The question was, who would be next?

The baker, Mr Pane, as I have just described, is a man of about the same age as the deceased Mr Salter. He raised his family in the village and his daughter now runs the baker's with him. His vices include cigarettes and alcohol and he is often found in The Badger's Holt. When he's not in the pub, he's working late preparing dough for the next day or he's in the bookie's on Kent Street, much to his wife's chagrin.

Mr Rawlinson ran the butcher's on the High Street. His claim to fame was that the local bobby lived above his shop. He joked that if it weren't for the reliable supply of bacon butties, Tuesbury would be an unattended centre for crime. Recent events would suggest that Tuesbury is fast becoming a black spot on the Met. police's list, despite this. The result: Rawlinson will soon need to up his stocks of bacon. Rawlinson is an excellent butcher and I often partake of pork chops, the odd lamb shank and, on special occasion, a fillet steak or homemade beef Wellington. As far as I know he has no enemies and, if he did, who would risk it with the constabulary living above his shop?

The greengrocer, Mr Davies, has struggled recently with the advent of a new supermarket five miles out of the village. There have been complaints that his produce is no longer kept in date. Limp lettuces, shrivelled mushrooms, and leathery apples are a few of the examples cited when people are justifying their move to the supermarket. The truth is, if you don't support your local shops, how can you expect them to survive for long enough to be there when you need fresh fruit in a Pavlova emergency? Mr Davies defended his empire against the force of the supermarkets and despaired at the attitude of the villagers. No, Mr Davies was more likely to be inclined to murder than be murdered.

Now Mr Dockerty, who owned the bookie's: there was a man with enemies. A tight-fisted, shrewd man, he would have put Scrooge to shame. Who can blame him when the sole purpose of running a bookmaker's establishment is to relieve punters of their money? Unfortunately there are those that do not know to quit when they are ahead and although I do not know for definite the condition of the regulars' finances, I shouldn't wonder that there are a few that do not have a clean slate. Depending on the quantity owed this may be motive enough for murder. But why steal the other models? Did the murderer owe money to all these establishments? I quickly shook off this thought, as ridiculous.

Lastly, Mr Kinney is the owner of our splendid fish and chip shop. Shortlisted several times for the *'Fish and Chip of the Year Awards'*, but not yet winning, they were robbed, in my opinion. The fat is never too greasy, heavy or old and the lightness of the batter is sublime. A recipe Mr Pane lays claim to but in fact belonged to Mr Kinney's grandmother. If you ask Kinney, you will be told, that she brought it over from Ireland. I have had the great privilege of being shown the document, which is normally kept in the safe. It's amazing what a bit of well placed flattery and the mention of an interest in family history can get you. In short, who would want to kill the purveyor of such delights?

I am, of course, assuming that the disappearance of the models, at the same time as that of the newsagent Mr Salter, suggests that the other models will meet the same fate. It could be coincidence, and they will not. It could be just a prank by one of the local teenagers. With raging hormones come vivid imaginations and they may have thought it funny to send the village into a tizzy. The good burghers of Tuesbury will probably say it was the youth of Bestall, when in actual fact we have trouble enough with our own delinquents: all happily blamed on Bestall.

Of course it may have nothing to do with the shop owners themselves. Instead the theft of the figures could even have been aimed at Mr & Mrs Tudbury. They have been known to call the police in an incident where a slightly rowdy teenager decided to re-enact Godzilla in the middle of Little Tuesbury.

Corn dollies and models of mini Tuesbury residents were a whirl in my mind. I couldn't help but feel there was some significance in all these effigies. Corn dollies were used to appease the gods of the harvest all those years ago. What if someone had stolen the models to appease their own gods? Again a theory I quickly dismissed as ridiculous.

It's not necessarily the theft of the models that concerns me but the follow-up cross on the door of the newsagent's. It's all just a little too coincidental. The question is: what links them all? Were they Freemasons? Something to consider; Freemasons in London have approached me but I was not aware of any in Tuesbury although it is not beyond the realms of possibility.

Did they all play golf? Who knows what goes on up at that golf club. Perhaps I should get myself a lesson.

I was definitely floundering now and as I made my way through the gate to the allotment, up the little path to the shed, I entered, croissants in hand, and set about putting the coffee to brew. I listed the missing models once more. Newsagent, chip-shop owner, greengrocer, bookmaker, butcher, baker…

All we needed was a candlestick maker and Tuesbury was not without one of those. Elroy Tuvay the antiques shop owner made candles, but he wasn't on the list. The thought of the antiques shop reminded me of the imminent arrival of Delilah's birthday. I had seen a charming necklace in the window of the shop last week that would suit her perfectly.

I started up the fan heater and laid out my tools ready to continue my work on Lord Blackwood's hat. I was attaching the headband and the fan. The trick was to secure them firmly, without a stitch showing.

I continued with my work, reluctant to take my coat off until I had warmed up. I made a mental note to visit the antiques shop tomorrow and purchase the necklace. I could call in on Steve too while I was on the High Street. The newsagent's hadn't been open since Harold's death; hardly a surprise. I knew they had a flat above the shop and for the first time since I heard the news, I felt the urge to offer my condolences. I am not a heartless man but I don't like to intrude on others' grief. Nevertheless, it was possible that I could offer him some comfort, having dealt with death so frequently myself, and indeed having known the pain of losing a wife.

I often found that as I got older my previous experiences of death imposed themselves once more on my brain and in an effort to restrain them I would push any thoughts of condolence as far away as possible. However, if I could offer comfort then it was my duty.

I resolved to visit both Steve and the antiques shop tomorrow and after coffee and croissants, I stitched into the afternoon, happy with my plans for the next day.

4.

The Collier

A Collier is a type of close fitting necklace. In some religions such as Voodoun it is a ritual necklace worn by initiates.

I'd spent the following morning finishing the fabric fan on Lord Blackwood's fedora. The stitches I'd employed were tiny stab stitches and my eyes had become used to the closeness of my work.

I now squinted in the bright sun that washed the High Street. I was outside Tuvey Antiques considering Delilah's potential present.

I had only seen the necklace in passing, not having had the time to inspect it previously. It had looked heavy and close fitting, but I'd seen Delilah wear things like this before. Now, standing on the pavement viewing the necklace, I saw that it was almost a choker and did not look as heavy as I remembered. In amongst the delicate filigree that covered what looked like a heavy tubular, silver frame, a snake entwined itself. It reminded me of the *'Garden of Eden'* and Delilah was not particularly religious, perhaps spiritual was a better word for Delilah's faith. I wondered if it was appropriate at all now I saw it up close.

My attention was caught by a figure appearing, out of the corner of my eye. I looked up to see Steve changing the headline on the newspaper board outside the newsagents. *Ladies' Luncheon moved to a week next Tuesday'*. So that's what made for breaking village news a week after a murder. I checked my cynical thoughts. There was of course no way Steve would want a constant reminder of his partner's death in the form of a headline board outside his shop.

The newsagent was about two hundred yards further up the High Street and I watched him in the hope he'd turn around and then I could wave. I've never been one for shouting down the street. I didn't get my chance though as the door of the antiques shop gave a *'ting'*, followed by a friendly:

'Hello Mr Hetherington, fine day, isn't it?'

Elroy Tuvey was a businessman, through and through. He never missed a sale. Everyone knew if you so much as paused to sneeze outside his shop you'd leave with something. I wouldn't say he was a lurker as such but he seemed to have a sixth sense for the customer. I'd spent too long looking in the window and, now he had come out to greet me, there was no escape.

'Can I help you with anything?', he beamed.

Tuvey was the only black man in the village but he did not let the minority label hinder him. He was an eternal optimist, never gloomy nor depressed. He set up his business on the High Street in 1989. A young man in his twenties then, the village had been suspicious, but he persevered and over twenty years on he was still here.

Passing tourists loved to rummage through the bric-a-brac for old cups and saucers that were suitably English and twee. He indulged them by making candles of telephone boxes, London buses and beer tankards to place in the cups, giving their souvenirs a purpose on their return home. Never one to miss an opportunity, Tuvey also sells little wax candle houses to Mr and Mrs Tudbury to stock in the model village shop. A skilled and lethal salesman, I was in his trap.

'Well…' I started.

'How about you come in and have a look. I see you are interested in the necklace, a fine piece. That one came from an auction house in Bestall.'

I followed him into the shop as he talked. Leaning into the window he picked up the navy blue leather case that held the necklace.

'Some might call this a collier. It's an elegant and finely crafted piece. Not at all heavy, made to adorn the necks of the finest ladies, it's a lovely piece, Mr Hetherington,' he ploughed on, regardless of my reticence.

He handed it to me. The first rule of sales: get the product in the customer's hands. I was surprised to find the metal warm against my hands where it had been sitting in the sunlight. It was, as promised, very light. Tuvey stood patiently, watching me inspect the item. His keen brown eyes watching the creases in my forehead and movement of my eyes as I turned it over. I could see the silver mark. The filigree vines and the snake wrapped themselves around what I now saw was a semicircular, flat backed, hollow piece of silver about sixteen inches in length. It reminded me of the Grecian jewellery Delilah so often admired in her textbooks. It was a lovely piece but I couldn't get over the snake. I handed it back to the patient salesman who placed it back in the case. The velvet lining of the case was worn with the years and it was a little shabby compared to the necklace it held. I would have to find another case for it if I were to purchase it.

'It is beautiful, is it not?'

'Yes.' I couldn't disagree.

'Shall I wrap it for you?'

You had to admire the man's techniques.

'I'm looking for something for Miss Delibes' birthday, and as beautiful as that item is, I'm not sure how she'd feel about a snake wrapped around her neck.'

Tuvey paused and fixed me a look, considering his prey. He was a very particular gentleman, deliberate in his mannerisms and his facial expression was more often than not neutral. Now, he was frowned as he began his final pitch.

'The snake is an interesting symbol, it cannot be denied. It has so many meanings. I prefer to think of it as my mother did. The great *Damballa*, sky god and protector of all life, circling the wearer.'

His perfect English accent broke as he pronounced the name Damballa although I could not tell what accent he had reverted to. Despite my recognition of a sales pitch when I heard one, I was intrigued.

'Damballa?'

'He is the Voodoo god of the sky. A protector.'

'Voodoo?' I wasn't sure that was much better.

'Rada, of course.'

'Rada?' I was beginning to regret stopping by the window.

'Good Voodoo! Not all Voodoo is bad, my friend.'

There it was again: that accent; as if quoting an old friend's wisdom. Unwilling to debate the pros and cons of gods and ultimately the role of snakes in religion, two things occurred to me.

How was I going to leave the shop without this necklace and, being a deeply un-superstitious man, did the symbolism of the necklace matter? Ultimately, did I think Delilah would like it? The answer to that was yes. Just because I wasn't keen on the idea of a snake as an adornment, certainly didn't mean Delilah wasn't.

Tuvey saw my face relax and went in for the kill sealing his deal.

'I'll wrap it for you Mr Hetherington and I have a new case I can put it in for you. Free, of course.'

I tried not to indicate that his prediction with regard to the case was alarmingly accurate.

The necklace was wrapped up in no time with a few pleasantries along the way. I eyed the waxed London paraphernalia at the till with gentle amusement. Tuvey proudly told me how he was designing a new line in candles for the model village. This time, he was making, the people that went with the houses. I couldn't help feeling there was something rather sinister about tiny burning people but he seemed to think the tourists would love them and come the summer they'd, be flying off the shelves. Tuvey knew his market and I wasn't going to argue. I must confess I tuned out of the pleasant small talk, thinking instead of Steve and the newsagent's board. He had clearly decided to open up today, which made my visit all the more easy and it felt a lot less intrusive.

I thanked Tuvey and took hold of the handles on the paper bag that contained my purchase. Last year the Village Retailers Association had pledged to use paper bags instead of plastic, to lessen the impact on the environment. It took me back to the days when paper bags were all you had. You rushed home clutching the bottom of the grocery bag hoping that nothing would fall out as the moisture from the veg soaked through the bottom. Now of course they were lined with some form of sealant. I pondered at the irony of this. Surely sealing the bags made it harder for them to decompose making them once again less biodegradable?

I bade Elroy Tuvey goodbye and stepped out of the shop and into the sun on the High Street once more. The bulbs in the containers had grown another centimetre or two overnight and I hoped a late frost wouldn't cut short their bid for freedom.

The board was still outside the newsagent's but the headline had changed. This time, *'Met Office predicts record highs this Summer'* it announced. How very British – last week murder this week the luncheons and the weather. I pushed the door. There were no other customers only the familiar shape of Prince nestled on his favourite beanbag. For a moment I wondered what the little dog thought of it all. One minute happy as a sand boy, walking in the woods, the next minute missing an owner.

Steve was out the back and, at the sound of the door, appeared through the rainbow ticker-tape curtain that separated the office from the rest of the shop. His eyes were puffy and he made a valiant effort to smile but he was fooling no-one. I had my excuse sorted: a birthday card for Delilah.

'Morning, Mr Hetherington.'

'Morning.' I nodded. 'I was very sorry to hear about Harold.'

Steve's smile faded and he tugged the bottom of his pink and grey Argyle cardigan.

'Thank you.'

Not wanting to create any kind of a scene and sensing his discomfort, I walked to the other end of the front counter to choose a card from the stand. It squeaked as I turned it, punctuating the awkward silence. It can only have been a few seconds before Steve spoke again, but it felt like an eternity. He had sat himself down on a small stool behind the counter and was looking out of the window. Had I not been the only person in the shop I would have questioned whether or not he was speaking to me.

'Is it true?'

I looked up from the card stand and raised an eyebrow.

'Is it true you solve crimes, Mr Hetherington?' This time he turned to look at me.

'I wouldn't say that.' I smiled as kindly as I could without being patronising. I didn't question why the newsagent might think this. Delilah's and my antics had been in and out of the local papers for the last year: not something I'm necessarily proud of.

'But you have done, and your website says you do?'

'My website? Does it?'

At the end of last year when I decided to retire, Rob and Delilah had helped me to set up my bespoke hat making business in the shed. They had helped me in so many ways, insulating the shed, making curtains, donating a rug; Delilah had argued it must look halfway homely. She had been particularly instrumental in dragging me into the twenty-first century with a website. I rarely had reason to look at it as she had thrown herself into the project updating it with any photos of hats I made and diverting any direct enquiries to my e-mail: a partnership that had worked very well. Little did I know that Miss Delibes had called the website, *'Hetherington's Mystery Millinery: Bespoke Hats and Investigative Services'*, a fact Steve now informed me of.

I stood in stunned silence.

'…So do you think you could help me?'

'Ermm…' was all my usually eloquent self could muster.

Steve stood up, 'You can't help but read the papers, working in a newsagent's, and I read about those murders up at the allotments and how you helped the police solve them an' all, so maybe you could help me?'

'Well…' I coughed and walked back down the shop to where Steve sat behind the till. 'I'm just not sure I'm your man. Sometimes it's best to leave the police to these things.' I said rubbing my shoulder. A painful reminder of my last dramatic encounter and, as if to re-enforce this memory, Jane's words were ringing in my ears: *Leave it to the police Dad.*'

Steve's shoulders sagged and he looked like a kicked puppy. Prince raised his nose from the beanbag and whimpered. A sorrier pair I have never seen. The dark circles around Steve's eyes were even darker close up and his eyes were bloodshot. His lip had obviously been chewed. All the signs of anxiety and tension oozed from him. It occurred to me I knew nothing of this man, not even his surname. He was the silent partner of a now dead man: a man I had known for years and yet I knew nothing of his partner. I felt awful. My idle curiosity in the case was one thing, but to actively start an investigation on behalf of someone was entirely different.

'Er… Steve,' I paused embarrassed at having to use the first name of a man I hardly knew. 'I'm sorry but I really don't think I can help. I apologise if my website misled you but I was not aware of the by-line attached to my business. It's simply not possible for me to get involved.'

Steve looked back out of the window and for a moment I thought he was going to cry. Goodness knows what I would have done then. A grown man crying in public is not something I relish the thought of, let alone the thought that I caused it! Taking a deep breath he turned back towards me.

'Well, thank you anyway, Mr Hetherington.' And he smiled.

I have no idea what he was thanking me for, but it had the desired effect. Guilt!

'If I can help any other way, then I gladly will. I'm at the shed most days if you just want some company.' I knew what solitude was like. I knew what it felt like to start talking to someone who wasn't there. These next few months for Steve were going to be hard.

'Thank you, you know Harold didn't have any enemies. I can't understand it. He didn't even have any family; all he had was this business and me. That's why I moved here. I couldn't make him give up the shop.'

'He was a good man,' was all I could think to say and I placed a card I had picked up on the counter.

'He was, wasn't he?' Steve replied.

I paid for the card I had selected randomly from the carousel and left the shop feeling very uncomfortable. After refusing to help him, I felt it inappropriate to ask any further questions of Steve.

I hadn't looked at the card until now. I'd felt the need to buy something in order to continue my subterfuge. I'd just picked up what was to hand. Standing outside the newsagent I looked at the photograph on the front. It had two donkeys conversing. One had its head in a trough of what had been photoshopped to look like beer and the other was saying *'Steady Neddy, don't make an ass of yourself'*, entirely appropriate for a woman that runs headlong at life.

It occurred to me that I too was behaving as rashly as Delilah. What was I doing kidding myself that I'd gone to offer Steve my condolences? I wanted to know more about Harold Salter. I wanted to know what had driven someone to murder him: to murder a man who to all intents and purposes was thoroughly good. I knew my daughter was right; this was best left to the police. What if my assumptions were correct and the killer would strike again? Self-preservation should prevent me from continuing but, as they say, curiosity killed the cat and right now, I was just too curious.

5.

Clairin

Raw rum, said to be the favourite drink of Papa Ghede who waits at the crossroads for the souls of the dead.

Thursday, I awoke to the sound of the telephone. With Lord Blackwood's commission finished, I had turned my alarm off and allowed myself the luxury of a lie in. This was not to be. Instead at five past seven I was treated to the excited voice of Miss Delibes.

'There's another one appeared.'

Although I often do my best work early in the morning when my mind is not occupied with the minutiae of the day, I do not enjoy conversation at this time and so my reply was a little terse.

'What?'

Silence.

'Delilah, *what* has appeared?'

'Did I wake you up? Oh no! I did, didn't I?'

'Perhaps…'

'I'm so sorry Blake, I'll ring back later.'

'No, no, I'm awake now. You'd better spit it out, whatever it is.'

Silence.

'Well?'

Silence.

Sigh.

'There's another cross on one of the doors!'

'Really?' Now I was awake. This was a development. An elaborate ruse by the teenagers of Tuesbury rarely went on this long. University students, possibly, but it was a long way for them to come from even the most outlying London colleges. There was also the fact that since their invention, traffic cones have been the hallmarks of undergraduate pranks.

'Yes. Apparently Bernard found it this morning when he dropped in after milking the cows.'

'Really.'

Two syllables was about all I could muster this soon after waking. 'Really' seemed to cover everything although I did wonder how she had come upon this information. I was not aware she socialized with Bernard.

'Yes, Rob got a phone call this morning. It's on the greengrocer's shop this time.'

She must have read my mind. 'Peculiar,' I managed. Four syllables, I must be waking up.

'X marks the spot!' Delighted Delilah.

'Indeed.'

'I think we should go and have a look!'

Voyeurism is not a hobby of mine and all I could hear was the resounding voice of my daughter: *'That Delilah is trouble Dad!'* She was right, but Miss Delibes' enthusiasm was invigorating and difficult to resist.

'Haven't you got work to be doing?' I rubbed my eyes and scratched my stubbled chin.

'Nope! I'm having a couple of weeks off before I go to Haiti. I know you've finished that commission and this is far too interesting.'

'I'm not sure how interesting a cross on the door of a miniature greengrocer's shop is, Delilah.'

'You humbug, Blake. This is the most interesting thing that's happened this year!'

'It's only February!'

'Well I'm going! I'll pop by after walking Bertie. Come if you like or don't. Suit yourself.'

And with that, she put the phone down. Delilah has never hung up on me before, maybe because I usually go along with whatever crazed scheme she has. She always made it sound so innocent: *'I'll just pop by...'* There was nothing *just* in regards to what Delilah was about to do.

I'd only been awake ten minutes, I hardly felt able to discuss the pros and cons of visiting a potential crime scene. I sighed. I'd better go, if only in a supervisory capacity, to prevent Delilah and Bertie from stomping all over the clues. Not for my own benefit of course, but for the benefit of Sergeant Claringdon. I can only imagine the embarrassment of having one's girlfriend destroying evidence connected with a crime scene.

I walked to the bathroom to wash the sleep out of my eyes. Whom was I kidding? Delilah knew what she was doing. She was an archaeologist, for goodness sake, she was used to preserving sites. No, I had to admit it, Delilah was right. This was interesting!

I hurried about getting washed, dressed, skipping my usual breakfast of Special K. Rushing out of the door, I grabbed my flat cap for protection against the cold and hurried across the village to its model twin. In my haste I forgot my cane, and by the time I got there, my foot was aching. The cold certainly made it worse.

Standing at the gate with Bertie, Delilah was talking to Mrs Tudbury who was manning the ticket booth. I could hear her as I approached.

'Such a shame we can't go in.' She was smiling politely. Bertie sat watching Mrs Tudbury as she explained once more that the police were in the model village and so they'd decided not to open in the afternoon to give them a chance to put the vandalism right.

'But it's only a silly little cross, surely?' Delilah shrugged, feigning disinterest in order to wheedle more information out of Mrs Tudbury. A technique I'd seen her use on other occasions when she wanted her way.

'Yes, but the police still insisted on coming down and 'aving a look. Turns out, an'i-social behaviour in rural settings, is high on their list. That and the fact that Mr Davies didn't come back from work yesterday,' Mrs Tudbury replied.

I'd noticed she often dropped her consonants, which I found an overwhelming urge to correct. I resisted.

'They think it's connected?' Delilah almost whispered. She leant forward, her head and shoulders now almost in the booth with Mrs Tudbury.

I coughed as I stopped beside her, out of breath and huffing little clouds of moisture into the cold air.

'Mr 'etherington! Fancy seeing you here on a Thursday. Well, this is a busy day for us.' Mrs Tudbury smiled knowingly, I assume looking at my flushed complexion and unshaven visage that compounded my flustered arrival.

'Indeed. Come on, Delilah, let's go and get coffee. I assume the coffee shop's still open?'

'Of course,' Mrs Tudbury replied.

'Mrs Tudbury was just telling me Mr Davies has gone missing.' Delilah resisted.

'Do the police know?'

'Yes, I told you. It was Rob who rang me! That's why they are here.' Delilah pointed at the pair of uniformed officers huddled together on the model High Street. The tiny houses came to mid-shin on the six-foot men and, as I looked across, one was taking a photograph, one foot in the High Street and the other in Huckspeth Road, where the greengrocer's was situated. Mr Tudbury was being questioned and the second police officer was taking notes in a small black book.

'I see.' In my early morning haze, I'd forgotten this piece of information.

'It's a queer one, Mr 'etherington, that's for sure. We've never 'ad problems like this before. Bernard found it this time. 'e often comes in early to do any little repairs. Loves this place, 'e does.'

'So the police think there's a connection between the cross on the greengrocer's and Davies going missing?'

'They didn't say that, but it's a bit of a coincidence, innit? Just like the cross on the newsagent's just after poor 'arold was killed.' Mrs Tudbury gave a dramatic shudder. I was resisting the urge to shudder, myself. The missing consonants were beginning to grate.

She leant forward out of the booth and in a half whisper added, 'It's not like Mr Davies ain't gone missing before though, is it?'

'Really?' Delilah replied. I had heard the gossip that had circulated the village at the time and waited for Mrs Tudbury's revelation.

'He ran away with that Tupperware saleswoman last year. Wife took 'im back, no idea why. She told everyone he'd been visiting 'is mother but he 'adn't.'

'So he might not be missing then?' I ventured.

'Nope. Fact I reckon he ain't missing at all. Reckon he done a bunk again.'

'Nooo!' Delilah was enjoying this far too much.

'Well, that solves that then,' I said taking advantage of a break in the conversation. 'Come on, I need some coffee, it's freezing. Take care Mrs Tudbury, I hope this little bout of vandalism doesn't last. It's amazing what people will do for a bit of attention eh?' I started to walk away in the direction of the coffee shop situated behind Little Tuesbury. I hadn't gone far when Delilah hurried alongside me tugging my coat sleeve and whispering:

'Never mind coffee, Blake, we need to go and see Mrs Davies!'

'I don't think…'

'Come on Blake, we've got a case!' she said, turning around and crossing the road to walk back in the direction of town.

'Yes I've been meaning to talk to you about that, Miss Delibes.' I followed. There was little else to be done. Who knows what she'd get up to without my staying hand?

'Oh?' She stopped on the other side of the road and waited for me to cross.

'Yes. Since when did I become a private investigator?' I joined her on the pavement and started to adjust my jacket, realising that in my haste I had done the buttons up in the wrong holes. No wonder Mrs Tudbury had given me that smile. She probably thought I was going a bit senile. I started to redo the buttons in the right holes.

Delilah was silent. I looked up. At least Delilah had the decency to blush when she'd been found out.

'You need qualifications for that sort of thing! I don't think you should be encouraging people to approach us in matters that essentially concern the police, Delilah!'

'Right!'

'It's not on.'

'Right.'

'Really it's not.'

'Okay, okay. But what do you call grappling armed art forgers, wrestling escaped prisoners and rescuing Bertie and me? All within the last year I might add!'

'Eighteen months actually, and I call it self-preservation!'

'I see. So think of this as self-preservation, Blake. It could be your shed with a tiny cross on it next. Then what?'

'Well, then I shall leave it to the police. Besides, I promised Jane.'

'I might have guessed Jane had something to do with it. She's no fun, that woman. She'd wrap you up in cotton wool if she could. You've got a brain, Blake, and I know your brain, it likes to be used and what better way to use it!' She finished with a triumphant wave of her hand and an echoing bark from Bertie. Turning, she stomped down the path towards the top of the High Street.

'That's my daughter, Delilah,' I replied, but it was rather lacklustre. She was right. Since the loss of my wife ten years ago, Jane had transferred all of her worrying to me. It wasn't that she was no fun, it was that in the last eighteen months I'd been shot in the foot, and broken my collar bone. She didn't want to lose another parent prematurely: I think most daughters would be a little alarmed at these events.

Delilah wasn't used to having parents around. Her father left when she was young and her mother was on the run without even a postcard or a care for her daughter's wellbeing. I sometimes felt she resented the relationship I had with my daughter, but there was little I could do about that.

I watched her walk down the street and decided to follow. I couldn't let her go off on her own.

'Hang on Delilah, I'm coming too.'

She turned around, beaming. Bertie did a little jig and whined, impatient to get on with the stop-and-start walk.

It didn't take us long to walk back down the High Street to the junction with Huckspeth Road. I had been in the greengrocer's only yesterday for some grapefruits. With a New Year's resolution to eat more fruit, I found pink grapefruit complimented my Special K nicely.

Entering the greengrocer's I was surrounded by the familiar smell of bleach mingled with fresh produce. A fastidiously tidy woman, Mrs Davies bleached the greengrocer's floors twice daily. *'You can't be too careful, Mr Hetherington. There was an incident with a mushroom two years ago, killed a man. It was all over our professional magazine 'The Vine'. Slipped and banged his head. Killed outright they reckon. Well that won't happen here.'*

I waited for Delilah to secure Bertie's lead to the bike rack outside. There were a couple of people at the till and I took a bag from the reel and started to pick out a couple of lemons. You should never be without fresh lemons in the winter and I may as well stock up as I was here. In the main, I bought fruit from the greengrocer's. My allotment kept me stocked with vegetables. Delilah joined me by the citrus fruits, and taking a bag, started to fill it with limes while looking across at the till. On placing the fifth one in her bag she noticed me looking at her with raised eyebrows. Who needs that many limes?

'I like lime in rum.' She grinned.

How many gallons of rum was she planning on drinking? The image of the birthday card popped into my head and I once more thought how appropriate it had been that my subconscious had chosen that it.

The customers at the counter were served, their bags packed and they left. That left Delilah and me. Delilah saw her chance and approached the till. At that moment Mrs Dellaware entered the shop and made a beeline for the lemons, and me. There was no escape.

'There's been another one you know!' She said loudly.

'Yes,' I said eyeing Mrs Davies respectfully. I was hoping Mrs Dellaware wasn't talking about what I thought she was talking about. I was pretty sure Mrs Davies didn't want to be witness to any gossip with regard to the shop or her missing husband.

'A tiny cross, just like the first one: sinister…' Mrs Dellaware's voice trailed off. Her eyes glazed over and she stood rigid, looking right through me.

'Are you okay, Mrs Dellaware?'

No reply. Delilah and Mrs Davies were looking across now.

'Mrs Dellaware?' I tried again.

Nothing. Mrs Davies tried now. She came out from behind the counter.

'Can I help you Mrs Dellaware? Are you okay?' She put a hand out and touched Mrs Dellaware on the shoulder. This got a reaction.

She jumped and let out what can only be described as a hiss and then realising it was Mrs Davies, gave a perfectly beatific smile.

'Yes, yes, yes I'm fine, sorry, just one of my moments. Now where's the broccoli?'

'At the back under, the Savoys, do you want some help?'

'No, no I'm fine, I'm fine.'

All three of us were completely perplexed. We'd still have been staring at Mrs Dellaware if it hadn't been for the shrill demands of the phone. Mrs Davies returned to the till.

'Do you mind?' she said to Delilah, who was still stood by the till. She looked rather comical standing there with half a dozen limes. Delilah shook her head. I joined her with my lemons and Mrs Davies answered the phone.

'Well, that was weird.' Delilah was talking under her breath but clearly about Mrs Dellaware.

'Who are we to question?' I replied looking at the bag of limes.

'Rum!' She said a little louder, raising the bag of limes and shaking it.

I rolled my eyes. Mrs Davies hung up the phone. I hadn't been paying attention to the conversation. She hadn't said much but it now became clear that whatever it had been about, it had not been good. She went to start checking in the price of the limes. Her hand hovered over the till and she burst into tears.

Delilah hadn't even started asking inappropriate questions! There was something in the air in the greengrocer's this morning and it wasn't just the bleach.

Delilah, as always, knew exactly what to do and rushed round the counter to put an arm round Mrs Davies. I was glad she was there. Crying women and me do not go well together, especially as I did not have access to tea and biscuits as a distraction. Mrs Davies was inconsolable. She was gasping for breath and I was a little concerned we might need an ambulance.

'Blake, could you turn the sign please, I'll take Mrs Davies out the back. Mrs Dellaware could you come back later', Delilah said as she passed her on the way to the back of the shop. Mrs Davies was ushered along with no resistance.

'I could be of some help?' Mrs Dellaware ventured, flourishing a floret of broccoli at the two women.

'I think it's perhaps best if we give Mrs Davies a little space,' I said, holding the door for Mrs Dellaware. She left obediently and I turned the shop door sign to *'Closed'*. I couldn't lock it but at least this might dissuade people.

I walked to the back of the shop in time to hear a pause in Mrs Davies' sobbing, followed by a wail.

'He's *dead*!'

6.

Ventailler

The ritual of 'airing' chickens, or swinging them, by their necks, in the air, before they are sacrificed as a way of capturing the evil spirits. From the French: to ventilate.

Entering the back room office, I was relieved to see a kettle.

'I'll make us some tea,' I said, and busied myself while Delilah comforted the distraught Mrs Davies.

Mrs Davies was not able, yet, to tell us from whom the phone-call had been. Her seismic sobs rendered her speechless. I found it hard to believe it was the police. They'd hardly drop you a line to let you know your husband was dead. Even with the recent budget cuts I'm sure they could send an officer for this sort of thing.

I stirred sugar into Mrs Davies' tea and handed it to her. She had stopped crying and was fiddling with the box pleats of her tweed knee-length skirt as she started to tell us about the phone call.

I was right. It wasn't the police. It was a garage in Bestall; they had rung about the Davies' car. Mr Davies had a Morris Minor. It was his pride and joy. Sage green with a walnut interior, it was easily recognisable in the village as his. The owner of the garage, where Davies had his car serviced, had seen it on his way out to a breakdown. It was parked in a lay-by on the London road and he'd recognised it immediately. Knowing that Davies would never have left the car in a lay-by unless there was a problem, they rang the shop to enquire. Now Mrs Davies suspected the worst.

'He'd never leave that car, ever. He loved it more than... more than me!' She blew her nose loudly.

'I'm sure there's a reasonable explanation for it. We should go and have a look.' Delilah still had her arm around Mrs Davies and she squeezed her shoulder as she spoke.

'And prudence would require us to ring the police?' I said, trying to convince myself that I didn't want to get involved in a drama this year, something that so far wasn't working.

Mrs Davies had a look of horror on her face. 'What if he's not dead... what if he's... run off?' she wailed. 'I'm not sure I could bear it if the police were there to witness that!'

'Is the car still in the lay-by?' I asked.

Mrs Davies nodded. 'The garage left it where it was. They wanted to ring us first. I didn't know what to say. I just told them I'd ring them if I needed them to come and get it.'

I looked at the two women's contrasting faces. Delilah's eyes eager for action, Mrs Davies' forming a pleading kicked-dog look. There was only one thing for it. I was going to have to go with them to find the car.

Two women with equally compelling motives, against one man was no contest.

'Come on then,' I said resignedly, placing my untouched tea on the counter next to the kettle.

'We can go in my car!' said Delilah. 'You're in no fit state to drive, Mrs Davies.'

Mrs Davies nodded and stood up. Wiping her eyes and nose one more time, she gathered a large fur coat from the back of the door and picked up the shop keys.

Delilah had parked on the High Street opposite the allotments. She often parked there to take Bertie for walks or to visit me at work in the shed. It was a short walk from the Huckspeth Road and thankfully we didn't encounter anyone who may have commented on Mrs Davies' puffy red face or bleary eyes.

There was silence in the car as we drove to the lay-by on the London road. Twenty minutes felt like two hours. I was dreading what we may find. Something in my bones was telling me this was not good.

'That's it.' Mrs Davies broke the silence as the lay-by and the car came into view.

It was a large lay-by with a burger van as a permanent fixture. Next to it was an old black and yellow AA box, with a pitched roof on each of its four sides and neat yellow stripes down the length of the four corners. The elegance of tradition looked pompous next to the burger van.

Delilah pulled up behind the Morris Minor. In pristine condition, the only hint that it was in use and not a museum piece was the red clay mud in the tyre cleats. There was only one place locally that had this kind of mud and that was Martins' farm near Deerton. I knew the greengrocer's did some business up there, as that's where most of the eggs in the area came from so it was perfectly feasible that this is where Mr Davies had been.

A mock 1940's *'dig for victory'* style advert for the greengrocer's filled the rear windows. The front windows were steamed up, I assumed from a night out in the cold instead of being tucked up in its garage in Tuesbury. Mrs Davies did not make this assumption; she made another.

'I'll kill him!' she announced as she strode across the rough surface of the lay-by, not noticing a puddle as it covered her shoe and stained her tights. 'I'll kill him!' a little louder this time in case we hadn't heard it the first. The transformation from grieving widow to murderous wife was terrifying and I hung back a little, waiting to see what would happen next.

The burger van owner appeared from behind the van where he'd been smoking a cigarette. Several years cruising lay-bys had given him a nose for gossip and a show. He leant against the side of the van, arms folded, watching.

'Mrs Davies, I don't...' I didn't get any further before she picked up half an old house brick that had been used to fill in one of the more minor potholes and launched it through the passenger side window.

The glass made a wholly satisfying noise as it shattered inward. If anyone had been in there it would definitely have caused them serious injury if not, as Mrs Davies had threatened, killed them. A blow to the temple with a brick is not something the human body is designed for.

Still five feet from the car, Mrs Davies' fury continued.

'Patrick Davies, get out here now!'

In her blind anger she could not see, as I could, that there was no one in the car. The seconds between her shouting and the realisation he was not there spread out before her: an ocean only she could sail.

Delilah had locked her own car and hurried towards us in time to see Mrs Davies smash the window. At the sound of the smashing glass Bertie had started barking and jumping up and down on the back seat of the Fiat.

The burger van owner had now taken up a seat on one of the plastic chairs that accompanied his haute cuisine. I took my opportunity in Mrs Davies' silent realisation. I stepped forward and poked my head cautiously through the gap that had been the window. A strong smell of damp upholstery and perfume hit me. Mrs Davies did not wear perfume. I had only ever known her to smell of bleach.

'The keys are still in the ignition,' I said, my voice muffled from inside the car.

I heard Mrs Davies start to cry again. Removing my head from the car, I turned to see Delilah with her arm around her once more.

'He wouldn't do that,' she sobbed.

'I think it's time we rang the police, don't you?' I said sternly. There were no arguments this time.

I made a rare call on my mobile to the authorities before furnishing us all with hot beverages from the burger van. After my rude awakening and complete absence of breakfast, I indulged in a bacon buttie. The morning's events had worked up an appetite. As we sat on the cold plastic chairs I realised I still had the lemons in my pocket. I must have shoved them in there in the rush. I still had to pay for them but I concluded there must be a more appropriate moment to do this. Instead I asked the burger van owner if he wouldn't mind cutting me a slice off one of them for my tea, instead of adding milk. As you can imagine he was most perplexed by this request.

Two uniformed officers I had not met before arrived half an hour later. They took their time walking around the car, looking underneath and finally asking Mrs Davies a few questions, which culminated in 'Have you tried to start the car?'

'No,' I replied on Mrs Davies behalf. She was starting to get upset again. 'I did not want to destroy any evidence.'

'But you said you smashed a window?' was the reply.

I stayed quiet. That was not my story to tell. I wasn't sure Mrs Davies wanted the police to know that she suspected her husband of adultery.

'What makes you think this is a crime scene, Mr Hetherington?' The younger of the two asked trying to keep a straight face.

'Three things.' I listed them on my fingers. 'Mr Davies would never leave his prized car in a lay-by, Mr Davies would never leave the keys in his car, and Mr Davies is missing!'

Mrs Davies nodded in agreement.

'He hasn't been reported missing. Mrs Davies?'

'Well, I er… he er…'

'What Mrs Davies is trying to say is that unfortunately her husband has disappeared before, but this time it's different. His car's still here,' I said patiently.

Mrs Davies nodded.

'Mr Hetherington, if you could let Mrs Davies tell us herself, we'd be very much obliged,' the older police officer interjected. He was clearly nearing retirement and he smiled benevolently at me. I've never seen benevolence executed in such a menacing fashion.

'Mr Hetherington's right, it's different this time. The keys are in the car.' Mrs Davies' bottom lip began to quiver once more.

'And how long has he been missing?'

'About a day.'

'I see, and have you tried ringing anyone he might have seen yesterday?'

'Yes… he was up at the Martins' farm signing a new contract.' Mrs Davies' eyes started to well up again.

'But… he… he didn't come back and they said he left there at four p.m. yesterday.' She finished with a sniff.

'Have you started the car, Mrs Davies?' the second officer continued.

'No, Mr Hetherington said we should ring you.'

The officer looked at Mrs Davies, back at the car, and then back to Mrs Davies once more. 'Would you mind if I started it?'

'No.'

Now we were all intrigued. The officer walked over to the car ten feet from where we were all sitting and, finding the driver's door unlocked, he opened it. It was a wonder it hadn't been stolen. Sitting in the drivers seat, he turned the key.

Nothing!

He tried another couple of times before emerging from the car and shouting across to us, 'is there a knack to this Mrs Davies?'

'No,' she shrugged.

The officer tried again before closing the door and walking back to the burger van.

'I think the problem is your husband's car has broken down.' He said.

'Why didn't he call the AA, then?'

'I have no idea, Mrs Davies.' The officer reached into his jacket pocket for a notebook. 'Would you still like to report your husband missing?'

'Yes… I think so.' A confused Mrs Davies looked up at the officer.

'I'll take some details now and then you can call in at the police station in Bestall to make a report.'

Mrs Davies nodded.

'Can I have his full name and date of birth, please?'

This didn't feel right. The condensation on the windows told me the car had been here overnight but there was nothing else to show where Mr Davies had gone. Surely he wouldn't have started to trudge across the fields homeward if he had had breakdown cover? Not on a winter's night like last night. It had been minus three. Why hadn't he rung the AA?

I was getting cold, so I stood up and walked to the farthest end of the lay-by where the AA box stood, to get the circulation going again. The uneven ground was still hard from the frost, and the puddles in the shade were laced with ice. I turned to walk back towards the group and I could hear the police officer continue his questions.

'Does your husband have a mobile?'

'Yes but I tried ringing it. It's off.' Mrs Davies replied.

So many people had mobiles these days; there was hardly any need for old AA boxes like this one. And then it hit me. What if Mr Davies' mobile wasn't off? What if it had just run out of battery? I was guilty of that. My mobile was off more often than on and mainly due to a dead battery. That being the case, surely he would have used the AA box. I paused, turned again and retraced my steps.

Standing in front of the proud wooden box once called *'the lighthouse of the road'*, I hoped I wasn't right. I reached out and took hold of the black metal handle of the door. I could feel the cold metal under my gloves. The door opened easily, as if something were pushing against it. As it opened two Brogue-clad feet pushed forward over the threshold of the box and a body slid down the back of the AA box. Following the Brogues upwards, green cords, a beige mohair jumper and a wax jacket clothed the man. His chin rested on his chest, a bloated blue face and bulging eyes reminded me of a rabbit with myxomatosis. The circle of his white collar was soaked with blood and a thick noose of wire echoed the line of the collar digging into the folds of skin on his throat.

'Officer!' I shouted, 'You might want to come and have a look at this.'

Mr Davies was the second to die.

7.

The Poppet

Old English word used to describe a small child or a doll.

The next day was Delilah's birthday. In the drama that preceded it I had almost forgotten that we were going out for dinner. We'd found a new restaurant. The Snicket just wasn't the same after last Christmas. Poison pen letters arriving at your table, have a tendency to spoil a place, for one. Instead an Italian restaurant named Grande Amore would be the setting for Delilah's celebrations this evening. A rather upmarket pizzeria, that did a sublime tiramisu.

My head felt groggy this morning: I'd had five hours of sleep. Not nearly enough: my brain had refused to switch off and the vision of Mr Davies' face loomed heavy every time I closed my eyes. I'm not one to dwell on the grotesque. This was the third dead body I'd encountered, but something about this one was different. Throttling someone took a particular type of person: someone who could look you in the eyes until they glazed over, someone who paid no heed to the thrashing and the fear, someone with absolutely no empathy. I shuddered. In my youth I had acquired a GCE in Psychology. I'd read about sociopaths. I understood that they did not feel emotions as others do, but to see the result up close like that; surely you'd have to feel something?

I went back over the events of yesterday. As soon as the two officers saw what the AA box held, their demeanour changed. Professional, curt, coded radio conversations heralded the arrival of the scenes of crime officers, an inspector, and Sergeant Claringdon. Delilah was comforting a hysterical Mrs Davies and an ambulance was called when she started to hyperventilate. A wide-eyed burger van owner was already on the phone to the paper with a story that would put his van on the map. He then started videoing the situation on his phone. Needless to say the police were not amused and seized his phone as evidence. Cordoning off the area as a crime scene meant the burger van owner had to close up for the day. With shouts for compensation, the generator was eventually silenced and the lay-by suddenly felt very empty.

Sergeant Claringdon had shaken his head in despair when he saw Delilah and I were there.

'I might have guessed,' was all he'd said.

In what I assume was an attempt to gain some professional distance, Sergeant Claringdon practically ignored Delilah not speaking to her until she was in the back of the ambulance with Mrs Davies. Even then he'd simply stated:

'Ring me when Mrs Davies is able to talk to us,' and closed the ambulance door on a fuming Delilah. Her face said it all; she was livid.

In the cold light of the next day, I could see it from his point of view. All sorts of questions would be asked. I'm not sure he could have dealt with it any other way. He was, of course, joining us this evening so I hoped they had made their peace with each other before we met.

Pulling my dressing gown on, I walked to the kitchen to boil the kettle. I sighed, as I waited for it to boil and for a brief moment my eyes drifted closed. The vision of Mr Davies' body loomed and I snapped them open them again.

It was six-thirty in the morning and still a grey dark outside: that magical time between the moonlight and sunshine. The blackbirds always started calling out first, next, the cackle of magpies, then the rooks and then the pigeons: clockwork. I tried to switch my brain off and think of something nicer than the slumped bloated body of Mr Davies.

Delilah's birthday! Birthdays were always a special time in our family, although not so much these days. The distance between my daughter and myself was not just a physical one. Despite her concern for me she still found it very difficult to tell me what was concerning her, in her life. You'd think it would get easier as your child becomes an adult. Instead, a whole new set of problems appears: grandchildren and the guilt associated with not seeing them enough, and husbands and the irritation they so obviously display at your presence in their house.

Delilah still loved birthdays. The tragedy was she had no parents to celebrate with. This year, she had Rob, and I was truly happy for her. Over the last few months she had a new enthusiasm for life. Admittedly the, *'Rob this'*, and *'Rob that'* conversations were tedious at times but I was a curmudgeon when it came to romance. Eleanor had always complained that I never bought her flowers or chocolates. But I showed my love in other ways. Fixing the guttering is a labour of love if ever there was one.

I sat on the sofa with my tea. I took the bottle of Talisker off the shelf beside the sofa and poured a capful in the tea. On retirement I had promised myself I would always get dressed and not sit around the house in my dressing gown simply because I could. For me, there madness lies. But here I was. I told myself it was the shock and let the whiskied tea slide down my throat and warm my chest. My head rested back on the sofa and I started to think about today's chores.

I had a shirt to iron for this evening. Lord Blackwood's hat needed to be delivered, as he had not sent someone fetch it for him yesterday evening as promised. The house needed vacuuming. Balls of dust had collected in the corners, one of the problems with a wood floor. The dust just seemed to ball up and float about the room like tumbleweed. I also had some e-mails to reply to. Several more quotes for commissions had been requested. One for a wedding in London, no less than five for Royal Ascot and a local college had contacted me to see if I'd be prepared to take a fashion student on work experience.

I liked the idea of imparting my worldly knowledge to a new generation; making a difference and teaching someone who was interested in my craft. Another of the wedges between my daughter and me was her refusal to continue the family business. But I knew I was wrong to expect her to give up her life in Devon for the sake of a hat shop that, with London rates, might not have survived the next recession.

Leaving my empty mug on the coffee table, I stood up to go and get dressed. Sitting around wallowing wasn't going to solve anything. I was drinking whisky at six thirty in the morning. This was not good. It occurred to me that in abiding by Jane's wishes and denying myself the outlet of enquiry, I was in fact becoming depressed. My brain needed to work things out. I couldn't just leave it with the awful memory of Mr Davies in the AA box. I needed to give it some closure. I needed to solve the case. Not just for myself but for Mr and Mrs Davies. Injustice is something that I have never ever been able to tolerate. That's what was making me maudlin, not the horrible vision that loomed close every time I closed my eyes.

This murder differed so much from Harold Salter's. It took a different kind of psyche to look someone in the eye and strangle them as opposed to hitting them over the back of the head. Or did it? Maybe I was assuming again. Had the killer approached Mr Davies from behind?

Had they even been premeditated murders or had the killer simply seen their opportunity? If so who would be passing the layby, who possessed wire strong enough to strangle: a poacher, perhaps? The wire could have been the sort used to catch rabbits. Possibly even a farmer. There were plenty of those around.

The only similarities were the sinister crosses on the doors of their Little Tuesbury establishments and an apparent absence of motive. Who wanted to kill Mr Davies, apart from Mrs Davies?

Standing in the middle of the lounge I placed my hands in my dressing gown pockets, closed my eyes, and took three deep breaths in and out. Mr Davies' bloated face was there for a second and then it was gone. Instead the faces of Mrs Davies, Mrs Dellaware, Mrs Tudbury, Steve and Delilah, along with the limes, the corn dollies and The High Street, all replaced it. The memories swirled and danced all the way back to the model village and the police officer standing amongst the tiny buildings. Opening my eyes I smiled. I was starting to feel better already.

I walked with renewed vigour to the bedroom. Once dressed and on the way back to the lounge with the shirt I needed to iron for this evening, I noticed Delilah's present sat on the small telephone table in the hall where it had been sitting since I bought it. It was still unwrapped. Picking up the brown paper bag I took it with me into the sitting room and placed it on the coffee table. I draped the shirt over the back of the chair ready to iron later.

I went to the drawer in the kitchen and found some wrapping paper. A pretty lilac colour with small black birds sitting in silhouetted trees, adorned with pink blossom. I felt sure Delilah would approve. Taking the Sellotape and scissors with me I went back into the sitting room.

I tipped the paper bag slightly and pulled the case with the necklace in it, out. As I did there was a thud on the coffee table as something hit it and bounced off onto the floor scudding under the sofa. It left a smudge on the glass and I was thankful it hadn't broken. I had only bought the necklace and I had seen Tuvey put that in the box, so what had fallen out? I placed the box back down on the glass table and lowered myself onto the floor. I could see a white shape towards the back of the sofa and was just able to slide my hand under to retrieve it.

Using my free hand to lever myself back up and onto the sofa, I stared at the little object. Brushing the dust from it I saw it was one of Tuvey's new range: a little wax person with a wick protruding from his head. A generic male face was sculpted into the wax, however the apron suggested that this was Mr Pane the baker. Fascinated, I turned it around and upside down and found that I was correct. On the bottom of the figure, carved into the wax was the name PANE. The model allowed for little else but if the aim was to sell them in the model village shop, then it would be enough for the tourists.

The model village, the dolls, the crosses on the doors, it all smacked of the occult and I was reminded of a film from my childhood. I don't remember the name of it but unbeknown to my parents I'd watched it through the stair rail, peering over their shoulders as they sat on the sofa. The 1950's horror movie had stayed with me. The pale faces, the dancing and the chanting around a fire, the tiny dolls, the pins and the victims writhing in agony. It was an image that had never left me, even now, almost sixty years on. I'd been ignoring it before: never one to be superstitious, but two crosses and two deaths coupled with the disappearance of the models echoed the Voodoo I'd seen in that film loud and clear. A clumsy cliché, but whoever heard of a subtle sociopath.

Turning the model in my hand I was reminded of the conversation I had had with Elroy Tuvey and the accent that had crept into his voice. I hadn't paid much attention before. It was crass of me to think so now, but it was the only avenue that rang true with me. Now I thought about it, his accent had sounded like a cross between Jamaican and French, an accent synonymous with the Antilles and of course the Antilles are synonymous with the Voodoun religion. Maybe I was way off beam but he had after all talked about Damballa and Voodoo when he sold me the necklace for Delilah.

Perhaps Elroy Tuvey might just know what this was all about.

8.

Juju

Juju dolls are seen as good luck and a way to keep the evil spirits at bay.

The bell tinkled frantically as I entered the shop with more purpose than usual. Tuvey looked up from his paper that was laid out on the large Georgian desk that served as a counter for the shop. I was reminded of my days at Hetherington's Hats, my ten a.m. coffee and reading the paper. He was a man after my own heart. In my rush to get out I hadn't even bought a paper this morning.

The 1960's bar stool that he was sitting on squeaked as he stood up. 'Well, hello Mr Hetherington, what can I do for you?'

'Well…'

I was at a point, when my thoughts were about to be vocalised, that I had no idea where best to start. I suddenly felt foolish.

'You found my gift, I see?' Elroy smiled

'Yes.' I hadn't realised I was still holding the little wax doll in my hand and I raised my eyebrows, surprised at myself. 'It was this I wanted to talk to you about actually.' I smiled, approaching the desk.

'Yes?' His dark eyes sparkled. The conversation about the necklace returned in a flurry of words. I remembered the mention of the god Damballa. Was it just a sales pitch? Or was there more to it?

There were so many thoughts circling in my brain vying for attention that it was only a matter of time before the next one that passed by was going to come out; 'I was wondering about Voodoo dolls, Mr Tuvey.'

'Voodoo?' The word hung in the air.

'Yes, you see I've been thinking about these murders and…'

'Murders?'

'Yes. You must have read the papers this morning,' I said, indicating the one lying the counter. 'Mr Davies has been murdered too.'

Tuvey folded the paper closed and continued to look at me with his intense brown eyes. Not a flicker of emotion on his face gave away what he might be thinking.

'I wanted to ask you about the models in the village and….'

'Do you think I murdered someone, Mr Hetherington?' Tuvey interrupted. His words were deliberate and slow, his caramel skin creasing across his forehead. 'With a tiny wax doll-candle?'

A man not unused to prejudice and accusation, he held himself with the utmost dignity under what were some very clumsy and crass questions on my behalf. I'd let my guard slip, become focused on one thing at the expense of all others. My mother's voice rang in my ears: *'be careful what you say Blake, no one knows what you are thinking unless you tell them.'*

I imagine the years of embarrassing observations, from the impertinent and brutally honest child that I was, led to this chastisement. And she was here in spirit to chastise me once more.

'Of course not, please accept my apologies, I shouldn't have come. Of course it's not Voodoo, it's just a candle.' I shook my head and started back towards the door.

'It's a little bit of juju, Mr Hetherington,' Elroy said with the same level tone except, that is, for the word *'juju'*. With that word came once more the accent that had led me here.

I turned back. 'Mr Tuvey, please don't get me wrong and goodness knows I do not wish to insult you again, accidentally or otherwise, but you do seem to be knowledgeable on the subject.'

There was a long silence, as Elroy looked me up and down. His neutral expression, yet again, giving nothing away. Scratching his temple he said, 'Would you like a cup of coffee Mr Hetherington?'

I did not feel I could turn down such an offer, given the way I had burst into to his establishment, and I replied: 'That would be very nice thank you,' and removed my gloves, placing the little wax figure on the counter. I was still curious to know if the machinations of my mind were in fact correct.

Elroy disappeared to make the coffee and I gathered my thoughts. This was not going altogether well. I'm not sure I'd have been so happy if someone had come into my shop and blurted out the words Voodoo and murder, with the implication that I knew something about it. No, I would not have been happy at all.

Elroy seemed an entirely different kettle of fish. He hadn't lost his temper and he had offered me coffee. Anyone who shares food or drink with another human when they have just accused them of murder is not a grudge holder. Unless he planned to poison my coffee? I pushed that thought quickly away. No, a man that had stayed in a village that at first offered him so much resentment and now embraces him, is a man that does not hold a grudge. It was almost as if he lacked the impetus for grudges. Perhaps his life was simpler this way? Maybe he was happy to stand back and see the bigger picture, happy to accept people's faults.

'So what do you want to know, Mr Hetherington?' He handed me a mug of black coffee and I blew the steam from the top before taking a cautious sip.

'I'd better start at the beginning, I suppose.'

He nodded.

'I take it you have heard that both Mr Salter and Mr Davies have been murdered?'

Nod.

'And that the models from the model village have gone missing?'

Sip.

'And that there are little crosses on the doors of the model greengrocer's and newsagent's in the model village.'

Frown. 'I see now, why you might think this is Voodoo, Mr Hetherington. Hollywood has a lot to answer for.'

'Right,' I replied, remembering the macabre face of the Voodoo priest in the horror film from my youth. 'Good, that's what I thought,' I continued, 'so I remembered what you'd said about the necklace and I thought perhaps you knew about Voodoo?'

'I know a little, yes,' he smiled. 'My mother was of the Voodoun religion. Her mother, my grandmother, was a Mambo.'

'Mambo?'

'A Voodoo priestess. She carried out the rituals for the villagers. Only Rada, of course.'

'Rada?' It came back to me now he'd mentioned it last time. 'Ah, the good Voodoo.'

Elroy nodded. 'That is good *juju*,' he said pointing at the little figure by the till; there was that accent again.

'Do you come from the Antilles?'

'I do, Mr Hetherington. I was born in Kingston.'

Thank goodness I'd been correct in at least one of my conclusions. I was beginning to doubt myself. I was also glad Delilah wasn't here as I felt sure the human jukebox would have burst into *'Kingston Town'* with very little encouragement.

'I moved here when I was two,' He continued. 'So I know very little of their ways.'

'So you learnt from your mother?'

'Yes. Voodoo is called Obeah in Jamaica and in most places it is banned. In my mother's village it was still celebrated, privately of course. Her parents wanted her to have the chances they had not and they sent her to a school in Kingston. The village made them outcasts, thinking they had abandoned their religion. But my mother was a proud woman, proud of her roots. She was determined our traditions should live on. In Kingston she was not allowed to practise Voodoo. At eighteen she fell in love with an Englishman. They married quickly and had me. It was hard at that time. My mother was married to an Englishman and she had no loyalty to Kingston, so when he suggested a move to England, she did not object.'

'Do you think these murders have anything to do with Voodoo?'

'If it does, it is no Voodoo that I know of. You'd need a Mambo or a Hongoun to tell you what it is that curses us.'

'So you think it's a curse?'

'Nothing happens quickly in Voodoo, Mr Hetherington. It's all about the preparation, about the timing and appeasing the gods. In Voodoo, revenge is a dish best served cold. There is no resolution without the will of the gods. Murder is not the will of any god my mother told me of.'

I finished my coffee, placed the cup on the side and looked at Elroy who was moulding the little figure back into shape.

'So what you're saying is, if you want to murder someone, Voodoo isn't the quickest solution.'

'Exactly.' He said, smiling at me once more. 'Voodoo is misunderstood. It's to protect not to destroy. The gods do the destroying all on their own.' He laughed.

'Well Mr Tuvey, you've been very helpful, thank you. Apologies again for the clumsiness of my initial questions.'

'Tell me, Mr Hetherington, are you trying to solve another mystery?' he grinned.

'Oh no, no, no. That's a job for the police isn't it?' I shrugged, reluctant to say out loud that I was very curious as to who had murdered the newsagent and the greengrocer, and in fact who would be next.

He laughed. 'I'm sure, but you are interested are you not? And please, call me Elroy,' he said extending his hand. 'You have an enquiring mind, Mr Hetherington, that is a good thing. Life should be questioned! You have not offended me. I will give it some thought. My mother's old books may have an answer for you.'

'Thank you,' I took his hand and shook it firmly. 'You're very kind to humour me.'

'There is plenty of humour in Voodoo, Mr Hetherington.' He smiled back. 'Papa Ghede who guards the crossroads is the biggest joker there is. According to my mother, that is. Come back next week, I will find the books and we can look through them.'

'That would be fantastic, thank you. 'I became aware that I was beaming at him. I was back on the case. The brain was working once more. What would Jane have to say about this? Frankly, I didn't much care.

I left the shop feeling altogether more positive. I was still not sure how much I believed of Voodoo. I didn't know enough to know if this had anything to do with it. As Elroy said, any Hollywood film would have you believe that crosses on doors and tiny models stuck with pins were the epitome of Voodoo but not for Elroy. For him Voodoo was more spiritual. The way he spoke about it was with affection and sentiment in his eyes.

Or was it all a smoke screen: a cover to divert attention away from the true motive for the murders? I couldn't help feeling that the models had to have something to do with it. Even if Voodoo wasn't the way to efficiently murder a person, but then, if someone believes in something enough then anything is possible. A belief that the gods want someone to die, whether or not that god exists or it is their true nature is irrelevant. The belief might just be motive enough for someone to kill. Further investigation couldn't be a complete waste of time. It all just seemed to add up.

My phone started to ring in my pocket. It was Delilah.

'Happy Birthday!' I answered.

'What? Oh, thank you. Never mind that, Rob's just told me he's going to be late to dinner this evening and…

'Shame, you'd think he could get the day off for your birthday.' I interrupted.

'Never mind, never mind, guess why!'

'Why?'

'I just saw Mrs Tudbury while I was walking Bertie.'

'Yes, so why is Rob going to be late?' Delilah's rapid change of subjects was exhausting.

'Well that's why: because there's another cross!'

'Oh.'

'On the baker's.'

'Oh.'

'Well?'

'I hope it doesn't mean the same as the others, I'm rather fond of Albert's almond croissants.' The absence of my almond croissants would be too much to bear. The ones found in the supermarket were not the same. Surely Jane would understand me wanting to solve the case under these circumstances. She enjoyed the croissants as much as, if not more than, myself on her visits to see me.

'Blake! Seriously, can you not think about your stomach for one second? I have no idea how you stay so thin. One look at Albert's croissants and my thighs are two sizes bigger.' Delilah huffed 'What are we going to do about it?'

'I suggest you don't eat the croissants.' Winding Delilah up was too much fun.

'About the cross Blake, as you know damn well.'

'All right, all right no need for that.'

A heavy sigh came from the other end of the phone followed by a beep that indicated my battery was on the way out.

'I've got to deliver Lord Blackwood's hat to him. He hasn't collected it yet, despite his promise to send someone and I'm concerned that with only a week to go I need to know if it needs any adjustment. Could we talk about this together over dinner tonight?'

No reply.

'Delilah?'

No reply.

I pulled the phone away from my ear: no battery. I considered my options. Deliver the hat and incur Delilah's wrath, or go to the model village. I didn't see what staring at another little red cross was going to achieve. I couldn't very well *warn* Mr Pane, it would probably scare him half to death. It was more assumption and coincidence than actual fact. If the police felt he was in danger then it was their job to inform Albert Pane, not mine. I had to draw the line here. No, the warning of victims was surely up to Sergeant Claringdon and I did not want to be arrested for inciting a riot. Besides I could talk to him about this at dinner this evening, presuming he would still be joining us. Delilah was going away to Haiti in two weeks and I doubted very much he'd miss her birthday.

The fact remained that I relied on my commissions to keep me in almond croissants and to allow me to go gallivanting around the village solving mysteries, and therefore protecting the makers of said products. No, there was only one option and that was to take my commission to Lord Blackwood. The third cross would have to wait.

9.

Cheval

**The cheval or horse in Voodoun is used as a metaphor to represent possession.
The spirit is thought to ride the possessed, as a horseman rides his horse.**

Putting the phone back in my pocket, I continued walking back down the High Street to the allotments and my workshop. My journey was delayed further when I noticed Mrs Dellaware and her nephew. They were on the other side of the road by the bus stop, but it was their body language that distracted me from my mission.

Mrs Dellaware was perching on the tiny metal shelf, under the bus stop canopy, that served as a bench and had a hand at each of her temples. Her nephew was bent over her with his hands in his back pockets saying something I couldn't hear. Perhaps it was the awkwardness of the hands in the pockets, the hunched shoulders, the low voice or the pained expression on Mrs Dellaware's face but something about the way he was standing over his aunt made me cross the road and enquire if there was anything I could do to help.

'We're fine thank you, Mr Hetherington.' Mrs Dellaware's expression contradicted her words.

Her clenched jaw, bloodshot eyes and the occasional plucking of her cardigan made me uneasy. It was a cold day and she didn't have a coat on. Neither did her nephew for that matter, in fact he appeared to be wearing slippers; although I am not up with the latest footwear fashion. He was clearly nervous. His hands never moved from his pockets and he barely acknowledged me instead fixing his aunt with a hard look, chewing his lip.

'Are you sure? It's awfully cold out here, how about I walk home with you?' I smiled, painfully aware that her nephew was capable of this, but something in his manner meant I couldn't allow myself to leave the situation.

'My aunt 'as one of her 'eads. She's just resting for a few minutes and then we'll be 'eading 'ome, won't we?' The whole sentence was directed at his aunt.

'Yes, dear.' Constance started to unbutton her cardigan.

As he leant forward slightly with his hands still in his pockets as if restraining himself, Don's voice was also strained; 'You don' want to take that off, it's cold out 'ere.'

I looked at the two of them. Clearly this was something I did not understand. I did not know Constance well enough to intervene further and I definitely knew very little of the nephew.

'Okay. I'll leave you to it then,' I said finally. Awkward didn't quite cover the situation and I didn't want to become a spectator to whatever kind of domestic this was. I had walked a few feet away when the response came from the nephew.

'Thank you, Mr Hetherington.'

I turned and the look of quiet desperation on Donald's face almost made me turn back but he'd made it very clear that this was not my situation to solve, no matter how much I wanted to. What was I going to do: drag Mrs Dellaware off the bus stop seat and down the High Street?

'You're welcome', was all I could reply and I touched my cap.

Don nodded and moved to sit beside his aunt on the bus stop shelf, hands still in his pockets, his slippered feet in a dwindling puddle. He didn't seem to notice.

I walked on down the High Street to the allotments, continuing my journey to collect Lord Blackwood's hat. Mrs Dellaware was certainly a character, there was no denying that, but I'd not seen this behaviour from her before. Apart from the occasional trip to the High Street to catch up on the local gossip, she was somewhat of a recluse. The behaviour I'd just witnessed was as odd as the behaviour in the greengrocer's the other day and I was beginning to worry that maybe Mrs Dellaware was ill.

Arriving at the allotments, I put it to the back of my mind. On entering my shed I noticed the red light on the phone blinking at me, indicating a message. I pressed play and went across to the workbench to pick up the box that enclosed Lord Blackwood's hat. I was very pleased with the way the fedora had turned out and I hoped Blackwood would also be pleased.

'You hung up on me, Blake!' Delilah's voice interrupted my moment of reflection and pride. 'It's my birthday! I'm going out for a walk with Bertie, I'll deal with you later.'

I laughed at this last comment. I'd never heard Delilah so affronted. I had to laugh; it was, after all, her birthday. And what could I honestly do about it? Time was getting on and I did not wish to delay my task further. I knew she would be out, she had just told me so, mobile reception in her village was next to non-existent, so I decided to ring her when I got back from Lord Blackwood's to apologise.

I set off up the road once more towards the Blackwood's estate, stopping in at the house to collect my cane. The walk wasn't far but my foot was beginning to ache from the yo-yoing trips up and down the High Street. My daughter had given me a new cane for Christmas. It was from New Zealand, where she'd holidayed last year, and the handle was carved in wood from a tree called a Tawa. A very handsome totem carving composed of little faces, which, I am reliably informed by Jane, is called a Tekoteko. A twist in the wood follows the stick down to a very practical rubber ferrule. Through the hole in the top of the stick is a leather strap and threaded onto this is the thing I love most about the stick: a little bone charm in the shape of a leaf. I think she'd been rather pleased that she'd been able to give me something suitable for a man of my age. I'm not sure how I felt about it but it was a work of art and useful to boot: beautiful and practical.

The persistent cold wind made for a bracing walk and by the time I arrived at the Blackwood estate I was pink cheeked and my extremities had lost their feeling. The trees on the estate had no buds as yet and the bare branches were still spider-black against the clear blue sky of the afternoon.

I could hear the snort of a horse and the scratchy sweep of a tough bristled yard broom as I entered the stable complex situated to the side of the house. I hoped to find a member of the yard staff to take the hat off my hands. Instead I found Lord Blackwood himself leaning against a half open saloon stable door: even better. He was talking to a chocolate brown horse. It had a star of white hair just above its nose and its ears were listening intently. Little clouds of warm air left its nostrils as it huffed its reply.

Hearing my footsteps, he pushed himself upright with the foot of his bent leg on the stable door. My smart brogues had not been the best idea I thought as I negotiated the horse manure littering the path. It took me by surprise; Blackwood's stables were usually immaculate.

'Blake!' He extended a hand, his familiar dark eyes twinkling with a smile and his hair, once dark, now a silvery grey, just visible under his riding hat.

I met his hand as I stepped the last few feet towards the stable.

'Lord Blackwood.' I hadn't called him Rufus since we were children.

'Rufus please, you know I don't like you calling me that. We've known each other long enough.'

I nodded. The Blackwood family estate had been here for centuries. Rufus had spent most of his working life travelling, occasionally returning to the village for holidays on the estate. Finally he had returned to Tuesbury on early retirement. Unfortunately for Rufus, his wife of thirty-five years had died in a riding accident only two weeks after they arrived. Over a decade ago, it still made the estate a sad place to be. Childless, Rufus invested his time in his horses.

'I see you've brought my hat. That's very kind of you. I meant to send Danny down, but I've had to let him go.'

'Really?' Danny had been one of the Blackwood's longest standing members of staff. He'd run the stables for almost twenty years and consistently trained Rufus' thoroughbreds to win.

'I caught him hitting Tipingee', he said reaching out to stroke the muzzle of the chocolate brown mare. She snorted. 'Damn shame, he was a fine trainer and yardsman, I doubt I'll find another like him but I won't have my animals abused, Blake.'

I smiled. I knew this was true. When we were young he would rescue worms from dry banks, placing them back in the long wet grass and carefully capture moths as they flapped against a closed window and release them.

He had even had a pet squirrel that he fed diligently every day. The man was a veritable Dr Doolittle.

'Well, let's have a look at your masterpiece then.' He reached forward for the hatbox.

He took it and I took the opportunity to rub my hands together and regain some of the feeling.

'I'm sorry, where are my manners, you'll come in for a drink, won't you?'

'That would be very nice,' I said and checked my watch for the time. 'I'd best be back in the village by four thirty at the lastest though. It's Delilah's birthday and we're off out for a meal to celebrate.'

'Still hanging around with that young thing, are you, Blake? I don't blame you, keeps you young, I just wonder where I might get a young filly like that from?'

I did not reply, Rufus knew very well the relationship between Delilah and me was purely friendship and nothing more, but he liked to tease me about it. Protesting would only encourage him.

Once inside, we entered the very grand drawing room. An inglenook fireplace had the smouldering embers of a fire, which soon roared into life as Rufus threw another log on. A big ginger cat was draped across the back of an exquisite velvet-upholstered, mahogany-footed sofa, and it lazily opened one eye to examine us as we entered. The pale blue faded fabric was covered in a waterfall of ginger cat hairs. The parquet floor was covered in what Rufus had told me were replica Victorian chinoiserie carpets; in keeping with the house's one hundred and twenty years of occupancy by the Blackwoods.

Rufus was a firm believer in the preservation of history and tradition. He also believed in harnessing natural energy. Much to the villagers' disgust, three years ago, Rufus had turned his field at the far end of the estate over to solar panels. The field backed onto Druid Wood and the panels ran the power to the stables. The local dog walkers had been up in arms at the change of use of the field. Rufus had, up until that point, turned a blind eye to their regular walks across private land where no footpath existed. Consequently, he had a few disgruntled villagers to contend with if he ever ventured onto the High Street.

'This is splendid, Blake!' Rufus was sat on the sofa with the cat lounging behind him. 'Sit down, sit down, don't stand on ceremony,' he said, indicating the Edwardian mahogany upright chair. The tired and worn dark green upholstery added to its charm. The same furniture had been in this room for as long as I could remember.

'Whisky?' he asked, standing up and walking towards the little teak drinks cabinet on the far side of the room. He'd abandoned the fedora on the sofa where it was in grave danger of ginger fur falling from above. I tried to ignore it. It was his hat now, to do with as he pleased. The grandfather clock chimed half past the hour breaking my obsession with the troublesome cat hair.

Three-thirty. Not too early to have a drink with an old friend I thought.

'Yes, that would be very nice.' I leant over the arm of the chair and held my hands to the fire to warm them. I took in the history of the room once more and Rufus poured our drinks. I hadn't been in this room for possibly forty years. A painting of Rufus' great grandfather hung above the drinks cabinet. His austere and sombre expression denounced the room. A vase of Alstroemeria had been stood on the small writing desk, the exquisite marquetry of which had fascinated me as a child.

'Can I take your coat?' He handed me a nip of Talisker. I'd always liked the smoky taste of the island whisky and Rufus always had some to hand.

'I think I'll keep it for now, it's cold out there today and I haven't warmed up yet.'

'It's our bones, old friend,' he said. 'Not as good at holding the heat as they used to be. You'll soon warm up by the fire,' he smiled. 'Can't beat a good fire.'

I smiled back. He placed his whisky glass on the mantelpiece above the inglenook and went back to the fedora. Placing it on his head he stood in front of the six-foot by three-foot mirror hanging over the fireplace. Pulling it forward slightly he admired himself.

'It's rather wonderful!' He grinned and took up his whisky again to take a sip. The fan of purple and royal blue fabric shone against the silk black of the hatband. His grey hair was almost silver against the fawn coloured felt of the fedora and his eyes creased in delight as he fingered the little tiny purple and blue fabric buttons. A fedora was the ultimate accessory for any man that fancied himself a peacock. You couldn't help but be reminded of the nineteen sixties gangster films, the square-jawed alpha male, trailing cigarette smoke from beneath the black-felted, white-banded fedora of his tribe. There were certain hats that demanded to be taken seriously. The fedora was one such hat.

I sipped my whisky and felt it warm my throat and chest.

'Do you remember the times we played gangsters on the lawn here?' Rufus said.

'I do, and I remember beating you.'

'A scandalous lie, Blake! I let you win! You're two years my junior after all.'

We laughed.

'It suits you, Rufus. I'm glad you like it. Does it fit comfortably?'

'Like a glove, Blake, I wouldn't expect anything else. You are the king of hats after all.' He winked. 'I'll write you a cheque, will that be okay?'

'Of course.' I finished the last of my whisky as Rufus wrote the cheque still wearing his new hat. It was wonderful to see that kind of schoolboy joy on a customer's face. It was a milliner's job to capture a client's personality and crown them with it. I'd done my job.

The clock chimed quarter to. I'd only been there fifteen minutes; just long enough to get the feeling back in my hands. The whisky had gone to my head slightly and Rufus was offering me more. I could easily have stayed there all afternoon reminiscing over old times, getting to know each other again, but I had a birthday meal to attend, despite Delilah's threats.

'I'd better be going, I'm afraid,' I said, as Rufus approached, whisky bottle held forth.

'Ah yes, the lovely Delilah.' He winked.

'Ruuufus!' I stood up, adjusted my jacket and put my gloves back on.

'Bring her to Cheltenham. I have a spare ticket and, while you're at it, ask her if she's got a friend who likes Talisker and horses.'

'You always were a ladies man, Rufus. One track mind.'

'Winning, Blake, that's my game. Winning and women.' He chuckled to himself.

'I have no idea how your wife put up with you.' I knew there was no way Eleanor would have put up with a wandering eye.

'She was a good woman,' Rufus replied, downing another shot of whisky. Sadness had returned to his countenance. 'The best.'

I nodded.

'Nevertheless, I think Delilah may wish to take Sergeant Claringdon to Cheltenham rather than myself.'

'I see, you have a rival! Well, I'm sure we can get him a ticket too, if he wants.'

I ignored the obvious attempt to bait me once more, 'Okay, you're on,' I smiled. It would be nice to have a day out together, and Rob surely couldn't object to a free ticket to the races.

'Don't leave it so long next time,' Rufus continued, 'it's always good to see you up here.'

'And you're always welcome at the Little Acorns.' I returned.

'Touché,' he acknowledged. Neither of us were good at keeping up our friendship despite the conversations we enjoyed when we did meet.

I left the warmth of the Blackwood's drawing room with a cheque in my pocket and a glow in my heart. That's why I made hats. The joy on Rufus' face made all the tiny stitches worthwhile.

I was home by five past four. The table at Grande Amore was booked for seven p.m. I went to ring Delilah to apologise. Picking up the phone, I could hear the familiar intermittent beep of the answer-phone. I rang one-five-seven-one and listened.

'So you're out. I've been trying to ring your mobile for the last hour but it's off. I suppose you've run out of battery. No wonder Jane gets so annoyed with you. Ring me when you get in - it's Delilah.'

I rang. Thankfully Delilah had recovered from her sulk and was once more excited about her birthday meal. Rob had secured the evening off although he would have to leave if work called. No rest for the wicked, as Delilah said, although I wasn't sure what she was implying. I explained the situation with the phone, the delight of my old friend on trying on his hat and the extra tickets to Cheltenham, and we finished our conversation on good terms once more.

I busied myself with the pre-dinner preparations: showering, ironing a shirt and wrapping Delilah's present. I ordered a taxi and went out to wait for it. I was looking forward to a large meal and lively conversation with friends. Life was good and I'd almost forgotten the horrors of the AA box. In fact, I had almost forgotten about the whole grisly business of the murders; that was, until the next day.

10.

Rara

A Voodoun dance festival occurring in the spring.

Over dinner that night there had been the inevitable discussion about the new cross on the door of the miniature baker's in Little Tuesbury. Rob was keen to play it down as a childish prank and an unfortunate coincidence. He laughed at the idea of Voodoo and assured us that a coshing and a strangling were down to opportunity rather than the occult. I mentioned my thoughts about the differing methods to him and suggested that it required a different sort of person to commit each murder. His answer: *'In my experience, the mind of a psychopath is not always logical.'* I did not push the subject further mainly because the image of Patrick Davies' bloated body was not one I wanted while I was trying to enjoy my dinner.

Despite Rob's protestations, Delilah was altogether more interested in the Voodoo angle and questioned me intently. She chastised me for not taking her to see Elroy, especially as it had been her birthday. In her preparation for the dig in Haiti she had been reading about the culture of the area and in particular the Voodoun religion. She confirmed what Mr Tuvey had said about good and bad Voodoo. *'They are called Rada and Petro,'* she'd said, *'like black and white magic'*. She agreed that Voodoo was used to protect in the main and had gained a bad name from westerners, suspicious of its use by slaves, who were actually only trying to protect themselves from their oppressors. Not understanding the religion, they saw it as dangerous or evil. Hollywood, later, did nothing to contradict this opinion. Fear and misunderstanding, are far more emotive than embracing a new culture.

'But it can still be used for nefarious purposes.' I said as we were finishing our main.

'Of course, but Elroy's right - it's a slow burn. It normally involves possession, zombies and magical death stupors,' Delilah replied.

'Well, Harold and Patrick were definitely not in a stupor.'

The conversation changed. Rob stated firmly that he did not want to talk about work any more and was keen to impress upon us that we should not interfere with the investigation. I assured him we would keep a healthy distance and instead, started to ask Delilah about her birthday presents. As if by magic the waiter appeared with a tiramisu complete with sparkler and the whole restaurant sang, 'Happy Birthday'.

We returned to our respective homes sated and warm with wine.

The following morning, Delilah drove across from Deerton to take Bertie for his walk in the woods. I was to join them. Deerton had perfectly serviceable footpaths and walks but since the murder of Harold Salter in Druid Wood, Tuesbury had become infinitely more preferable to Delilah. Her excuse was that while she was away in Haiti I would be walking Bertie, and Bertie needed to get used to his new walk routine. I was pretty sure Bertie wasn't bothered which woods he was walked in, as long as there was plenty to sniff.

Getting up so early to walk Bertie had been a challenge after glasses of Prosecco and half a bottle of Delilah's favourite Gavi with the meal: a refreshing grape but somewhat less palatable the next day. It was Sunday and another fresh morning, with more clear, blue skies. We were tantalisingly close to spring and yet the bitter cold wind still whipped through the trees.

On the way through the woods, Delilah brought up Rob's dismissive attitude towards the Voodoo angle. I hadn't given it much thought. She clearly had. She was worried that Rob had offended me.

'Not at all, Delilah. Why on earth would he offend me? It's a fanciful idea, Voodoo, really, I think I need my head checked for even thinking about it.'

'I think you're onto something though.' She persisted. 'Rob's just being churlish because, after the murder of Mr Davies, Chief Inspector Gabbett took over the case.'

'Oh, so he's been taken off the case?'

'No, no, he's still working on it. It's just that this Gabbett's putting pressure on him. What with that and Knighton…'

I'd had the misfortune of meeting Inspector Knighton last year and if he was anything to go by, then two of him, was not something I wanted to have to suffer. I felt for Rob's plight and hoped I was not adding to it with my idle verbal meanderings over dinner.

As I returned to the village the church bells were calling for the ten-thirty family service. I hadn't attended church since Eleanor had died. Church always felt like a family occasion to me. I still enjoyed hearing the bells. Mavis Peterson had tried to cajole me into joining the bell ringers, but I had enough to do on the allotment: there was only so much physical exercise an aging body could take.

I had stopped at the shed to check for messages. I rarely had any on a Sunday but just occasionally someone thought I might be working. This meant we were approaching the green from the south side, from the direction of the allotments.

To the left of the green the local Morris dancers were practising. The tiny bells on their shins could not be heard over the clamouring of the church bells. A small pond lay between us and the orchard and Bertie now rushed towards it, sending a duck flying into the air quacking and squawking in indignation. A few pigeons were also startled and narrowly missed some of the Morris dancers in their trajectory. On the opposite side of the green is a small community orchard, made up of about thirty trees. There are two benches on the edge of the orchard facing the green dedicated to the orchard's benefactors, and I could see someone sitting on one of them. They had something on their head. It didn't look like a hat, but I couldn't be sure. Most peculiar. I put it to the back of my mind considering it might easily not be a person and instead a Green Man the school children had made in preparation for the May Fair. Even so, what was it doing just sitting on the green when the May Fair was over a month away?

Drawing level with the Morris dancers, I stopped to watch and Delilah ran after Bertie: an attempt to stop him leaping in the pond. She was only a few feet away and I could hear her shouting over the church bells as she stood by the edge of the pond.

'Bertie, no!'

I knew Bertie did not understand *'no'*, or if he did, he chose to ignore it, and knowing it would take her some time to retrieve him I settled myself by leaning against the maypole to watch the Morris dancers practise.

I focused on the men in their white suits, their rainbow tassels, the concentration on their faces, the rise and fall of the hankies, and I saw that Donald was amongst them. I was impressed that he seemed to have embraced one of the traditions of village life so easily. From my position I could also see people heading towards the church on the other side of the High Street and the figure still sitting on the bench.

Half past ten and the bells stopped, bringing peace once more to the green. The knocking of sticks indicated a second dance was about to start and, in between the bells, I could just hear Delilah shouting at Bertie.

'You're going to be in so much trouble when you get out of there.'

If he did understand full sentences, this was hardly an enticing proposition for the Jack Russell. Another minute or so passed and, due to an absence of ducks, Bertie finally dragged himself out of the pond. I went to walk over to join them but Donald called me from the other side of the Morris men. He was sitting, or rather standing this dance out and he was taking advantage of the break with a cigarette.

'Mr 'etherington,'

I walked round the group of dancers as he was extending a hand. To do anything else would have been rude.

'I didn't get a chance to introduce myself properly the other day. I'm Donald Yveny, Mrs Dellaware's nephew.'

'Hello,' I met his outstretched hand, 'and I'm Mr Hetherington, as you know.'

'Yes.'

His hands were warm from the dancing, unlike my own. His cheeks were pink and flushed with exercise and his blond hair ruffled in the breeze.

'Thank you for your 'elp yesterday; my aunt 'ad one of 'er 'eads. Sometimes she just needs to get out.' He smiled.

'I see.' This had been his explanation yesterday and I was still unsure as to the dynamic between the two of them. The need to get out was clearly strong if there was no time to change one's footwear. I was pleased to see Mr Yveny wearing more suitable shoes today.

'Are you a fan of the Morris men, Mr 'etherington?'

'They are very entertaining. Have you been Morris dancing long?' I continued, glad of the change of subject.

'Only a couple of months. They 'aven't let me loose with the sticks yet, just 'ankies. I don't blame them. You can easily break fingers with a misplaced stick.'

'Indeed!'

It wasn't until now, talking one on one, that I noticed he had a thick accent. It was almost French.

'Are you French, Mr Yveny? I only ask as I spent a lot of time in France myself,' I ventured.

'Creole, Mr 'etherington, not de same.'

'No, of course not,' I blushed at my ignorance and was saved from the growing embarrassment as my eye was alerted to Delilah and Bertie, now on the far side of the field near the orchard and the figure sitting on the bench. 'The Antilles, then?'

'Yes, Trinidad. I think your friend's calling you, Mr 'etherington.' Yveny was looking in Delilah's direction.

I squinted. She was waving both arms in the air frantically and Bertie was sitting with his back to us, barking at the Green Man on the bench, which was eliciting no response. 'I think she is.'

'Am I 'earing 'er correctly?' he said.

'I'm not sure.'

The clacking of the Morris men's sticks stopped and they all turned to see what the commotion was.

'I think she said *"elp, 'e's dead"*,' he finished.

'What?'

'Oui,' he replied mater-of-factly.

I started a brisk walk across the grass to where Delilah was standing. I could see her clutching the man's wrist and shaking his shoulder shouting, *'Mr Pane!'* He was not responding. Always the drama queen, I rather imagined when I got there, Pane would be cursing Delilah for awaking him from an afternoon nap.

The baker was slumped on the bench in his white apron. Cigarettes littered the grass beneath the seat, where they had fallen from an empty packet, also under the bench. A solitary cigarette remained in the stiff bent fingers of his hand. Possibly his favourite smoking spot, for I knew Mrs Pane disapproved of the habit. His white apron was, bizarrely, over the top of his wax jacket and black jeans and across the pocket was a red cross. Stranger still was the addition of a wreath of ivy on his head. A Green Man indeed, but not one made by school children, although Pane looked equally stuffed.

As Delilah shook his shoulder his head fell back and his eyes opened. I placed my hand on the side of his neck to feel for a pulse. His collar was stiff from the early morning frost. Mr Pane was, absolutely, dead, it did not take a medical professional to recognise the blue lips and blotchy purple pallor of a dead man and the total absence of a pulse.

Why was it always us? Why couldn't the Morris men have paid more attention and discovered Mr Pane. He had clearly been here for some time. Did nobody else notice? This was becoming an embarrassing habit and I felt sure the emergency operators must have known my voice as I rang the familiar number once more.

Thankfully there were over half a dozen Morris men to back up our story when Sergeant Claringdon arrived. This time he acknowledged Delilah and suggested that we all wait in the village hall where a police officer would come and take statements from us.

The village green was cordoned off just in time for the end of the church service and a healthy congregation of onlookers. A police officer did join us in the hall to take statements, which titillated the exiting congregation further. The village hall had a sudden increase in the use of its facilities until a second officer arrived and stood by the door, putting a stop to the weak-bladdered, rubberneckers.

Delilah was unfortunately suffering from what, if I were a little less compassionate, might be termed verbal diarrhoea. The effect of discovering Mr Pane, dead as a doornail, had sent her imagination into overdrive.

'I told you that little cross meant something, and now there's one on his apron too. Rob wouldn't believe me, but it's just too much of a coincidence,' she was saying. I was restricting my responses to nodding at various intervals, a) reluctant to join in with speculation at this point while a police officer was watching, and b) unable to get a word in edgeways.

'I wonder how he died? Was he just strangled like Davies? I didn't see any hand marks though, did you? And footprints, I couldn't see any although it is very muddy. Oh no! Did Bertie and I smudge them? I hope not. Maybe they are behind the bench. I didn't go behind the bench. That's how they would have approached if they were going to strangle him.'

I took a breath, about to speak, but wasn't quick enough.

'I know how important it is in archaeology to preserve scenes. I can't believe I just traipsed up to him like that. They'll probably only find my footprints now and of course little Bertie's.' She leant to scratch Bertie's head, but continued talking. 'Rob's going to have to listen to us now and we'd better go and see Tuvey again. I think there's something in this Voodoo. It's just too much of a coincidence: the models, the crosses...'

'Delilah!' I raised my hand and she finally stopped. Bertie shuffled beside her. The whole time he hadn't left her side, he just sat watching her, taking it all in. Perhaps he did understand full sentences after all. 'I really think we need to leave this to the police.'

'But....' She started. I took her hand and squeezed it.

'Three murders, Delilah! *Three!* I don't think this person's sane, do you? Do you honestly think they aren't going to consider a similar fate for us if we interfere?'

'That's what Rob said,' came a downhearted reply.

I wanted to get to the bottom of this as much as Delilah did but I didn't want to draw attention to ourselves any more than we already had. It was time to take an altogether more subtle approach to this investigation and, unfortunately, that might mean leaving Delilah out of the loop. I needed to keep her safe. If we could just get through the next week without another body, she would be in Haiti and out of harm's way.

11.

The Ancestral Loa

Loa are powerful spirits of the dead. Ancestral Loa are spirits passed down through the generations.

The day of the Cheltenham festival arrived: more crisp blue sky, but this time accompanied by threatening grey clouds. We'd agreed to meet Lord Blackwood at the racecourse and he'd left us tickets at the booking desk. Rob offered to drive.

Delilah appeared to have recovered from the previous day's events although I wasn't sure it had all sunk in. The persistent questioning from the police officer showed he was clearly interested in her association, not only with the victim, but also with Sergeant Claringdon. Questions like *'And how much wine did you consume with your meal last night?'* were a bit beyond the pale when establishing an alibi. I may have thought that he was trying to decide if she'd drunk enough to drive back and kill Mr Pane in between courses, or even suggesting that Rob had drunk enough to fall asleep early and therefore invalidate her alibi. However, he did not ask me the same questions and I could just as easily have been in the frame for this one.

She held up well in the face of these questions and throughout referred to Rob as Sergeant Claringdon. She was far from stupid and she knew how potentially undermining it was for Rob having his girlfriend questioned in a murder investigation.

Today, Delilah had not disappointed with her outfit. Unfortunately, the appearance of an atrocious hatinator had. Anyone who saw Delilah in her normal everyday work attire of jeans, Doc Martin's, a muddy fleece and long sleeved t-shirt would not expect her to dress in such a frivolous fashion outside work. Despite my belief that first impressions are rarely wrong, they can also be deceptive. I learnt early on that should she wish to be, Delilah was the master of playing the damsel. Only once had I seen Delilah truly upset and that had involved a large amount of wine and a direct threat to her beloved Bertie.

Today she wore a cobalt blue shift dress with a lace overlay. I knew a little about women's fashion; one has to know about outfits in order to find the correct hat. Many a day in the shop spent listening to ladies describing ensembles and what sort of hats they wanted to go with them, provided me with ample information to recognise an expensive shift dress when I saw one. I was also pleased to see she was wearing the necklace I had bought her for her birthday and the tiny, silver, Jack Russell earrings that Rob had given her. It was still cold and she wore a smart beige tailored jacket with shoes and clutch bag to match. It was a lovely outfit until, that is, one looked at the hatinator.

In the same colour as the dress, the hatinator comprised a flouncy bow that would have taken some skill to make that ugly. At the centre of the bow was what I think was supposed to be a rose shape with white piping to edge it. Now perhaps I'm being mean-spirited, after all, Delilah could make most things look good. But the fact that money can be made in making something that looks quite so shocking is a real bugbear of mine: not a hat and not a fascinator, just ugly. I don't like fascinators either! For me there is no fascination. Hats make much more of a statement. Of course, a hatinator does too, just rarely the right one.

Rob was wearing a pinstriped double-breasted suit with brogues. Myself: I'd dug out my tweed suit. An old favourite bought for me by Eleanor the year before she fell ill. It still amazed me that it fitted. In fairness, it is so much easier for men when dressing for occasions. It normally involves a suit and you either wear a hat or you don't, none of this half-hearted flouncy hatinator nonsense.

I don't normally wear hats, other than my cap to keep out the cold. Ironic I know, but today I had chosen to wear a dark brown trilby. I'd made it for myself last year as a retirement present. I'd kept it fairly plain. I used a very fine brown felt and a silk forest green ribbon with a tiny gold yellow feather tucked in the band. Gold had always been Eleanor's favourite colour. I'm not sure why I had never bothered to wear a hat before. Could it be that spending my days surrounded by them satisfied my need to wear one?

This was the hat's second outing and it was proving rather useful. It was shading my eyes from the sun as I read the programme. When it did break through the clouds it was bright and angry, affronted by the commotion below on the racetrack as it sauntered east to west.

Tipingee was running in the fourth race, which gave us plenty of time to visit the hospitality suite for gin and tonic. It was starting to feel like spring. The smell of fresh grass was in the air and the general din on the course was cheery and hopeful. We finally caught up with Rufus. It was his hat I spotted first and its proud silk fan, a peacock of silk in a sea of heads. Bets were placed and he took us to a private box he had hired especially for the occasion, where we were introduced to some of his friends before we settled. The diplomatic corps certainly provided you with a good pension if you could afford private boxes and racehorses.

The programme informed me that the first race was to begin at one-thirty and that this was the jump race season. This was only my second visit to a racecourse but the experience of a private box was luxurious compared to the jostling and cheering I'd experienced along the side of the course. This experience was definitely more civilised. There were still about twenty people in the box. Trainers (Danny was conspicuous by his absence), sponsors and friends were all there for Tipingee's debut.

There were five of us sitting in a group of lounge chairs to the back of the box and we talked as the first two races thundered by, the pounding hooves echoing in the box. Rob was sitting on the edge of his seat looking uncomfortable as he listened to Delilah. His knee wouldn't stay still and he kept checking his phone. It is my understanding that, during murder investigations, you are never off duty.

Delilah was making conversation with the other ladies in the box. She was entertaining them with amusing quips about her archaeological endeavours: an animated Miss Baltimore-Whitby whose mother and father were sponsoring Tipingee, and a silent, interesting woman called Mrs Darensky. I was later to learn the latter was Rufus' fiancée. A fact he'd kept very quiet. Easily twenty years his junior, her manners were impeccable. Sitting with her knees together, not crossing her legs, holding a Martini delicately between the thumb and forefinger of a white lace gloved hand, smiling and nodding occasionally. I recognised a woman who didn't work when I saw one. And Mrs Darensky was just that. Her career was being a kept woman. Her French manicured nails beneath the see-through gloves indicated she did not partake in manual labour.

My observations were interrupted by a shriek from Miss Baltimore-Whitby. Botox prevented her face from creasing, and in turn the observer from gaining a clue that she was in fact laughing: an odd effect as she dabbed her eyes with a tiny silk hanky. The little dog in her handbag jumped.

'That's a riot, darling, how do you cope with all those men?' she gasped. The dog barked. 'Shush Wilson, someone will notice you,' she gently pushed the tiny head back into the bag and fussed over it.

'Did I hear a dog?' Rufus appeared from the front of the box where he'd been extolling the virtues of Tipingee and reassuring Mr and Mrs Baltimore-Whitby that the loss of his trainer would not mean the loss of the race.

Miss Baltimore-Whitby, her hands in her lap, looked up at Lord Blackwood. Rob was still looking at his phone, oblivious to the commotion.

Delilah coughed, 'I have a terrible cold I'm afraid, Lord Blackwood. Must be the weather.'

'Sounds quite bad; please, call me Rufus.' He leant forward and peered at the bag, which Miss Baltimore-Whitby had clasped almost shut.

'Ver did you say you were from, Delilah, dear?' Mrs Darensky spoke. Her accent was soft, and her manner was languid.

'Deerton.'

'And dat is…?' Her gloved hand waved delicately in the air, demanding elaboration.

'About two miles from Tuesbury.' Delilah was now sitting up straight, knees together, mirroring Mrs Darensky's body language.

'Ah, Tuesbury. Rufus tells me there have been some terrible murders there. T'ree, I read this morning, correct?'

'Yes. We found Mr Pane yesterday.'

It had been in the morning papers. *'Star baker, found dead.'*

'We?' Mrs Darensky emphasised the 'w' but remained unmoved.

Miss Baltimore-Whitby was transfixed, hands clasped on the bag

'Yes, Blake and I.'

Mrs Darensky turned her eye to me. She could see I was uncomfortable. She had ignored Sergeant Claringdon and myself completely until this moment. Rob was nearest to her and was now looking disapprovingly at Delilah, who had the good sense to stop talking. It appeared that his anxiety had not been unwarranted.

Mrs Darensky leant forward, lips parted slightly to speak again, but whatever she was going to say, was never said.

'I can assure you all, the police are dealing with the investigation and are currently pursuing a variety of avenues.' Rob said. The phrase was mechanical, off pat. His voice cut through the surrounding conversations with authority.

'Oh, how masterful.' Miss Baltimore-Whitby chimed, fanning herself with her hand.

'And who are you?' Mrs Darensky asked.

'Sergeant Claringdon, Madam, of the Warwickshire police.'

'I see.' She delicately tidied the edge of her skirt and shuffled her feet to the left, leaning closer to Rob. 'You can enlighten us then, Sergeant Claringdon.' The last two words were elongated, deliberate.

Delilah was looking decidedly uncomfortable in the presence of such unabashed flirtation, but Rob was unmoved.

'I am not at liberty to discuss the case.'

'Well then, we shall have to make up our own little stories.' Miss Baltimore-Whitby's voice chimed in.

Rob did not rise to this challenge.

'Come on ladies, I think we should leave the sergeant alone. He's here to enjoy himself.' Rufus said from where he stood beside me. He had been as silent as I had, in this whole exchange. 'Matilda dear, it won't be long until Tipingee's race, come and watch with me.'

Mrs Darensky rose from the chair, gliding effortlessly to take Rufus' outstretched hand.

'You coming, old man?' Rufus said, winking at me.

I followed; we were, after all, here to watch the horses. I left Delilah at the mercy of Rob's glare and the undiluted thanks of Miss Baltimore-Whitby for saving her dog from eviction.

At the front of the box there were several other people drinking and talking, waiting for the fourth race to start. Mrs Darensky moved to speak to a gentleman in his forties wearing a navy blue windowpane suit and holding a glass of champagne. There was a cacophony of hooves and snorting they horses went by to line up for the race. I could just about hear Rufus when he said,

'Lovely, isn't she?' he said looking at his fiancée rather than Tipingee, as I was.

Momentarily confused, all I could think to say on both accounts was, 'Very exotic, Rufus.'

'She'll look after me Blake. She knows which side her bread's buttered on.'

Looking in the direction of Mrs Darensky, I raised an eyebrow.

'Oh come on, I'm not stupid. I have no children, no wife, who's going to look after me in my old age?'

'You could be honest about it and employ someone.' I said.

'Who wants an interfering nurse? No, Matilda is a far more interesting option.'

'I see.'

'I often wonder what would have happened if I'd had children.'

I said nothing. What do you reply to that?

'There's no one to take on the estate, once I'm gone. It makes me sad to think Matilda would probably sell it, but what else am I to do?'

'Just because you have children doesn't guarantee they will follow in your footsteps,' I said remembering my own daughter's reaction to the suggestion she take over the millinery business.

'True, true. But if I'd had a son, at least there'd be another Blackwood somewhere.'

'That I can relate to,' I said. There would be no more Hetheringtons either.

'I should start being honest with myself. There is something I can do about it.' He frowned, raising his binoculars to his eyes. 'They are lining up. Tipingee's raring to go. That's my girl!' He was excited and happy again.

'Look. Look, there they are!' The distinctive voice of Miss Baltimore-Whitby announced her arrival with Delilah and Rob, at the front of the box and everyone jostled for position.

Bang. The race was off.

12.

Morts

The collective noun for the dead

A week on and the papers seemed to know more about the case than the police. The seven days had not gone by without various complaints voiced by Delilah at her ban from amateur sleuthing. Rob had told her straight, that it was embarrassing that his girlfriend had such a fascination with dead bodies and a propensity for finding them. She'd suggested that part of being an archaeologist meant she encountered plenty of dead people and he didn't mind that. Rob remained unmoved on the matter, and consequently went up in my estimation. Any man who could remain unaffected by Delilah's persistent nature had my utmost respect. Delilah did heed Rob's warning shots: for me, an indication of her feelings for the sergeant, and she stayed well away from the murder investigation.

Instead, our time had been filled with long walks in Druid Wood with Bertie and, at Delilah's insistence, the occasional stop at the scene of the first murder, which was now looking much as it had for the last hundred years. The tape was long gone and all that remained was a fallen tree, which Delilah rested on to take in the atmosphere. I despaired.

This morning I had a new a commission I was working on, for a sixtieth birthday. A rise in temperature signalled the arrival of spring. Today I relied only on tea for warmth rather than the expensive fan heater.

I was indulging in a little deduction as I worked the stitches on the brim of the extravagant Derby-style hat. Thinking couldn't possibly interfere with Rob's investigation, surely? I had been surreptitiously removing articles from the paper with regard to the three murders and keeping them in an envelope in my bedside table. I say *surreptitiously* because I knew it would only take the slightest provocation, the mere notion that I may be still interested in the murders, for Delilah to resume her investigation. I fear this would land her in the custody of her paramour as he fought to maintain his official role. I admit I have the capacity to blunder into situations; I still cringe at the thought of my conversation with Elroy Tuvey, but I have age and experience on my side, and subtlety, contrary to appearances, is not beyond my capability.

My papier-mâché style investigations were almost discovered yesterday when Delilah and Bertie had lunch with me at Little Acorns. I was making the sandwiches in the kitchen and I heard my name. Returning to the living room I discovered Delilah peering at me through a hole in the obituary section of yesterday's Evening Standard.

'What's this?' she said. The smirk on her face indicating she thought she had found me out.

Thankfully the old brain cells were working on a hundred per cent that day, 'An old school friend died, thought I'd send a card.'

'Oh, sorry.' She looked suitably embarrassed and pretended to read the opposite page - the dating columns. I was relieved to get away with it so lightly.

Tomorrow Delilah would be off to Haiti and this evening she was holding an exhibition of her work in the village hall as a going away party. It would have been foolish to stir the whole thing up again just before she went away.

When she and Bertie left, the paper was still open on the coffee table. My interest had long been with the obituaries. Age brings with it a certain level of morbid curiosity. The dating columns held no interest to me. The obituaries and the lost and found sections had so much more story behind them. My eye was drawn to the bottom of the page and to a small *buy and sell* section. Again, I'd never paid attention this section before, but the words PRINCE and SPANIEL leapt out at me.

FREE TO GOOD HOME
Cocker Spaniel named Prince
five years old. Needs a new
loving family due to change
in owners circumstances.
Ring Tuesbury 355 266

The newsagent's number: I knew this because I often ordered my paper over the phone. I had cut the advert out and placed it with the other newspaper clippings in the drawer. It seemed strange to me that Steve would want to get rid of a beloved pet.

Now, as I stitched the brim of the Derby, I pondered the significance of this advert further. It had been almost a month since the first death. I'd seen Steve in the newsagent's a couple of times since he'd asked for my help, but thankfully the subject remained closed. Prince was asleep on the beanbag where he'd always been. Admittedly he had looked as dejected as any dog might after the loss of one of its pack, but he hadn't seemed to be any trouble. There were many options that ran through my brain at the time. Could it be that Prince was a reminder of Harold, or maybe Steve had never liked dogs and it was Harold's idea to have one? Either way Prince's days in the newsagent's were numbered.

The death of Harold Salter was still unsolved. The papers had quickly become bored with the hate crime angle and started to dig further into Harold's personal life. Amongst other vagaries, the newspaper claimed he liked to bet on the horses and that, in his youth, he'd worked as a stripper in a nightclub in London. There was a garish photoshopped picture of someone that if you squinted may have been Harold but I very much doubted its authenticity. It didn't ring true. The only person who could tell me was Steve and questions such as this would either offend or suggest that I was investigating as he had requested. Neither were good options.

The face of Mr Davies still haunted me in the early hours of the morning and I'd wake in a cold sweat needing water. It was the violence of his death that had stayed with me. When I finally visited the greengrocer's again, the other day, Mrs Davies had told me, without provocation that the police had found that the car had been tampered with. How had the killer known the Davies' car would break down in that spot? Had the killer instead flagged Mr Davies down and then tampered with the car after the murder to make it look like a breakdown? In which case, was it someone the victim knew? This made the killing even colder, coupled with the proximity required to garrotte someone.

Pictures of Albert Pane soon followed. A nostalgic sepia picture of Pane as a ten year old in a school baking competition, accompanied a harried picture of his wife appealing for any help in the investigation. The paper proffered the notion that it had been a poisoned cigarette that had killed him. They wrote a lengthy description of how this could have been carried out. Delilah said that Rob had not denied this but it was possible that he was just not engaging in that topic of conversation. Now, when people bought cigarettes from the machine in The Badger's Holt, the occasional voice from a regular at the bar would announce, *'They'll kill you they will.'* The third death in three weeks and it appeared the villagers were becoming desensitised.

At the news of a third murder, the nationals were all over the village. Rehashed headlines like *'Who Killed The Tuesbury Three?'* and utter lies such as, *'Recession Sees Village Turn To Violence,'* littered the news stands.

The one thing that continued to stand out for me was the violence and immediacy of Davies' death: so unlike the others. You don't need to look someone in the eye to hit them over the back of the head. Poisoning a cigarette would only mean doctoring the victim's own supply or handing them one specifically for the purpose. So, why such violence in Davies' case?

There were the similarities in the modus operandi. The first case appeared opportunistic but you'd have to know when Mr Salter walked Prince and what route he took. This would require just as much planning as tampering with a car, or poisoning a cigarette. They all implied malice aforethought, premeditated murder.

I still kept coming back to the goings on in the model village: the models themselves going missing and the crosses on the doors. Three times there had been a cross on the victim's door. In two cases these were definitely there before the murder. But still, no one was very sure how long the models had been missing for: the newsagent, the baker, the butcher, the bookie, the greengrocer, and the fish and chip shop owner. There were ten to twelve other shops on the High Street and two others on Huckspeth Road that didn't appear in this line up: why? What did these six have in common that the others didn't?

It wasn't their homes that were marked with crosses, it was their place of business; this had to be the link. Perhaps there was some kind of rivalry?

Last year a large supermarket had tried to develop a piece of land about half a mile out of the village in an attempt to usurp the existing supermarket already on the London road. There had been uproar and the plans had been kiboshed: there were too many *'not in my back yarders'* in Tuesbury. A high proportion of the population was over retirement age and they didn't like change. If they did want to visit a supermarket, they had only to take a short drive or bus ride and they'd be there. The second supermarket had, of course, appealed but failed again. Was this a further, unofficial, subversive appeal? I dismissed this thought as quickly as it appeared. A multinational business wouldn't conduct this sort of campaign, would it?

Rival businesses aside, the most obvious similarities I could see between the shopkeepers were their age and gender: all were males between the ages of forty and fifty-five. I needed to know more about their history and their business, if indeed this was to do with their business. Perhaps they all had debts?

Assuming the missing models were not just coincidence then those left were Mr Rawlinson the butcher, Jim Dockery the bookmaker, and Terry Kinney the fish and chip shop owner. I was sure Rob had his theories, but I had been reluctant to talk to him about it since that day at the races.

A sharp stab from my needle brought me back to the Derby in my hand. I hadn't been concentrating. I dropped the hat onto the workbench to avoid staining the soft beige felt with blood. Sticking my finger in my mouth to stem the flow, I looked up and out of the window.

The bright desk light had blinded me and it took a while to focus on the allotments outside. The peaceful plots of bare turned earth were full of the promise of spring. My onions and garlic were doing well and the potatoes had soaked up the recent rains, meaning there were plenty more new potatoes for me to dig for. I would have to plant the runner beans soon.

The light outside was going as the evening started to draw in. I looked down at my watch. It was almost five. I was meeting Delilah at the hall at six to help set up the exhibition. This was her first exhibition outside her little Limehouse Basin museum and she was keen to get it right. The villagers of Tuesbury were a tough crowd. I had just enough time to go home, get changed and walk down to the hall.

13.

Loup Garou

In Haitian folklore the Loup Garou is a werewolf.

The hall was cold when I arrived. With no regular patrons on a Friday to warm the place up it took a while before the damp musty smell dispersed. I'd been surprised when she suggested that she wanted to do this the day before she left. Most people would be far too busy worrying that they had everything packed, making sure their currency was exchanged and booked tickets printed out. Delilah rarely left things to the last minute.

Delilah had received some lottery funding for the museum and she had thought an exhibition would be a good way to promote her work. She had told me she'd be spending the afternoon setting up the display cabinets with an old friend from her student days. The same friend had offered to look after the museum while Delilah was in Haiti. A godsend, considering the Easter holidays fell during the time Delilah was away. Holidays, as always, were a time when school children, accompanied by their parents, desperate for a distraction, flocked to the museum. Delilah also wanted to encourage more adults to visit the museum and this was the point of this evening.

She was hoping for a good turnout. There had been posters placed on the church notice board and in local shop windows, and with the current interest in Tuesbury's serial killer there should be a few tourists.

A big blue baize board on legs had information about the forthcoming trip to Haiti, what they hoped to find and what they might bring back. She had a mobile display case that was full of Roman hairpins, coins, beads and other little finds she'd painstakingly retrieved. Some of these items were easily found by your average Joe with a metal detector but Delilah had carefully cleaned each one and labelled them with stories, bringing history alive.

A lot of them had been from her student days, when she'd gone out on her own with a metal detector. Some were even from when she was a child. According to Delilah, her mother had never understood her need to take these things home in her pocket. Bits of flint shaped like arrows and an even larger piece that turned out to be an axe head. At the tender age of nine she hadn't known what it was, she'd just liked the way it felt in her palm, the undulation of the smooth flint.

'I'm glad you are here, Blake.' She walked across from the far side of the hall, Bertie trotting after her. Her hands were still in cerise mohair gloves that matched her scarf. I too had left my coat and scarf on. 'Can you work out what's gone wrong with the heating: It's like an icebox in here? I can't get hold of the caretaker and people will start to arrive in an hour.' She touched one of the bottles of Cava with the back of her gloved hand. 'I suppose the one good thing is we don't need to put these in the fridge.'

'I'll see what I can do.' I said, walking in the direction of the heating panel, situated by the stage at the far end of the hall. It was set at fourteen. No wonder it was freezing. I pushed the buttons into submission and watched the numbers climb until they reached a healthy twenty-three. I felt the warm air start to filter out of the vents as the heating hummed into life.

'Great, what was wrong with it?' Delilah appeared from the kitchen with some trays of canapés.

'It was set too low.'

'Oh,' she frowned.

I wondered sometimes how such a practical woman could be so impractical at times.

'Where's your friend?' I asked, 'I thought she was meant to be helping you?'

'She was, but she had a family party to go to this evening so she can't be here. It's a shame; I would have liked to introduce her to people, especially you, Blake, in case she needs help while I'm away.' She turned back to the blue baize board where she was arranging some photographs. 'So, come on then, tell me what you've found in the paper today. There's some more canapés in the kitchen you could get if you don't mind.'

I did as I was told and headed to the tiny kitchen. I suspected she hadn't believed my story of the old school friend after all and I wanted to avoid answering the question. On the side were two more catering trays full of canapés. A last minute change had been required, as Delilah had arranged for the catering to come from Pane's Bakery. Given the recent events, this was no longer possible. A recommendation from the local Arts Society had proved a useful resource. Salmon blinis, duck spring rolls, goat's cheese tartlets; there was something for all. I noticed in the kitchen that even Bertie had a little stash of Bonios.

I walked back to the table in front of the stage and left the canapés on there still covered. We had a little while until people would arrive.

'Have you got any plates?' I asked.

Delilah tutted, 'It's finger food, Blake, we don't need plates.'

'Well napkins then, surely?'

'Yes, there's some in my bag over there.' She pointed to a hessian reusable shopping bag with *Live Life Recycle* written on the side of it; an interesting take on reincarnation.

'So, come on…' She looked up at me. 'Anything in the paper?'

Hoping to avoid the subject of the murders, I went for: 'Well, I did see Steve at the newsagent's is advertising for a new home for Prince.'

'No!'

'Yes.'

She finished arranging the photos on the board and walked towards me as I was on my way back from the bag. 'Well, he must have a good reason for it.'

'I suspect so.'

'You can ask him, he's coming this evening.'

'Why would I want to ask a grieving man why he's giving up his dog?'

'Concern, obviously.' She said into the bag. Retrieving a pen and some small pieces of card, she returned to the table.

'Perhaps *you* should ask him.' I said.

'Yes but he might ask me to take Prince. He knows I love dogs, but I can't take another one on. Besides I'm about to go away.' She was concentrating on the card now, using tiny cursive letters to label the canapés.

'He might ask me!'

'I think it's a good idea.' Delilah said, standing one of the little cards beside the duck spring rolls.

'Is it?' I had a feeling I'd just been talked into adopting a dog. The manipulation that women so often employed was such a primitive drive, passed down from generation to generation, that I was pretty sure they didn't even know when they'd done it. Sometimes you didn't even know. Like a blind junction, suddenly a *'Give Way'* sign is glaring at you and you have no other choice.

She stood up straight, twisting the pen in her fingers and looked at me. 'You walk Bertie with me often enough and you'll be looking after Bertie while I'm gone. You said yourself you enjoy the company.' She smiled.

There it was: *'Give Way'*.

I didn't reply. There was nothing more I could say. It wasn't altogether a bad idea; I just wasn't sure how

Prince would feel about it, stuck with a doddery old codger like me. Bertie has the patience of a saint when his favourite dog biscuits are deployed but even so, my pace frustrates him on occasions. Prince was a spaniel. Spaniels needed exercise and lots of it. I assumed that when he was not out for a walk he was dreaming about them.

The next hour passed quickly and by quarter past seven, people were starting to arrive at the hall. There were even some of the older children from the village who were completing a school project on the Romans and Delilah was enjoying herself by showing them all the finds.

By eight, Rob Claringdon had taken up position by the kitchen door with a glass of orange juice. I assumed, due to the lack of Cava, he was still on duty. I went to join him under his sanctuary arch.

'Safest place to be,' he said looking up at the doorway, 'accounts for all eventualities: escape, earthquake, and sustenance.' He indicated the kitchen behind him with a thumb.

I agreed.

'How's the investigation going?' I said trying to appear friendly rather than nosey.

'So, so. How's yours?' He looked at me, not a glimmer of emotion on his face: a policeman's face, deadpan. I had no hope of knowing whether or not he was serious. I couldn't be sure how Rob felt about my contributions.

He'd seemed happy to listen to my hypothesis last year, but that was before he'd become involved with Delilah.

I moved past him into the kitchen and picked up the carton of orange juice on the side, filling my Cava glass. I was too lazy to find a tumbler and also fully aware that I would be on washing up duty later. Was he humouring me for her sake or did he genuinely appreciate my fevered insights? I decided to err on the side of caution.

'I've been rather preoccupied with some commissions. A rather nice Derby as it happens.' I said leaning on the wall to the right of the doorway.

'You surprise me, Blake.' He smiled. 'I would have thought you'd take an opportunity like this evening with both hands. All these people you could subtly interrogate.'

'I prefer to observe.' I replied

'I see.'

'Exactly!'

'So you haven't got any hypotheses you'd like to share?'

'Oh I have plenty of those, but I'm not sure you're interested in the postulation of an amateur. I say leave the professionals to it on this one. I don't want to be the fourth victim.'

'Very wise, Blake, but I'd be interested nonetheless.'

So he was interested. It surprised me and I found myself hesitating as I once more felt foolish in the face of having to voice my thoughts. Steve interrupting the conversation saved me.

'Hello, Mr Hetherington, Sergeant Claringdon.'

'Mr Pensthorpe.' The sergeant nodded.

I fully expected Steve had come over to talk to the sergeant and I went to make my excuses and find an exhibit to occupy my mind. The hall was full and warm with bodies. I started to remove my coat and scarf in preparation for hurling myself back into the fray when Steve stopped me.

'I wondered if I could have a quick word, Mr Hetherington.' He said.

I stopped, nervous that he might bring up the subject of the investigative services, something I wasn't sure Rob knew about or would appreciate.

'Yes, of course.' I tried to appear confident and this time it was Rob's turn to leave; he made his way over to the display where Delilah was eulogising over the axe head her nine year old self had found.

'It's about Prince.' He looked down at the dog, which he had brought with him.

I waited for him to continue. I had a feeling I knew where this was going. Taking my smile as an indication he should continue he did.

'Delilah said you might be able to give him a home.'

'I see.'

'He's not happy without Harold…' he stopped, and looked down at the dog, his glass twisting in his hands.

'I'm not sure he'd be all that happier with me.'

Steve looked up. 'I don't know what I'm going to do, I can't keep him in the shop all day, he's started growling at people.'

'I see.'

'Harold would hate it if he went to strangers.'

'He's growling at people?' I said.

Steve saw his opportunity and continued with renewed determination, 'Oh yes, he growled at Mrs Dellaware the other day, now she won't come in the shop.'

'I see.'

'He howls in the night as well. The tenants above the florist have complained. He just won't settle.'

'He does sleep a lot in the day.'

'He's just waiting for Harold to come home, but he's not going to, is he? It's just hopeless.' I could see the tears welling. He drained the last of his Cava.

'I'll get you another drink.' I said.

We threaded through the clusters of people until we reached the table by the door. There were still a couple of bottles of Cava left and I filled his glass.

'It feels wrong drinking this.' Steve huffed a little laugh and stared at the bubbles. 'I miss him.'

I poured myself a glass. I was going to need one if we were going to do emotions, man to man.

'Of course you do.' I said 'You've had hardly any time to adjust, you need to give yourself time.'

'I know.' He looked at me again, those piercing blue eyes imploring me to do something. 'I just feel so wretched every time I look at him, Prince that is.'

Now I am not a man of steel, I do not have an iron heart. I feel for the plight of another human in so much pain and I feel for the plight of Prince, but I didn't want to tie myself down to a dog. At five years old, Prince could need another ten years companionship at least. Maybe it was Prince with that curious look on his face, head cocked to one side, wondering what on earth the exchange meant, or Steve's RADA worthy version of a damsel in distress, who knows but I found myself saying:

'Perhaps I could take him for a couple of weeks, as a trial you understand. See how we get on?'

'I'm so pleased. Thank you so much Mr Hetherington,' and then to Prince, 'well, what do you think of that, Prince? Mr Hetherington's going to look after you now'. With that he handed me the lead. A complete change had come about Steve's countenance as he gulped his Cava.

'Hang on a minute, I don't have any food for him!' A slight lie as Bertie was due to come and stay with me for three months, tomorrow, and I had bought in a huge supply of dog food and Bonio in anticipation for his arrival. Even so, I felt I should protest at the immediacy of the exchange.

'I've brought some with me,' he said pointing at the plastic bag stashed under the drinks table. Next to it was the familiar beanbag, from the newsagent's, complete with doggy indentation.

'I'm looking after Bertie for the next three months, what if they don't get on?' I said.

'Oh don't worry about that, I saw Delilah walking Bertie in the woods yesterday. I was up there with Prince. They got on like a house on fire.'

And then it hit me. This whole thing had been planned. Delilah's surprise at Steve's advert: fake. She too had read the paper. She had arranged this. I was incensed at the manipulation. I was now the owner of a howling *'loup garou'*. I did not kid myself further that this was a temporary exchange. I watched Steve float off into the crowd, smiling and laughing. Far from the grieving widow he'd been five minutes ago. My anger allowed me to think for a moment that a man who can turn emotions on and off like a faucet, may in fact be capable of killing his lover. But then why would he have asked me to investigate Harold's death? Nevertheless, his card was marked

'Well, Prince,' I said to the caramel coloured spaniel now sitting at my feet, 'I guess we'll have to make the best of it, won't we? I hope you like Bonio.'

14.

Ti-bon ange

A person's guardian and conscience, in a spirit form. This is separate from their soul. It is thought that if person is questioned in their sleep, their Ti-bon ange will speak and they cannot lie.

For the remainder of Delilah's event, I quietly seethed. Prince and I took up position in the kitchen doorway once more and I observed the theatrics from a distance.

The Reverend Lambert was standing by the display of Roman beads and was talking to the, thoroughly obnoxious and sycophantic, Olea Faba: a woman who, unfortunately for the reverend, was also a member of her congregation. Her cassock swished over the top of her shoes as she opened and closed her hands in slow motion clap in time with her undulating sentences. An occasional nod from the reverend brought forth a frantic nodding in return from Mrs Faba.

The children attending the exhibition, had gone home about half an hour ago. Most of them had school tomorrow, that is, apart from Tommy Carstairs whom I had noticed knocked back two glasses of Cava while his mother wasn't looking. He turned green and proceeded to run in the direction of the toilets. Sergeant Claringdon had also seen this display and spoken to Mrs Carstairs who had gone a shade of crimson I have rarely seen.

Rob was now standing with Delilah in front of the blue baize boards looking at a map of the Antilles. Heads together, Rob had his arm around Delilah's shoulders and she was talking to him, pointing occasionally at various parts of the islands. I am not sure why it surprised me that she had arranged a press gang adoption of Prince. Her love of dogs coupled with her *'I know best'* attitude lent itself to such subterfuge.

After another glass of Cava my indignation gave way to resignation. Behind me Prince had curled up on his beanbag. I'd placed it next to the little radiator in the kitchen and he was happily snoring away. Perhaps they were right: he did need a change of scenery and he would be company for Bertie while Delilah was away.

Seeing my more relaxed manner, shoulders more at ease and smiling at Prince over my shoulder Delilah finally approached me.

'Am I forgiven?' She asked. I jumped, still expecting her to be over by the baize board.

'No, Miss Delibes, you are not.'

'What have you been up to?' Rob said appearing behind her.

'That's what she's been up to.' I said, pointing at the sleeping Prince.

'Ah.' Rob said. 'I told you.'

'So you knew, as well?' That just took the biscuit. I had expected some kind of solidarity from the sergeant.

'Not exactly,' he replied, 'but I had an idea and I told Delilah not to interfere.'

'But look at him, Blake. He's been through such a lot, he just needs a loving home.' She entreated me to agree as she bent down to stroke the sleeping spaniel.

'He howls in the night!'

'I'm sure he'll be fine.'

'He growls at people!'

'Well he's not growling at you, I think he likes you, and he loves Bertie! It'll be good for them.'

'Really? Why didn't you take him, then?'

'Yes really!' she said, ignoring the obvious question, 'now stop sulking and come and help me clear up.'

I looked across the hall and it was now empty, save for the Vicar and her congregation of one. I sighed, picked up a tray, and followed Rob to the tables by the door, to collect the glasses.

Delilah looked up at the clock. 'Nine o' clock. We've got an hour before the fish and chip shop closes. I'll treat us all to chips if we can get this cleared up in time.'

Chips did sound good, but she still wasn't forgiven. The next hour went in a flurry of washing, drying, packaging up, dismantling and folding. The cardboard boxes of artefacts were to be locked in the office overnight where Rob would finish packing them up and take them back to the museum on Friday.

The hall was returned to its usual state and a small pile of dust swept into the corner ready for the cleaners.

'Right!' Delilah's voice echoed in the empty hall, 'Who's for chips then?'

Rob's shoes clicked on the floor as he stood the broom up in the corner. Bertie had been hindering the process by chasing the broom around the room as Rob swept. For the first time since he'd settled on the beanbag Prince lifted his head and opened an eye. *'Chips'*, was clearly a word he recognised. It was reassuring to know he still had an appetite.

Leads were attached, coats put on and scarves and gloves applied to ward off the cold night air that waited outside. It was a short walk across the green to the fish and chip shop on the High Street. The white and blue glow of the sign could be seen from the front door of the village hall: *'Kinney's Cod'*, a beacon to all. As we entered the chip shop I noticed Elroy Tuvey closing up in the dark. Late for an antiques dealer, but perhaps he had some accounts to catch up on.

Kinney kept a good shop. The oil was never old, the batter never too stodgy and the chips were always fresh. I was hungry from the evening's exertions and opted for a large plaice and chips. Not the haute cuisine I usually prefer, granted, but you can't beat chip shop chips.

Delilah and Rob were keen to get home and after making arrangements for the next day and Delilah's departure, I said good-night to them and I headed home up the High Street, passing Prince a chip.

Two doors up, the noisy voices of the mid week drinkers in The Badger's Holt drifted out through the front door. A curl of cigarette smoke floated out from the front door. There was someone standing outside, pint in hand. They were talking to another person and as I got closer I could see it was Donald Yveny. He was talking to Elroy. I drew closer and I could hear their voices. The smell of beer mingled with cigarette smoke. I heard the words, mort, ami, mère and honte, but I could not catch the whole conversation.

I passed them and Prince sniffed at their shoes.

'Good evening, Mr Hetherington.' Elroy said

'Good evening.' I replied.

'Those chips smell good.' He said.

'They are good.' I offered them both one. Chips are for sharing after all. Prince waited for his patiently and we moved on with friendly goodnights.

Death, friend, mother and shame, that is all I'd heard. Not unusual. I'd lived in France for several years to study millinery and once you've learned a language it never completely leaves you. The French accent Elroy and Donald had used wasn't the usual accent I was used to. There was another undertone to it: the same sounds as I heard in Elroy's voice when I had been talking to him about Voodoo. I already knew Donald spoke Creole, it was entirely possible that Elroy Tuvey did too. He had said he was from the Antilles.

I finished the plaice and chips and rounded the corner at the top of the High Street. Almost home, I scrunched up the paper and went to throw it in the bin. I had seen something. I'd almost completed the throw into the bin but a replay in my head told me not to. Stopping for a moment in the light of the lamppost I unfolded the squares of greasy paper and peered at it. There, in amongst the splodges of grease, was a message. Written in red biro, it was barely visible in some places. In half inch high capitals were the words

PLEASE HELP!
T KINNEY
355 243

Astounded, I folded the paper neatly, grease inwards and placed it in my pocket. How on earth did Terry Kinney think I could help him? I hadn't even noticed him in the chip shop as we'd been served. More interestingly, what did his conscience need to get off his chest? Had he too seen the by-line on my website?

'Well, well, well, Prince,' I said, 'someone else who's on the net.'

15.

Renvoyer

A ritual performed in order to send away a loa.

The plea for help got me thinking about its author, Terry Kinney. Did the whole village now see me as an amateur sleuth, or had gossip amongst businessmen meant that Steve had told him about my by-line? Did he know his counterpart model was missing? Was he asking for my help because he knew why the murderer might be after him, or was he just assuming, given the fate of the last three?

Terry Kinney's home was not in the village but his business was. He also had five other fish and chip shops in neighbouring towns and villages including Deerton, where Delilah lives. He had spent the last year working at the Tuesbury branch. He was a hands-on boss. All of his new shops had a years input from him. I'd seen him less and less in the shop this year but he had been there this evening. He couldn't possibly have known *I* would be in there. He'd clearly seen his chance and taken it, but why had he not wanted to speak to me then and there? Was he trying to avoid the gossip, or was there something he didn't want to admit. Especially not in front of a Detective Sergeant. Rob's presence had a way of silencing people.

The business wasn't the only thing he had in common with the previous victims. He fitted the demographic; forty-five year old, male, business owner based in Tuesbury. It was this little set of similarities that were gnawing away in my brain. Why was a killer targeting male business owners in their forties?

Three murders on, there were so many questions, and still no answers. I went back to the beginning again: Mr Salter, Mr Davies, Mr Pane, Mr Rawlinson, Mr Dockery, and Mr Kinney. Mr Salter, Mr Davies and Mr Pane were dead; fifty per cent fatality. If the similarities could not enlighten me, perhaps the differences could. The greengrocer is on Huckspeth Road and the bookie is on the Kent Road not the High Street. This meant it wasn't about the High Street, so was it about the shops at all, or was this coincidence? I started to think about the other shops and businesses in Tuesbury. There was the florist on Morimer Road, with the dentist next door. On Huckspeth Road the hardware store joined the greengrocer's and there was a launderette on the other side. The bookie on Kent Road had empty premises next to it and nothing else business-wise. Making up the rest of the High Street were the beautician's, the hairdresser's, a convenience store, the Post Office, which doubled as a bank, and the library. The old café, Frascatis, was permanently closed and two other units on the High Street were empty, a sign of the recession. The florist, dentist, beautician's and hardware store, were all owned by women. The Post Office and the library were

Government Organisations. Jimmy Malani owned the hairdresser's but he was nearing retirement. I had no idea whom the empty units were owned by. This left me with another question: was it only men or did the killer intend to move on to the women shop owners in due course?

It kept coming back to the same facts: all the models stolen represented business owners in the same demographic.

I was almost home. The night was cold and the warm satisfaction of the chips was wearing off. I'd be glad to get back to a warm house. Prince was of the same opinion, as he did not stop to sniff the lamp post on the corner of my street. Then it hit me. I tutted at my stupidity. Elroy was in that demographic. Why wasn't he included? The only difference was his skin colour. Perhaps that was it. All our other men were white.

The conversation I had just overheard popped back into my head. Elroy had been speaking to Donald, a relative stranger to our village, in the same demographic as our victims, but not included. However, he would not yet have a model to be stolen and, setting him apart from the others, he didn't have a business here. In fact what was his business here? He'd come to visit his aunt but why after all this time? I'd never seen him before and Mrs Dellaware had been in the village many, many years. The language Donald and Elroy had been speaking wasn't French so it must have been Creole. Did they know each other or was it coincidence?

I had no desire to blunder about with more insensitive questioning of Elroy's roots. I could ask Donald instead. He had made an effort to introduce himself to me, so all I needed to do was find a way to bump into him again and ask him a few pertinent questions. I wasn't sure my foot would take joining the Morris men. No, a trip to The Badger's Holt might be in order instead. They did very good dinners. As of tomorrow I would have two dogs to exercise and would be in need of decent sustenance after a long walk.

I reached the front door of Little Acorns and placed the key in the lock.

'So fella, here it is.' I said.

Prince looked up at me and licked his nose. He wasn't a bad little chap. I scratched between his floppy, curly ears and his big brown eyes looked up at me with a gratitude rarely found in humans. Once the door was closed, I let him off his lead to explore. It was then I realised that I had left the beanbag and the food at the village hall. I would have to go back tomorrow to collect it. I hoped Prince wouldn't be too upset. I had food in the cupboard for the morning. I watched from the lounge doorway as he explored the nooks and crannies, huffing little dust balls out from under the sofa. He spent some time investigating the spot on the rug where Bertie sits on his visits. I went into the kitchen to make myself a hot drink to take to bed.

He was up the stairs before I'd even realised. I heard his footsteps and dashed up after him to try and prevent him from going in the bedrooms. I arrived in time to see him curl up on the end of my bed, settled down for the night. Head on his front paws, he opened one of his big brown eyes and raising an eyebrow enquired as to how I could move him when he looked so comfortable. I didn't have the heart; it was my fault after all. I'd forgotten his beanbag and I hadn't stopped him going upstairs. Just for tonight, I thought. I went back down to finish making my hot drink. Tomorrow I'd get the beanbag back and Bertie would be here so he could set an example and they could both sleep in the kitchen. I'd have to see if the old stair-gate was in the loft. It had been almost forty years since it had last been used, when Jane was a tottering toddler and I hoped that it was still working.

Prince slept soundly on the end of the bed. No howling or growling, just a soft doggy snore. Ten years without another soul by my side each night and it was good to have company for a change, but I couldn't allow myself to go soft on him. Dogs needed to have their place in a household. Tomorrow I would have to exercise some discipline.

The next morning and we were going to see Delilah off to Haiti. Rob was coming at zero six hundred hours and we'd all go to the airport together. It was only just getting light outside and my body complained. Knees creaking, I got up, trying not to disturb Prince, but the jangle of his collar told me he was awake.

I dressed and let him out into the back garden. We ate breakfast together and at six o clock sharp I heard a car pull up outside. Taking hold of Prince's lead, I took my flat cap off the side and headed out.

Delilah was excitable and talking at a million miles an hour, as usual. Bertie sensed his impending abandonment and was sulking on the back seat. Things were not improved by the arrival of Prince who woke Bertie up with a sharp bark of welcome. Compared to the dark silence of the morning, dotted with the odd kitchen light, the interior of the car was like a discotheque.

'Morning,' said Delilah. The noise hit me square in the face as I entered the car.

The radio was playing some kind of pop music while a dashed blue line of lights intermittently lit up the console. Rob was silent, listening to Delilah, his fingers tapping on the steering wheel, the only indication that he heard any of the ruckus.

'How did you get on with Prince? He looks happy enough,' she continued without allowing a reply. 'I think you two will get on just fine. It makes me so much happier knowing there's someone to keep you company while I'm away.'

I fear I grunted, but there was little room in the mêlée for anything else. Delilah continued talking at a hundred miles an hour and, seatbelt secured, Rob started the car.

The cacophony continued throughout the half hour journey to the airport. Prince laid his head on my lap, pushing his nose and ears under my jacket, I suspect an attempt to hide from the noise. The peace I felt when the engine was turned off and the radio silenced was indescribable. I closed the car door and caught my reflection in the window. The hazy morning light haloed a face that was far from angelic. My shoulders were tense, my face creased and my ears were ringing. How could anyone listen to music that loud? I hadn't imagined Rob tolerating that kind of nonsense.

Bertie and Prince had to stay in the car. Abandoned, they were now sitting together in perfect symmetry looking at their departing masters.

Gate five was Delilah's flight. Standing by the security check in we said our goodbyes.

'Now, Blake, you need to let me know if anything else happens. He won't.' She said, nodding in Rob's direction.

'I look forward to hearing all about your finds when you get back.' I replied

'I've started a blog, here's the address,' she said, scribbling it down on the back of the receipt for the coffee we'd just had. 'You can read all about it here.'

I smiled. It was just like Delilah to expect me to use technology as deftly as she did. I had no idea what a blog was. Still, it looked like a website address that I could easily type in, so I resolved to give it a go at some point.

'Take care of yourself, Delilah,' I said, reaching forward to hug her. Hugging wasn't something I usually did, but when someone's about to travel half way around the world, you need to let them know you care.

'You too, Blake.' She said. 'And look after Bertie for me.'

'Of course.'

I walked across to some seats in the middle of the concourse so that Rob had space to say his goodbyes.

There were some tears that were kissed away, more hugs, some whispered promises and Delilah was off through security on her new adventure. I'd miss her crazy theories and gung-ho investigation style. I was sure from the look on Rob's face he was going to miss her even more.

We walked back to the car in silence. I know when a man needs his space to process information and Rob was just such a man. Back at the car the dogs greeted us with joy until they realised Delilah was missing, at which point they returned to sulking on the back seat. Turning the key, the radio roared into life again,

'Shit!' shouted Rob as he jabbed the radio off. I looked at him.

'I hate that rubbish that Delilah listens to.'

I started to laugh and Rob joined me.

'Thank God for that.' I said once I'd caught my breath. 'I'm not sure I could have coped with another journey like the last one.'

He stopped laughing and smiled. 'Don't let on though eh, Mr Hetherington, I haven't had the heart to tell her.'

I nodded. 'Of course, and please Rob, call me Blake for goodness sake.'

Rob pulled a CD from the glove compartment and soon some innocuous modern folk music filtered through the speakers to accompany us on our journey home. The dogs, unimpressed by Delilah's absence settled down to sleep on the back seat.

We were almost back to Tuesbury when the phone rang. I hadn't seen it before amongst all the lights on the dashboard. Now it lit up like the Milky Way amongst a galaxy of lights. As it rang the music stopped. Technology never ceased to amaze me.

'I'm sorry I should get this' Rob said.

I could see from the screen it was Inspector Knighton. I'd only come across the man once and I knew it wasn't going to be good news.

'Claringdon,' Rob answered.

'Claringdon, Knighton.' Knighton's voice boomed over the speaker attached to the sun visor. 'There's been another murder!'

'Okay, I'll be there asap.' He said, running the a.s.a.p. together as one word.

'Yesterday, Claringdon, yesterday. This is the fourth murder on our patch and things are not looking good for us. Gabbett's going mental!'

'Right, sir, I'm on it.' He said.

'Good.' Knighton hung up as abruptly as the conversation had started.

'No rest for the wicked, eh?' I ventured.

'Unfortunately not; I think I must have been very bad in a previous life.' Rob replied.

We rounded the top of the High Street and I was home once more. The commotion as both the dogs decanted was minimal considering the upheaval both the mutts had encountered over the last two days.

Before I'd got the key in the door Rob was off. This time lights flashed on the outside of the car and a blue light had been attached to the driver's side roof. The deafening sound of the sirens explained how he might be able to tolerate Delilah's music without complaint. The man had probably lost some of his hearing driving around in a reverberating tin box.

I needed a rest before I headed back to the village hall to collect Prince's beanbag. I'd take them for a walk at the same time. I let them both out into the garden and they proceeded, to my dismay, to dig up the primroses. Things were definitely going to be different around here.

My mind turned once more to the inspector's call. Who could it possibly be this time? Was it one of the remaining three and if it was, which one?

16.

Baka

Evil spirits in the form of animals

I tried my best to concentrate on the task in hand. I was attaching a very fine silk ribbon to a Derby. My head was pounding. Two paracetamol taken half an hour ago were not working.

Yesterday morning, I'd collected Prince's beanbag and food from the village hall and then taken both dogs for a walk in Druid Wood. Prince had refused the usual walk, which would have taken us past the fallen tree where Salter had met his maker. Hardly surprising, he was probably traumatised. Instead we walked around the edge of the wood along the path that follows a stream that flows through our village, curling around the woods before it leaves for greater things.

Bertie and Prince had enjoyed splashing around in the water and were wet through when we entered The Badger's Holt. We were just in time for a late lunch of sausage and mash. I had a pocket full of Bonio to keep the boys occupied while I ate and waited to see if Donald Yveny would appear. He did not. I was going to have to be more organised if I was going to happen upon Yveny at an appropriate moment for a spot of innocuous questioning.

I paid my bill and as I did, asked the landlord, Braydon Deveraux, with as little purpose as possible, if he'd seen Donald lately. He had not been in today, more of an evening visitor, came my answer.

The Badger's Holt was a family-run business; a Freehold pub that had belonged to the Deverauxs for generations. Braydon Deveraux had a jolly face. His veined nose was indicative of too much drink with a pot belly to match. His Grateful Dead t-shirt echoed the unspoken feeling of unease in the village at the recent murders. In his forties, he was a man whose body had had far more wear than his years required.

'He'll no doubt be in when the morris men meet next Friday, ' he said helpfully, handing me my change. 'They always come in here for a pint afterwards.'

That was almost a week away and I resolved instead to try one evening in the coming week.

'Awful business, these murders.' He said

'Yes.'

'Talk of the village.' He went on. 'Don't suppose you have any theories, do you, Mr Hetherington?' He rested his hands on the bar, his arms straight and his shoulders hunched as if he were about to commence CPR. The man was very serious.

'Hats are my business, Mr Deveraux.' I replied.

'That they are,' he said, 'but word has it you're a bit of a detective on the side.'

I wasn't sure the cerebral machinations and hypotheses that floated around my brain constituted detection. If I could detect crime, there would not have been four murders already. I could feel my cheeks burning. Bertie and Prince sat at my feet looking up at the bar, one on either side, heads cocked, fascinated by the petechialed nose of Mr Deveraux.

Folding his arms on the bar and leaning forward he smiled. 'Heard about Rawlinson, I take it.'

'No.' I said, forgetting my embarrassment.

'Surprised, I thought you were friends with that Sergeant Claringdon.' He said, reaching for a tin by the side of the bar.

'He wouldn't discuss the details of murder with me.' I said quietly and firmly.

'Oh come now, Mr Hetherington, no harm in a bit of speculation.' He threw the two dogs a biscuit from the tin. 'Handsome little fellows aren't they?' He said, smiling down at them. 'Delilah gone to Haiti then?' He changed the subject.

'Yes.'

'We'll miss her in here. Life and soul she is.' He stood up again as a regular further down the bar waggled his pint glass in Deveraux's direction.

I could see I wasn't getting far, so I took the opportunity to leave and ponder the murder of Rawlinson, on my way to the shed. So the butcher was dead: the fourth of the models counterpart's to die. My initial thought was the lack of fine sausages and pork chops at my dinner table. Selfish perhaps, but for a brief moment I wondered if the murderer was intent on putting me on a diet. First my almond croissant supply was curtailed and now my free-range pork chops. I had not, as Deveraux had assumed, heard anything more from Rob and it would be almost twenty-four hours before I did.

Now, a day later and lost in my thoughts and my work, I squinted at the thin needle trying to make stitches less than a millimetre. I sighed, frustrated at the hat and the murders.

A snort from Prince reminded me of my two companions huddled in front of the oil heater. I looked across at the sleeping balls of fur that were Bertie and Prince. It was hard to believe the awful night that had preceded their now peaceful slumber. Prince had been gracious enough to let Bertie share a corner of the beanbag. It was a sight that warmed the soul, unlike their performance last night. The hooligans had kept me awake and after such a long day I assumed they would sleep. As always, assumptions are the route to many a mistake. I had attached the stair gate to the bottom of the stairs. Thankfully it still worked. A small amount of rust was easily sanded off and with a little WD-40 the mechanism was working once more.

All went well until the early hours of this morning. As payment for the dogs' extradition to the kitchen, I was treated to howling at two in the morning. Initially I thought it would subside. I was reminded of the times Jane had thrown tantrums and cried for attention. Eleanor had simply said, *'leave her, she'll settle herself.'*

Employing this technique on the dogs didn't work. They were possessed: possessed with the need for human contact, I feared. After forty minutes, enough was enough. I am a patient man but, in this particular instance, I doubted the neighbours were.

My appearance did not stop them howling. I stood in the doorway to the kitchen and shouted 'No!' The one word I knew they understood. They were silent and sat side by side looking at me expectantly. It was then that I could hear the dogs barking over on Blackwood's estate. A very still clear night meant the sound carried easily, with no clouds to absorb it.

'Look what you've started.' I'd said to the guilty pair.

They went to start again.

'No!' I said a little quieter this time but firmly.

Bertie trotted over to the back door. I immediately felt guilty. Had they been howling because they needed to go out?

Standing in the back door, with the cold of the night on my face waiting for the dogs to come back in, I'd heard the darndest thing. A rattling came from across the fields, from the direction of the woods. It was a grating noise like the sound of a football rattle: rhythmic and constant. The Blackwood's dogs' barking and howling was clearer now. It was an eerie atmosphere and I drew my dressing gown closer around me. Goodness knows what people got up to late at night in Druid Wood. Thankfully, the dogs had come back quickly.

They had followed me to the foot of the stairs as I closed the stair-gate. Their eyes begged for a pass to the upstairs realm but I had been determined not to give in. As I got back into bed, the howling started again. No one was going to get any sleep at this rate.

Relenting, I went downstairs, opened the stair gate and let Bertie and Prince upstairs. Prince took up position once more on the end of the bed and Bertie observed a distance by sleeping against the closed door. I had failed, but at least we would all get some sleep.

It was these two devil dogs that I had to blame for my headache and sluggish work rate this morning. Getting up, I moved to the small bench in the corner and turned the kettle on. This morning's paper lay on the bench. The headline read:

'Butcher fourth victim of the Tuesbury Killer.'

Factual; but I supposed *'Rawlinson Butchered'* would have been in bad taste. I chastised myself for such flippant thoughts and finished making my tea.

Deveraux's red face popped into my brain once more. Something bugged me about him and I wasn't sure what. He wasn't an unpleasant man. Occasionally the smell of beer and body odour became somewhat overwhelming but he always had a smile. I'd not been privy to his gossip before, then again I'd never asked for it. Working in a hostelry must encourage that kind of behaviour. He'd seemed concerned about the death of Rawlinson but not concerned enough. Mr Deveraux was in his forties, white, male and a business owner. Why was he not one of the models that had gone missing? Maybe that's what was bothering me. Was he even on the list of possibles? There must be something different about him. I thought once more about the models and their similarities. That was it! None of them had been in the village all their lives. Mr Deveraux had. But what was the significance of this?

A knock at the door interrupted my thoughts. I was rarely visited in the shed. Customers tended to contact me by telephone or e-mail. They only visited for measurements or to collect the finished product, neither of which I was due to happen today. The council's interest in the functionality of my shed made me cautious and I had placed a spy hole in the door, which I now used. I could see clearly who it was and I was a little surprised.

'Come in.' I said opening the door.

An elated Bertie and a 'Hello, Blake,' confirmed it was Rob.

'Have a seat,' I smiled, indicating one of the old, checked fabric, high back chairs, adorned with an old family picnic blanket. 'Tea?'

'I'd love one, thank you.' Rob replied.

'So how are you? Busy, I should think?'

'You've heard about Rawlinson, then.' Rob glanced at the paper on the worktop.

'Yes, a fourth model.'

'What?'

'Well, six models stolen, four of their counterparts dead.' I stated.

'Yes, when you put it like that, it doesn't sound so random, does it?' Rob took the mug from my hands and warmed his own on it. Bertie curled up next to his feet, his chin resting on Rob's polished leather shoe.

'No, altogether more methodical, I would have thought.' I said.

'I'm struggling with this case. Alston gone off on honeymoon, deserted me and I was relying on him for inside information.'

'Alston?'

'Yeah, he's our man in Tuesbury. He normally catches most of what goes on, living above that butcher's. Not for long though.'

'Oh?'

'Well, once he's married I should think he'll move in with her, I'm surprised he hasn't already.'

'Some people are still very traditional.' I replied, smiling at the thought of Alston marrying, I barely knew the man, but I'd never seen him with a woman and the idea of him on honeymoon in the middle of a murder case amused me.

Rob blew on his tea and reached down to scratch Bertie's nose. The little dog huffed appreciatively. 'Blake, I need your help.' Rob said.

'Really?' The surprise in my voice did not need the confirmation that my creased brow and raised eyebrows gave it.

'This one's got us stumped.'

'I'm not sure how I can help.' I said, taking a sip of my tea.

'I've spoken to Knighton and he agrees. He'd agree to anything at the moment just to get Gabbett off his back.'

'Agrees what?'

'That you're our man.'

'Your murderer?' I smiled. I was teasing him, but it was easy.

'No, Blake' Rob replied patiently. 'You've lived in this village virtually all your life. You know these people. You know what makes them tick. We want you to be a, sort of, police consultant. What do you say?'

'Well I'm flattered.' I took another sip of my tea and watched Prince, his eyebrow twitching as he dreamed. Jane wouldn't be happy about this. 'Surely this is a job for the professionals - four murders!'

'I know, Blake, and I know it's a big ask, but you were a lot of help with the Devine case and we think you could help us again.'

I stood up and turned the heater up a notch; I hadn't realised how cold it had got. Sitting in one position all morning was not good for the circulation and the barrier of fur between the radiator and me didn't help matters.

'An informant then?' I said.

Rob shrugged his reply. 'Sort of, I suppose.'

'Okay.' I sat back down. 'But I'm not getting into any sticky situations again. A gunshot wound to the foot and a broken collarbone are enough war wounds for one lifetime.'

'Absolutely, there's no way we want you put in any danger, it would be a consulting role only. Help us get a handle on some of the characters in this village. Find out who's doing this before they kill someone else.'

'I hope very much you can do that.' I said.

'So who should we start with?'

'I've been giving this a lot of thought.'

Rob gave a wry smile, 'Go on.'

'Well, the main things our victims have in common is they are all male, between the ages of forty and fifty and own a business in Tuesbury.'

'Good.'

'But that doesn't seem to be helping so I thought about the differences, the things that set them apart from others.'

'Okay.'

'Well, that didn't get me very far either and then I got to thinking about the people that fitted that demographic but did not have a counterpart model stolen.'

'Ah, now that's thinking. So who did you come up with?'

'Elroy Tuvey, Donald Yveny and Braydon Deveraux.'

'Okay, any ideas.'

'Well, I discounted Braydon Deveraux as, unlike the murder victims so far, he has lived here all his life. Elroy Tuvey…well…'

'Well?'.

'He's black. I'm not sure that has anything to do with it, but it is an obvious difference.'

'Sure is. Who's Elroy Tuvey?'

'The antiques shop owner.'

'Okay, so what about Donald Yveny?'

'Donald Yveny's new to the village. He wouldn't have a model yet, so it's feasible he could be a target.'

'Back to the models again.'

'Well, the theft of the models does seem to me to be the starting point for all of this.'

Rob nodded. 'So we need to speak to this Yveny, then?'

'I think so. I was trying to find a way to bump into him.' Rob laughed and I explained some more of my thoughts. 'I saw him speaking to Elroy Tuvey, outside The Badger's Holt.'

'And...'

'They were speaking Creole I think. It made me wonder…' I was interrupted by another knock on the door.

It was turning out to be a busy day. I got up to open the door. Peering through the spyhole I saw serendipity had been at work.

Opening the door the bright light of the day was a change from the shed and the smell of cigarette smoke wafted in. The back of a man's head greeted me. He was casually dressed in a checked shirt, jeans and black motorcycle boots. The figure turned, dropping his cigarette stub and grinding it into the path as he did and smiled.

'Mr 'etherington, you were looking for me I believe.'

'I was; what very good timing.' I said opening the door further and inviting him in. 'Sergeant Claringdon, this is Donald Yveny.'

17.

La-Place

A 'la-place' is an apprentice to a Voodoun priest.

Rob took charge of the conversation.

'Mr Yveny, I'm Detective Sergeant Rob Claringdon.'

'Hallo.' Donald replied, shaking hands with Rob. Donald drew his arms back in, folding them across his chest, and, shoulders hunched, he waited.

'Have a seat, Mr Yveny. Would you like some tea?' I offered.

'Thank you, but I'm okay.' Donald moved from the doorway and sat in the chair opposite the sergeant. He placed a hand on each knee and his right knee started to jiggle. Donald had thick rough hands with bitten and sore cuticles suggesting he had a manual job and a nervous disposition.

'You are aware of the murders we are currently investigating?' Rob started.

'Of course,' Donald said.

'We think you could help us?'

'If I can, but I am new 'ere, I don' know the people. I think someone like Mr 'etherington would be of more use to you.'

As he spoke I now noted his strong Spanish accent. Perhaps it wasn't French I had overheard. A lot of the romantic Latin based languages are so similar if you're not concentrating. He spoke English impeccably. As Rob talked, I observed, sitting on the stool by the workbench.

'How long have you lived in the village, Mr Yveny?'

'Eight months. I moved here from Santo Domingo to be with my aunt. I lost my motter in the earthquake two years ago.'

'I'm sorry.'

'Don' be. Her last wish was that I come to England and look after my aunt. So 'ere I am.' He shrugged.

'About the murder of Albert Pane.' Rob placed his mug down beside the chair and leant forward. Donald met Rob's eye. 'You were one of the ones who discovered the body.'

'Yes.' Donald sat up straight and rolled the cuffs of his jacket up. 'Mr 'etherington was there too and I told your colleague all I knew.'

'Did you know Albert Pane?'

'I did not. My aunt did.'

'But you never met him yourself?'

'No. I did not know Mr Pan. He made very good bread though. I'm sure I could not expect any less from a man called Mr Bread.' Donald laughed at this last comment and his knee started to jig once more.

'Mr Bread?'

'Yes, Mr *Pan*. It's Spanish for bread. It's funny, no?'

'I see.' Said Rob. 'So you speak Spanish?'

'Of course, I come from Santo Domingo.' He smiled.

'Do you speak any other languages?'

'Of course.'

'What are they?'

'I come from a group of islands, we must communicate well and so I speak a small amount of many languages.'

'Creole?'

'Yes, of course. My mother spoke Creole.'

Rob sat back in his chair, observing Mr Yveny. Perhaps he was out of questions or possibly it would be inappropriate to ask any more in front of a civilian, even if the had just been recruited to the force. Maybe he was just waiting, because the silence prompted a response.

'Sergeant Claringdon, I don' like to see you in blind alleys. If you want to know what this is all about then I suggest you speak to Elroy Tuvey.'

Rob sat forward, mirroring Donald's stance.

'Go on.'

'This is bad juju, sergeant. Bad! Elroy will help you.'

'And you won't?'

'I don' know these people. Elroy, he does. He knows.'

'Knows what?'

'Speak to him, I don' want to involve myself anymore.'

'Mr Yveny, there is such a thing as obstructing a police investigation.'

Donald observed the sergeant in a silent stand off. 'Enemies are hard to sway, sergeant, and I don' want any enemies 'ere.' He stood up and turned down the cuffs of his jacket once more. He pulled some leather gloves from his pockets and put them on, readying himself for the outside once more. 'Now, if I am free to go?'

'Thank you, Mr Yveny.' Rob said handing him a card. 'If you think of anything else…'

'You're welcome.' Hand on the handle of the shed door, he turned to me, 'It seems we did not talk, I 'ope it was not too important Mr 'etherington. Perhaps I will see you in The Badger's 'olt on Tuesday evening,' and he left the shed.

Rob and I listened as Donald took five steps along the path, his footsteps falling silent as he reached the grass surrounding the allotments.

'Mr Tuvey has answers, then.' Rob said.

'Possibly. I don't think he'll mind talking to you. He said he'd dig out some books for me, so that's a good excuse to drop in.'

I went to the little sink at the back of the shed and washed up the mugs. The dogs were still dozing. They had barely moved when Donald entered. As soon as Bertie had realised Rob had no treats he'd gone back to the beanbag and joined Prince.

'You'd never believe those two kept me awake all last night, would you?' I said.

'They were howling too, were they?'

'Yes,' I turned from the sink, 'How did you know?'

'We had several complaints actually.'

'But I didn't leave them that long.'

'No. Complaints about the Blackwood's dogs; howling all night they were.'

'I did hear them when I opened the door to let these two out for a minute.'

'I don't suppose you hear much where you are though: quiet in your neck of the woods.'

'Most of the time,' I said, 'But last night I heard a weird noise while I was standing there. Not one I've ever heard before. Most of the time it's just nightjars or owls but last night there was a rattling, like one of those football rattles.'

'That wasn't reported at all. That might explain the howling dogs.' Rob was concentrating on the tips of his bull-polished shoes. Snapping out of his thoughts, he looked up. 'Come on, let's go and see Elroy.' He started to pull his jacket on and then stopped. He looked at the Derby on the side. 'That's if now is convenient, of course.'

My hands were dripping on my shoes and I grabbed the towel hanging by the sink and dried them. I should carry on with the commission, heed Jane's warning and stay well out of this. I should listen to my *superego*, the part of my brain telling me that a sixty-odd year old man has no business gallivanting around the countryside, assisting the police in their investigations. However, working on commissions meant I could manage my own workload, and when did I ever listen to what my daughter told me or for that matter pay attention to my *superego*.

'These two could do with a walk.' I said, placing the towel back on the hook. At the mention of the '*w*' word,

Bertie and Prince looked up in unison. I turned the heater off and they were both on their feet by the time I'd lifted the leads down from the back of the door. Placing the hat I was working on in a plastic box to avoid any damage while I was out, I took my coat and hat off the back of the chair. Rob was checking his phone. I was surprised he got any reception here but he seemed to be engrossed in something.

'Hexalex.' He said, as he saw me looking at him. 'Helps me think.'

'I see.' I said, having no idea what Hexalex was. I didn't get to ask because as I put my hand in my coat pocket it fell on the crumpled piece of paper. I remembered the plea for help from Terry Kinney. I'd completely forgotten about it with all the commotion of seeing Delilah off, Prince arriving and then the howling in the night. The man went to the effort of hiding a message in my fish and chips, I ought to try and find out what it was he thought I could do to help.

'There's someone else we should talk to.'

'Oh yes?' Rob said, putting his phone back in his pocket.

'Terry Kinney. He gave me this.' I handed Rob the paper. He unfolded it and read the message.

'Interesting? How do you think he thinks you can help?'

'I suspect we have Delilah to thank for that. I let her design my website and unfortunately she created a by-line…'

'...She decided you should do a bit of detective work on the side?'

'Erm, yes. I think she meant well. He's not the first person to approach me.'

'No?'

'No, Steve Pensthorpe did too. I set him straight, I am no detective.'

'Ah, but you are now, Blake. Delilah suggested it, way before I talked to Knighton about it.'

'About what?'

'Getting you on board as a *'consulting detective'*, she called it.'

'I've always thought she watches too much television,' I said, attaching the dogs' leads as they hustled me.

'You might be right there. She hates it at mine. I don't have a TV.'

I laughed at the thought of Delilah torn between her man and CSI Miami. Another dichotomy of character; one minute glued to his phone and the next, no TV.

'I know!' Rob said in reply to my laughter. He looked at his watch. 'Almost time for lunch, maybe we should have fish and chips?'

'Agreed' I said, locking up behind me, ignoring the fact that this would mean chips twice in almost as many days. The dogs pulled forward and I checked them with a 'heel' that both obeyed. As we walked towards the gate of the allotments and the High Street beyond, I gave a wry smile at the irony of becoming a consulting detective. I'd always assumed Rob felt I was interfering;

that he tolerated me for Delilah's sake. Jane had no choice now. I'd been recruited. I must admit I felt a swell of pride as I entered the fish and chip shop, the dogs safely secured outside. The detective and his consultant were on the case.

18.

Barrière
An entranceway sometimes used to appoint gods to the cross-roads.

A warm blanket of air hit us as we entered the chip shop. The odour of batter and the noise of crackling fat swirled to meet us.

Terry Kinney's Tuesbury branch of fish and chips was one of the best. Deerston had been his flagship for many years but now Tuesbury was his pride and joy. In achieving loyal customers and a healthy profit within one year of business in a rural and intolerant village, Kinney was doing well.

The dogs raised their noses, breathing in the smell wafting out of the door as we opened it. Now they pressed their leathery snouts against the condensation on the windows with sorrowful chocolate box looks, absorbing the heavenly aroma of jumbo saveloy.

I have always prided myself on my palate, considering myself a lover of the finer things in life. Chablis, scallops, organic meat, artisan croissants, but Kinney's fish and chips were irresistible. The cuisine of fish and chips has been around for over one hundred and fifty years. A mixture of European fashions from France, Belgium, Portugal and Spain; who are we to argue with the lovers of food. It lost some of its charm with the banning of newspaper wrapping. A greasy piece of beige paper or a polystyrene box just doesn't have the same feel about it. It certainly wasn't as informative; unless of course Terry Kinney has wrapped your chips.

As if on cue, Kinney appeared from the back of the shop. He smiled at me and looked as if he were going to say something when he clocked Rob and turned back the way he had come. Rob's sharp black suit, manicured appearance and long dark mid-shin wool jacket marked him as unmistakably CID. I was not surprised. If Kinney had wanted the police involved he would not have wasted his time sending me such a clandestine message.

Kinney's teenage daughter, back from her first term at university, was serving the queue. The last thing we needed was a scene; that way, Kinney would never talk. Mrs Kinney arrived behind the fryers and, tying a red and white vertical striped apron around her tiny waist, she pushed her carefully coiffured dark brown hair into a white meshed trilby style hat, and began to take orders on a small order pad. An attractive look on such a handsome woman: her green eyes were strikingly beautiful under the bright white trilby. Mrs Kinney had always been a woman of high standards. Our turn approached. There had been an unspoken patience between the two of us, making the unconscious decision to ask to speak to Mr Kinney in an orderly fashion and without raising alarm.

'I wondered if I might have a word with Mr Kinney.' Rob said.

Mrs Kinney looked up from her order pad, 'I'm afraid he's just popped out.' She gave the detective a flirtatious smile, daring him to tell her otherwise.

'What a shame. Mr Hetherington and I were under the impression he wanted to speak to us.' Rob said.

'I'll tell him you called.' Mrs Kinney ripped an order off the pad and clipped it above the fryers. 'Can I get you gentleman anything, while you're here? On the house of course.'

'That's not necessary, Mrs Kinney…' Rob began.

'No, no, I insist. It's the least we can do for our loyal public servants.' She smiled with just a hint of a threat.

The cheap red pen scratched our order of cod and chips, plus plaice and chips with a pickled onion and we waited on the window bench.

So Terry Kinney had left the building. Not the action of a man who was desperate for help. More like the action of a man evading the police. Rob and I sat there in silence and I picked up the Tuesbury Gazette. It was folded on the sports page, and a picture of Tipingee dominated it. She had won all her debut races and was turning out to be an asset to the Blackwood estate.

Rob nudged me. He'd cleared a little hole in the condensation on the window and was peering out at the street.

'There he is.' He said, his voice a low whisper.

I made my own porthole in the steam and looked out. Terry Kinney was walking along the opposite pavement away from the fish and chip shop and towards the village green. Rob stood up.

'It might be better if I went,' I said. 'He'll speak to me,' and I too stood up.

Momentarily irritated by my forthright suggestion, Rob quickly regained his professional composure.

'Good idea.' He said, 'I'll wait for the fish and chips, that's the important job after all.' He smiled at his own humour and I left the shop. I left the dogs where they were, I could catch Kinney up much quicker without them and Rob was still in the chip shop.

I caught him up, half way across the green. Kinney was a tall man with a long stride, though thankfully, at six foot, I am too, although my stride is a little shorter these days. In my hurry to leave the shed I had not done up my jacket and it flapped in the breeze, allowing my scarf to begin unwrapping itself as I hurried across the grass. Kinney heard me breathing hard to keep up and thankfully stopped.

'You wanted to speak to me, Mr Kinney.' I said, stopping as I drew level. The cold wind was immediately noticeable and the back of my neck was sweating a little from the exertion.

'I did, Mr Hetherington.' His eyes glanced back across the green in the direction of the High Street. 'That police officer not with you?' He said.

'He's collecting our lunch.' I replied. Not a complete lie. Kinney obviously recognised the law, but why was he so keen to avoid it?

'D'ya have a moment?' Kinney said, nodding at the bench where we had found Mr Pane.

'I'd prefer to sit over there,' I said, pointing to a second bench placed at the back of the cricket pavilion. 'More sheltered.'

We made our way in silence and I regained my breath. There was only one other person on the green: Mrs Dellaware, who was making steady progress with two bags of shopping, presumably returning home to Poets Avenue, beside the allotments.

'So you're a personal investigator?' Kinney was very matter-of-fact in his words. He had a very soft Irish accent and his dark hair and green eyes gave away his heritage. His moustache and dimpled chin gave him a classic, Clarke Gable look. A slim man, but not thin, his appearance suggested he took care of his health and physique: he looked like someone who had a physical sport as a hobby: cycling perhaps. I was sitting with my hands in my pockets, my coat pulled tight around me and I was surprised Kinney was not yet shivering in his v-neck jumper and jeans. No scarf, no gloves, no coat. Something was definitely preoccupying his thoughts.

'Not exactly.' I said.

'But dat's what your website said.'

'We have Miss Delibes to thank for that.' I gave a wry smile. 'If I can help you, Mr Kinney, then I will.'

'T'ank you.' He looked out across the green. Mrs Dellaware had reached the other side and disappeared behind the hedge bordering the allotments. We were alone despite the hustle and bustle of village life around us.

'I t'ink dis was a mistake.' He said turning to face me. 'I'm sorry to have wasted your time.' He stood up and stepped off the veranda.

'You know what they say, Mr Kinney.' He turned back as I spoke. 'A problem shared is a problem halved. I'm a great believer in that and I'm a good listener.'

Running his hands through his hair he pushed his hands into his pockets and, shoulders hunched, he returned to sit on the bench.

'It's dese murders, you see Mr Hetherington.' Kinney put his head in his hands, elbows resting on his knees. A sigh sent a little puff of air out across the veranda.

I stayed quiet, choosing instead to watch a moorhen by the pond as it picked its way among the reeds. Kinney needed time to gather his thoughts. After a few minutes he sat up, crossed his arms and began.

'I know what links dem.'

I turned to look at him now, betraying no emotion. He was a rabbit in headlights. I didn't want him frightened by over-zealous interest.

'I heard about de models going missing. It's all over the village.' He started to list them on his fingers. 'Mr Salter, Mr Rawlinson, Mr Pane, Mr Dockerty, Mr Davies and *me*.' The last word was a hoarse whisper. He swallowed hard. 'Four of dem are dead already, it's only a matter of time before dey get to me.' His head returned to his hands, elbows once more resting on his knees.

'What makes you think they want to kill you?' I said.

'It's dat bloody horse! I should never have let de others talk me into it.' He said, his frustration pushing him upright again and into the bench. His forehead creased and his knuckles were white as he balled his fingers in clenched fists.

I sat forward slightly. I was fairly confident the aggression was not being directed at myself but I could tell I needed to be cautious.

'Which horse is that?'

'Tipingee.' He said.

'Rufus' horse?' I was surprised into using my old friend's first name.

'Yes. We all meet at de golf course, you see. Danny Barnette said we should put a bet on dis horse, he said it was a sure winner. Well you're not going to turn down an offer like dat are you?' He said, arms outstretched, hands upturned.

'She's a good runner.' I replied.

'She is, de best, dat's de problem. Barnette gives us the tip off and we keep winning.'

'I see.'

'Dockerty's not happy.'

Jim Dockerty, Tuesbury's only turf accountant, had a reputation for liking money and resented parting with it. 'I see.' I said.

'He said Blackwood must be fixing the races because he's never seen a horse with such high odds win so many times. He says dere's something dodgy about it.'

Now I turned to face Mr Kinney. Up until now, I'd thought nothing more of this than a man paranoid that he'd won at the bookie's too many times. Blackwood had sung Tipingee's praises. He'd never implied she wouldn't win. I'd never been a betting man and I hadn't ever paid much attention to odds. The odds had been high for Tipingees' debut, but I assumed this was because she was unproved. So why did the odds continue to be high? Surely they'd drop the more she won?

'High odds?' I said.

'Yes.' Kinney had his arms folded tight across his chest once more and was staring at his feet, his legs stretched out in front of him. 'De guys at the club say Tipingee's not from good stock. She's not a good jumper. Blackwood got her cheap. Dere's a rumour his winnings are not…honest.' Kinney hesitated over the last word.

'And Salter, Rawlinson, Pane, Davies and you, you've all been betting on the horse and won.'

'Yes.'

I thought I knew the answer to my next question but I had to ask, 'Who do you think is murdering people, then?'

Kinney chewed his lip and looked at me arms still folded. I could tell he knew that what he said next, there was no coming back from. 'Dockerty.'

I let the name hang between us for a few seconds. 'But surely Dockerty knows it's a risk of his trade, losing money.'

'He's lost a lot.'

'I see.'

'I went to boarding school with Dockerty. He's a nasty piece of work. He's always had his own way; no one's crossed him. He hated it when I made a success of my business. He hates it even more now we've taken money off him.'

Why did these things always go back to a childish grudge? I now knew the Irish joviality of Dockerty's manner hid seething repressed revenge.

'He accused us of race fixing. I haven't placed a bet for two weeks. Pane and Davies did and look what happened to dem. I'm not a greedy man, Mr Hetherington.' He stood up and rubbed the back of his neck. 'I best be getting back to de shop. Susan will wonder where I've got to.'

'Okay.' I stood up and joined him to walk back across the green. 'I think I should pass this on to Sergeant Claringdon.'

He stopped. 'But I don't want to be arrested. It's not my fault what Blackwood does with his horses, I was just acting on a tip. I'm a business man, Mr Hetherington, I have a reputation to uphold, you understand my predicament.'

'Mr Kinney, there's been four murders now and you've just told me you think you could be next. Don't you think it's time to let the police know? I doubt he'll arrest you for betting on a horse.'

He frowned. 'My wife will kill me,' was his ironic statement.

'If I tell the sergeant, it might give you some kind of protection. I can't promise, but at least it will mean we're closer to an arrest and stopping this murderer. He's more likely to arrest you for obstructing a police investigation if he finds out what you know.'

'Okay.' Kinney conceded and we started walking back to the High Street. He turned, 'don't tell Dockerty what I said, will ye.'

'You have my discretion on the matter, Mr Kinney. The detective sergeant is not a stupid man. He will want our villain caught. We don't want him to bolt.'

Kinney nodded. 'I knew he was a bully in school, but murder...? I still find it hard to believe.'

Reaching the edge of the green, I could see Rob and the dogs standing outside the chip shop. Both dogs looked up obediently and expectantly as Rob ate his lunch. I had a feeling mine may be cold but as I walked across the road back to the shop with Kinney I didn't care. There'd finally been a breakthrough, a new opening in the case, an entrance that may take us to the truth. At last something that linked the stolen models to the victims. How could I have missed the obvious? Dockerty was a greedy man. There was nothing Voodoo about that at all, just simple, greed and revenge. Is this what Tuvey had been trying to tell me? If you look greed and revenge up in the dictionary, they definitely came under the heading of bad juju.

19.

Asson

The Asson is a sacred instrument of the vodoon priest: a dried gourd filled with seeds or snake bones and covered with beads or small bones.

'So…?' Rob said as I reached the other side of the High Street and claimed my fish and chips. Although Kinney had returned to the warmth of the shop, I was aware we were on a public street and I apprised Rob of the conversation with short sentences.

'They all bet on the same horse. All the models.'

Rob nodded and scrunched up the greasy chip paper, throwing it in the bin beside the door. I took a chip and bit into the soft, fluffy, vinegar-soaked potatoey goodness. They were still warm: just. I gave Prince and Bertie a chip each.

'They've had plenty.' Rob said, 'although you'd think I'd kept them all to myself, the look on their faces.' He wiped the grease from his fingers on a tissue. 'Kinney too?'

'Yes. All of them.' I said, 'He thinks he's next.'

'I see. And he didn't want to tell me because…'

Miss Derby, on her lunch break from the infant school, approached the door to the chip shop. 'Don't tell anyone you saw me,' she said, cheeks blushing with guilt.

'We're teaching the kids about healthy eating this week,' and with that she ducked into the shop before she talked herself out of it.

'Allegations of horse fixing.' I said.

'Which horse?'

'Blackwood's: Tipingee.'

'I'd better go and check that out then.' Rob said.

'Kinney's worried: doesn't want anything coming back on him.'

'Fair enough, but this is murder.' Rob said, shrugging.

The batter on my fish had congealed. It hadn't been cooked all the way through; unusual for Kinney, and a sign of the busy lunchtime.

'Do you still want me to go and speak to Tuvey?' I picked the fish out of the batter with the tiny wooden fork. It was good fish. 'Only it would be polite if I did. It's been over a week since he offered to look out those books for me and if he's gone to some effort, I really should show an interest.'

Rob nodded, 'Guess it might not be Voodoo after all, Blake.' He said.

'Just my fevered imagination then,' I replied, smiling. But even as I said it, the idea still nagged at me. Folding the rest of the chips and empty batter into the wrapping, I disposed of the rubbish.

'Oh I wouldn't say that; just a keen mind, willing to explore the options. It's a good trait. I admire it.'

I wasn't sure how to reply to this. He wasn't patronising me, but I wasn't entirely sure it was a compliment either.

'Right then,' I said. 'I'll take these two with me, and when I'm finished at Tuvey's, I'll take them for a walk up at Druid Wood.'

'Okay. I best check in at the station and then I'll do a bit of digging at the bookies. Let me know if anything interesting crops up. Irish bookie's and Voodoo…' He laughed. 'I'm not sure I can see it myself.' I was prepared to take a bit of gentle teasing from a professional detective. I was an amateur after all and maybe Voodoo was a bit far fetched especially in the light of this new evidence.

Rob and I parted company. He walked in one direction and I the other. Tuvey's antique shop was three doors down. The window display changed weekly and in pride of place this week was a stuffed toy shaped like a black cat, arching its back. Its mother-of-pearl button eyes glistened in the early spring sunshine of the afternoon. A shabby pheasant feather was tied to its tail and pieces of French lace, silver and an enamelled butterfly brooch decorated the body. My granddaughter would think it wonderful, I thought as I entered.

The shop was empty and the sun shone through the window, picking out the dust on the antiquarian books.

'Mr Hetherington.' Tuvey greeted me with a bright white smile. 'Good to see you again.' He extended a hand, which I took. His handshake was solid and firm and his eyes compelled me to smile in return.

'I have the books I said I would find. I am glad you gave me cause to look them out as they have been sitting in a box since my mother passed away.'

Before I could reply he had disappeared out of the back of the shop, emerging once more with two thick A4 sized leather bound notebooks.

'These are my mother's special books.' That's what she called them and to me, they still are.'

'It's kind of you to share them with me Mr Tuvey…'

'Elroy, Elroy.' He interrupted with a dismissive flick of a hand and opened the books. 'This is *Dambala*…' He said, proudly turning the book so that I could see.

There on the page was a fine pencil drawing of the snake god Elroy had told me of when I had bought the necklace for Delilah.

'The great Sky god.' Elroy said.

I perched on a stool that had been placed by the till for customers and the dogs sat obediently at my feet, happy to be in the warmth of the shop after being made to wait outside the chip shop.

'And what about Voodoo dolls?' I ventured. 'Did your mother ever talk about them?'

'Oh yes…' he turned the pages until he was almost at the back of the book. 'She used them for protection. Here, here are the pictures of some of the dolls she made.'

Polaroids had been placed in the back of the book with pictures of dolls: some made out of straw, some of them fabric, others incorporating parts of old children's dolls. They were fascinating and I was lost for words as I studied the pictures and the carefully scribed annotations beneath each one.

'What's this one?' I was pointing at a picture of a very old doll. It had no arms or legs as such, just a peg doll head with wild hair and button eyes. Around the main body of the doll was wrapped string and feathers.

'Ah, that one. There's a story for that one.' Elroy needed little encouragement to continue. 'This is an heirloom doll. There's a rumour in our family that my great-great grandfather had a wandering eye. This doll was made by his wife to stop his philandering ways.'

'Did it work?'

'Who knows, but it's still passed down from generation to generation, to the first male born each time, just in case.'

'And you have it?'

'I do.'

'And this one,' I said, changing the subject and pointing to the black cat very similar to the one in the window. This one was smaller and didn't have the lace. Instead it had a small gold cross pinned to it.

'Protection of course. It sat on our mantelpiece at home and protected our home and our family.'

'The little cross is interesting.' I said.

'My mother was a catholic too; she went to church every Sunday. There are links between the Catholic Church and the Voodoun religion. Although of course, they wouldn't want you to say that out loud.' Elroy looked up from the book. 'Would you like a cup of tea, Mr Hetherington, while you look at the books?'

'That would be very kind of you, thank you…Elroy.' The salty chips had given me a thirst.

He went back into his office, leaving me to take in more of the photographs. I pondered the significance of the Voodoo mixed with Catholicism. Rob would definitely find that amusing. Perhaps Dockerty, whom I knew was Catholic, as I'd seen him attending the church on Huckspeth Road, was also an Irish Voodoo enthusiast.

He'd only been gone a few minutes when Mrs Olea Faba entered the shop. Not one of my favourite people in the village. Olea had a habit of stirring up trouble wherever she went.

'Mr Hetherington.' She said, taking her gloves off and stuffing them in a bobble hat she had also just removed.

'Mrs Faba.' I said, as politely as possible.

'Olea, please.' She replied, frowning at some china teacups.

'Ah Mrs Faba, you've come back for the teacups. I knew you couldn't resist.' Elroy swooped in from the back office, sniffing out the sale from several yards.

'Such delicate bone china, the gold highlights on these are beautiful and the handles will fit your fingers perfectly. What better home for them, than with a true English Rose.'

'Mr Tuvey, you are a charmer, but I'm still not sure fifty pounds is what they are worth.'

'A hard woman you are, but for the five, I'm afraid I can do nothing on the price.'

I was watching the interaction from the counter. Mrs Faba had not once looked at Tuvey and he fought bravely to gain eye contact. I remembered such customers from my own shop: browsers through and through. In normal circumstances I would have said the likelihood of a purchase being made, even with a discount, was slim. However, Mrs Faba, as Tuvey had said, had returned to look at these items. This was a sure sign of intent. She held the delicate china cup in her hand; looking but not looking, turning it over, tutting and then placing it back down on its saucer. All her body language implied she was not going to buy.

'An awful lot for a cup of tea, don't you think, Mr Hetherington?' She gave a determined look in my direction and it caught me off guard. My nose tingled with the embarrassment. She'd caught me people watching.

'They are very fine examples.' I scratched my nose. I felt for a shop owner on a path to no sale.

I placed my hand back down on the book to turn another page and it fell on rough edges. I looked down and I saw now what my hand had felt. Some of the pages had been torn from the book. I wondered if Tuvey or his mother had removed them and why? My thoughts were interrupted once more by Mrs Faba's shrill and intrusive voice.

'What do you think?' She said, picking one of the cups and taking a couple of steps towards me. She would have brought it right up close for me to inspect, but Prince stopped her. Up until now he and Bertie had wedged themselves beside the counter and were dozing. The large oak table in the middle of the shop was between them and the door. They had not woken when Mrs Faba entered the shop but now Prince was on his feet and he barked.

'SHUSH,' I commanded. He was obediently quiet. I was beginning to wonder what I had taken on, what with the howling the night before and now misbehaving in antique shops.

Mrs Faba almost dropped the cup and an anxious Tuvey wrested it from her hand.

'I'm not sure I will have them after all.' She said, placing her hat and gloves back on and hurrying from the shop.

'I'm so sorry, Mr Tuvey. I've only had Prince a few days and we haven't got used to each other yet.'

'No, no. No matter.' Tuvey said reaching down to scratch Prince's ears. Prince received the affection gratefully and settled back down beside Bertie, who had merely opened one eye during the whole ruckus.

'But I lost you a customer. I feel very bad. Here, I'll buy the cups, they would be a nice present for my daughter.' I got my wallet from my coat pocket. It was the least I could do. They were very nice cups. They reminded me of afternoon teas with my grandmother years ago.

'And the little cat in the window?' Elroy didn't miss a trick. 'I'll do it for half price.' Elroy said with a gleaming smile.

'Of course.'

There was no point resisting. My granddaughter would love it dearly.

With carefully wrapped teacups and good juju cat in tow, I gathered the dogs' leads and set off towards Druid Wood for a walk, which by now they deserved. I could stop at the shed and leave my new purchases safely there. I was not going to be able to throw sticks, control dogs and manage a bag full of fine bone china.

I had crossed the High Street more times than was good for my health today. The cars never slowed down to the thirty miles an hour required. It didn't help that there was a downward gradient into the village that crept up on an inattentive driver and by the bottom of the hill you could easily be ten miles over the limit.

The number sixty-seven bus was approaching the bus stop and I crossed the road behind it. The noise of the big diesel engine filled my ears. Thick grey fumes momentarily swamped my lungs. Stepping onto the pavement I could see Mrs Faba making her way across the allotments. I was reluctant to follow given Prince's earlier behaviour, but both dogs, intent on their walk, cajoled me through the gate. It was, after all, the quickest route to Druid Wood.

The activity of spring filled the little plots. Shoots reached for the sky, blackbirds fought for their territory and unfortunately, squirrels dug for bulbs. Bertie and Prince put paid to the plans of one furry monster setting about Delilah's tubs of daffodils. The shallot sets were coming on well, but still had a couple of months to reach their full potential. Soon I would plant the marrows: this year's attempt to win a first prize rosette at the Tuesbury Autumn fair. I had some seeds from a prize-winning marrow grown by an old customer. He had heard of the disaster that had befallen my pumpkins last year and sent me the seeds as a gift.

I undid the padlock and found some space in one of the cupboards to stash the cups. The dogs were past being patient and whined.

'Come on then.' I said and we headed to Druid Wood.

Druid Wood had covered almost two thousand acres in the mid-nineteenth century and belonged to the Blackwood's estate. It was sold off in the latter half of the nineteenth century to cover the debts of a grand tour. Now less than two hundred acres remained, thankfully protected. It's the haunt of many dog walkers at various times during the day and at this time of year when the trees are still naked you can sometimes see the odd deer. Interspersed with yew trees, the smell is one of the best I know. It reminds me of Christmas. I love the peace of the woods; the tranquillity it brings to the mind: no distractions, just the chit of a green finch or the rat-ta-tats of a woodpecker.

I let the dogs off the lead and, thrusting my hands into my pockets, breathed in the air heavy with pine. I caught the scent of bonfires and wondered who had chosen such a windy day to light a fire. I hadn't noticed any bonfires being prepared on the allotments. Most people were concerned with new growth; the old growth had already been cleared from the plots.

The dogs busied themselves inspecting the undergrowth, huffing at leaves and finding the best places to mark. Prince disappeared occasionally but once called he came back promptly, something I was glad of. Despite the episode of howling and the kerfuffle in the antiques shop, he was a very fine companion and was shaping up to be a very well disciplined dog. I was still puzzled as to what had caused the outburst in the antique shop. Had he been surprised? No one likes to be woken with a start. The howling during the night could have been due to new surroundings, but the fact that Bertie had joined in confused me. He hadn't joined in at the antique shop.

I heard the dogs start barking; in unison this time. I called them. I had to call three times but they came, eventually. Clipping their leads back on I wondered if it was a deer or perhaps a squirrel they had found.

But then I heard it too; a haunting whirring that drilled through the frigid atmosphere of the ancient woodland. Chainsaws had a throatier roar, birds sang high and shrill; this rhythmic rattle was new to me. Or was it? The whirring changed its tone and triggered recognition in my brain. It was the same noise I'd heard last night. Had this been what the dogs had been howling and now barking at? Whimpering, Bertie huddled into Prince. They looked up at me waiting for the next command.

'I think we've had a long enough walk, don't you boys?' I said to the expectant brown eyes.

I received no argument and we headed back towards the allotments. It was three p.m. There would be enough light to fit in a couple of hours work before heading home for dinner. It had been a long day already. Chasing fish and chip shop owners, discussing Voodoo, Victorian teacups, pictures of beheaded plastic dolls and now eerie woodland shenanigans. This case was getting to me. I was tired and ready for the normality that hat-making brought.

20.

Folklore

A community's traditional beliefs or customs, which are passed down through the generations.

I arrived home, after several hours working in the shed, to an e-mail from Delilah. It had taken me a while to get into the habit of checking my e-mails daily. But I now checked them with a cup of tea before dinner and it signified the end of the working day. I could relax with some music and a book. This evening I was looking forward to Vivaldi to accompany my Colin Dexter. I rarely watched television these days. I watched more when Eleanor was alive.

We had watched the Morse series together; it had become a Saturday night ritual. I much preferred the musings of Morse to the dithering old busybody, Miss Marple. When Eleanor died, I started to read a lot more. It took my mind off things much better than the television. I had read several of the classics, most of Peter Robinson's and now I was working my way through Dexter's novels. I liked to read a series, especially one that exercised the mind. *The Riddle Of The Third Mile*, was proving to be a puzzler. All the clues were there, I just couldn't see how to put them together. Not unlike the goings on in Tuesbury of late.

Tea in hand, I sat down to my e-mails, spurred on by the thought of a relaxing evening. Delilah's e-mail came with a story. She was very much enjoying her first week in Haiti and had quickly got stuck into the local culture of dancing and socialising. Her e-mail told me of a lady she'd met at one of these dances who told her of the different fairy tales in Haitian folklore. The one that had caused Delilah to prick up her ears was the story of Tipingee. She knew she'd heard the name before and she'd woken up this morning remembering where:

'I just had to write and tell you Blake. I mean, what a coincidence. Tipingee is the name of your friend's horse. I didn't think about its name. Who thinks about the name of a racehorse? They are all a bit strange but the tale of Tipingee's a good one; you should look it up. It got me wondering why Blackwood would name a horse after a story about doppelgangers. I know, I know, my overactive imagination again. Anyway read it you'll see.'

The e-mail went on to discuss the virtues of Haitian rum and the quirks of her team and of course, to ask after Bertie. She was having a whale of a time. I sent her a quick e-mail back, just two lines:

'Glad you are settling in nicely, Bertie's doing just fine. Tuesbury's same as always.

Good to hear from you,

Blake.'

I can't get on with writing in electronic form. I prefer the telephone or an old fashioned letter. Curious, I looked up Delilah's story. The wonders of modern technology meant there was so much information at your fingertips that I was often unsure where to start, but over the last ten years I had become used to searching for things via the Web when looking for particular stock items. Building websites, however, was still way beyond my capacity and, I left Delilah to deal with that. Although after the recent requests as a result of the website's 'subtitle', I think perhaps I may have to learn. I found the story referred to by Delilah and she was right, it was interesting.

Tipingee was a young Haitian girl who had a cruel stepmother. Don't they all? She overhears her stepmother telling an old man, who has helped her carry wood back from the forest, that as payment he can take Tipingee as his servant. He is to come to the well in the village tomorrow at noon. Tipingee will be wearing a red dress and if he calls out her name, she will reply. Tipingee gets her friends to join her in the village the next day, also dressed in red. The old man calls out for Tipingee and she steps forward saying *'I'm Tipingee.'* But then her friends step forward and say, *'I'm Tipingee, she's Tipingee and she's Tipingee, too.'* The old man is annoyed and goes back to the stepmother who promises Tipingee will be there the next day, this time dressed in black. The same thing happens, only this time Tipingee and her friends are dressed in black. The old man is very angry and goes back to the stepmother telling her that if she tricks him a third time she will be his servant instead. The stepmother assures him she is not tricking him and that Tipingee will be there, by the well, in a red dress. Tipingee and her friends, as you may predict, repeat their performance and her stepmother is taken into servitude. Tipingee and her friends live happily ever after.

A typical fairy-tale, you might think, but the cogs were whirring. I had been reluctant to believe the assertions Dockerty was making about my friend but now I found myself wondering. What if there was a ringer, like her namesake? I couldn't believe Rufus would have knowingly made the purchase of a duff horse. If the horse that was racing wasn't the horse that was entered, this could set the odds high for a sure winner, but how long could that continue? Surely the bookie's would change their odds soon enough. Tipingee would have to lose at some point? No, it just seemed too far-fetched. Rufus, although not always honest in his relationships, as far as I knew, was honest when it came to his horses. He worshipped them.

I turned the computer off, fed the dogs and put the oven on for dinner. I noticed in the hall an ear of white paper hanging from the letterbox. Pulling on it, I revealed two letters that had concertinaed themselves in the letterbox. Back in the living room, I poured myself a whisky and opened the first, official looking white envelope. It was a letter from the bank, with Blackwood's cheque attached. It had bounced. I couldn't see why. The name was correct and it was in date. The only explanation available was *'insufficient funds'*.

The second letter was from my daughter and I would wait until after dinner to read that. Opening the CD player I loaded Vivaldi's Four Seasons. Spring filled the air as the violin began the allegro of the first concerto. The dogs had finished their meal and came to sit in front of the mock fireplace. I obligingly turned it on for them.

Sitting down on the sofa I looked once more at the bounced cheque sitting on the coffee table. It was very confusing. I'd known Blackwood all my life and to my knowledge he'd never had any money trouble. Then what about his sacking of Danny Barnette? Danny had been with him many years. He'd never had any trouble with him either and yet, he'd fired him for hitting Tipingee. Hardly the behaviour of the stable-hand Blackwood sang the praises of. I filtered back through conversations I'd had with Rufus. I was starting to mistrust anything he'd told me, and all on the basis of a horse fixing rumour and a bounced cheque. What if there was a ringer and Danny Barnette knew about it, and told Kinney and his friends? Was that the reason he was sacked? I had three options. Wait to see how Rob had got on with Dockerty and run my ideas past him, talk to Blackwood's stable hand, or talk to Blackwood himself.

I did not fancy approaching my friend on the subject of a bounced cheque. Cowardly, I know, and it was not an insignificant amount. I had no idea how to find the stable hand now he was not in his employ. It could be he was a member of the golf club, but I was not and so could not gain legitimate access. This left only one course of action: wait and speak to Rob.

I got up to place my chicken and mushroom pie in the oven: it was one of Rawlinson's I'd had in the freezer. The dogs were settled for the evening by the fire and as *Summer* began on the stereo I sat back to read Jane's letter which was sure to include my grandchildren and their various endeavours. I was eager to see if Seb was walking yet. Blackwood and Tipingee could wait until tomorrow.

The following morning, Rob phoned me on my mobile at about nine thirty to find out how I had got on with Mr Tuvey. He wanted to compare notes and we agreed to visit the model village again today, to see if there was anything that had been missed. I had put in a good three hours work on the Derby and it was starting to look like a worthy sixtieth birthday present. I just had the last of three handmade mauve, silk roses to complete. Then the hatband could be attached.

Rob knocked on the shed door at eleven am, sharp, as arranged. His punctuality was a surprise, given the laid back nature Delilah took towards time keeping and I smiled at the thought of his frustration at her tardiness, as I've no doubt he would be. It was another sign to me that he was in love with her. The dogs dragged themselves away from the oil heater to greet Rob at the door. Today heralded the first day of spring but there was still a nip in the air.

'Good morning's work there.' Rob said nodding back in the direction of the shed as we crossed the allotments.

My face questioned him.

'Well you've got two silk flowers done since the last time I saw you. They must take time. It's looking very nice,' he replied.

'I have. Fiddly little things, but worth the effort.' I was surprised to see the sergeant had taken an interest in my hat-making on his previous visits.

I packed away my work, turned off the heater and we headed out. I was more than happy to take the time out for a walk on such a fine day and I was eager to discuss my ideas regarding Tipingee, and see what Rob had found from his conversation with Dockerty.

'So how did it go with Dockerty yesterday?' Perhaps I should have left the sergeant to volunteer the information but I was keen to discover the result of the conversation. Find out whether or not I was right in my hypotheses in regard to Blackwood's racehorse.

'For a man that hasn't found it necessary to report the matter to the relevant authorities, he was very forthcoming on the subject. He asserted his view that Lord Blackwood was race-fixing.'

'Did he say why he thought that?'

'He couldn't tell me how he thought Blackwood had done it, no, but he felt sure there was something *'dodgy'* as he put it about the amount of money the group of friends had won on the horse. He thought they must have had a tip off that it was fixed.'

'Danny Barnette.' I said.

'Who's that?'

'Blackwood's trainer.'

'Ah, well that's possible. But that still doesn't make it a fact.'

'He sacked him.'

'Who, Danny Barnette?'

'Yes.'

'Now, that is interesting. I suppose the only way to know for sure is to speak to Mr Barnette.'

'Yes...' Reaching the edge of the allotment, I got the dogs to sit before crossing the main road. Prince was getting much better at believing my sincerity when I told him to do something. 'Rob, you should know I've known Rufus Blackwood since I was a boy. He was, at one point, a very good friend of mine...'

'I know, we went to Cheltenham remember? He certainly doesn't strike me as needing money. Why would he risk his reputation?'

'That's just it, I think he *is* having problems with money.' I blushed, feeling incredibly guilty at the confession and the betrayal of my friend's finances. We continued to walk up the High Street towards the London road and the model village. I fell silent as some people bustled by, carrying on with their daily chores. The baker's was still shut and a customer outside the florist studying the gardenias forced us into the road in-between the parked cars. Once past, I took a deep breath in and I heard my voice say:

'The cheque he used to pay me for the commission bounced.'

'Awkward,' was Rob's one-word reply. He did nothing to assuage my guilt, with an echoing silence that stretched to the top of the High Street and back.

'I know, there's something else too,' I continued as the world started to come back into focus. I felt immediately better as soon as I'd said it, like a child with a guilty secret. 'Did Delilah say anything to you about Haitian fairy-tales in her latest e-mail?'

'No. She told me about the dancing and the rum.' Rob laughed.

'There's a folk tale in Haiti called *Tipingee*'. She thought I'd be interested because she remembered Blackwood's horse was called Tipingee.' I went on to tell Rob the story and as I reached the end he said

'And you think maybe Blackwood's horse is a real life Tipingee.'

'Yeesss.' I was a little too enthusiastic.

'Hmmm. I should go and ask Blackwood some questions. At least find out how I can contact Danny Barnette.'

'I wonder...I should go and talk to Rufus. I might get more out of him and I do have the excuse of the cheque.'

'Good idea. I doubt he'll admit any money worries to me, but you never know. Faced with a bounced cheque, he might tell you something.'

About two hundred yards from the gate to the model village I brought the dogs to heel. It was Mrs Tudbury in the booth today and she was looking flustered. She was talking into her mobile. The distance and the Perspex of the booth window meant I couldn't hear what she was saying, but the tone of her tone voice was urgent and official. She looked up as we approached, hung up the phone and leant out the window.

'That was quick, sergeant, I'm glad it's you. You never can be sure who you're gunna get.' And then noticing me, 'Mr Hetherington?'

'We were hoping to have another look round, if that's okay with you,' Rob said, as confused as I must have looked.

'You 'aven't just been called then?' Sensing its requirement, Rob's mobile started to ring. He took it from his pocket, looked at the screen and answered.

'Claringdon…yes…yes…I'm actually already here…yes.' And he hung up. 'So, you've had another disturbance?'

'Good, you're up to speed then,' said Mrs Tudbury, smiling.

I was not, but all was about to be revealed as I followed them both, clicking through the turnstile and into the expanse of tiny brick buildings.

We walked past the wood and the marshland to the west of the village and entered the High Street. There was no one else in the Little Tuesbury, beside Bernard, who could be seen working away at the far end of the village, polishing the tiny solar panels next to the riding stables. Ten paces and we were at the far end next to the florist, the charity shop and the hairdresser's, all opposite the bookie's, *'Dockerty's Turf and Surf.'* The recent introduction of Wi-Fi in the bookie's had resulted in what Dockerty thought was a catchy name change.

'There it is, same as the others.' Mrs Tudbury had stopped, hands on hips, chin jutting out, facing the bookie's.

We were looking at a small cerise cross in what looked like paint or perhaps nail varnish. According to Mrs Tudbury it was almost exactly the same as the crosses on the previous doors; those doors being the newsagent's, greengrocer's and the butcher's. I of course had not seen any of the actual crosses, only the remains of damaged paintwork after they had been removed.

'I see.' Rob took his mobile once more and he began to take pictures. 'When did you notice this?'

'We've been very vigilant considerin' the events of the last few weeks. I'd say it hadn't been more than a day at the most.' Mrs Tudbury replied.

'I'll have to get a team down here to dust the area for prints and I'll need your CCTV for the last few days.'

'Of course, I'll sort it out for you. I dun know that you'll get any prints. It rained last night, and if they wore gloves, there's no chance.'

We both looked at her.

'I've watched TV too.' She crossed her arms across her chest.

Rob cleared his throat, 'Well, none-the-less, we better do this by the book.'

'Could be a prank,' said Mrs Tudbury, looking at Rob again. 'It's a different colour see innit.'

Rob said nothing and crouched down to look at the little door. Bertie and Prince had sat quietly throughout the whole affair and now Bernard had come to scratch their ears and fuss them.

'Shall I leave you to it?' Mrs Tudbury offered.

'Yes that'd be fine thank you, Mrs Tudbury. Of course I'll need to ask you some questions before we go - you'll be around?'

'Yes, yes. Business doesn't run itself.' She replied.

'No. And the CCTV?'

'I'll sort that out for you now. Bernard, would you man the booth?' She said over her shoulder as she went.

'Sure, Mrs Tudbury.' Bernard replied, still fussing over the dogs.

'I better take these back to the gate and tie them up, we don't want doggy nose prints everywhere, do we?' I said to Rob.

'I'll do it.' Bernard volunteered, 'I don't mind. They can keep me company in the booth'. He smiled.

'Well, that's jolly good of you, Bernard, thank you.' I said, handing over the leads.

Bernard headed off around the top of the London road and the Martin's farm avoiding the High Street and was some distance away before Rob said anything.

'So, what do you think then, Blake?' He asked.

'Well, it's another cross.'

'Yesss.'

'The line of the cross going from top left to bottom right is on top of the line going top right to bottom left, suggesting they were right handed.' I said, 'See,' and I drew a little cross in the air.

'Very good.' Rob was clearly impressed but I often observed left and right-handed habits. Being left-handed myself, brought it into focus more.

'The nail varnish, if it is nail varnish, implies a woman. I don't see Dockerty as a nail varnish man. However that could be a ploy to put us off the scent…' I'd used the word *'us'* and paused to see if I got a reaction. There was none. Rob was clearly comfortable with this assumption so I continued, 'And then of course there's the fact that I understand the others were red but this one's cerise and…'

'And the others were painted right to left, suggesting a left handed person….' Rob interrupted.

I broke in again '…Another attempt to blur the lines?'

'And Dockerty could know we're on to him!' Rob finished.

21.

Servir A Deux Mains

To serve with both the 'rada' and the 'petro', right and left sides, of the Voodoun gods.

Between the Cricket Pavillion and the terraces on Kent Street is a tithe barn; it marks the beginning of the older section of the village surrounding the green. The Tourist Information will tell you that this part of the village dates back to the sixteenth century. What is not so freely mentioned, is that those cottages on the High Street, were once affectionately called *'Hot Street'* and were known for their ladies of the night. I love the irony of history; from scandal to highly desirable homes in just five centuries. The tithe barn itself was traditionally a place to pay taxes to the church or the landowner. That Tuesday, an entirely different form of payment had been taken.

Reverend Persephone Lambert was familiar with the dead. Part of her job was to see them into the next world. She rounded the corner of Kent Street, I imagine, enjoying the morning sunshine, cassock flowing out behind her, hymn books clutched tight, as she hurried onwards to commence her duties in the church that morning. I feel sure she would not have expected what she found slumped in the doorway of the tithe barn. I can only empathise with how she must have felt as she lent forward to wake the sleeping figure, hunched on the third step, head resting against the brickwork, still cold from the night before. I know how that skin will have felt as she searched for a pulse and I shudder at the memory of this action.

Jim Dockerty was not drunk. He was not down on his luck, bereft and depressed, unwilling to return home to a wife and family to tell them of his losses for that day. No, James Dockerty was dead, our prime suspect: no longer.

I was to discover all of this when Rob visited the shed later that evening.

'We won't be getting any more information out of Dockerty now.' He said as we sat down for coffee in the shed.

Rob had spent most of the day on the scene, organising interviews and negotiating phone-calls from a disgruntled chief inspector. Five murders and no solid case to arrest anyone did not look good. For the press, Tuesbury was fast turning out to be a hotbed of murder. Tuesbury itself had noticed a lack of people on the High Street. Villagers were choosing to stay in the safety of their own homes. Even the Post Office, a hive of activity on pension day, had noticed the reluctance of its regulars to come and collect their weekly allowance.

Detective Constable Alston was still on honeymoon for another week. Rob had of course been assigned another officer in his absence but he'd made it clear to me he didn't rate his colleague and was disgruntled that she would be cutting her teeth on this case.

I was just finishing the Derby, which was due to be delivered next week. When Rob knocked, I had left the last few stitches to complete tomorrow, in favour of boiling the kettle. We were drinking a very fine blend of Himalayan coffee beans and the smell invaded every corner of the shed.

'At least there are clear motives for killing Dockerty.' Rob continued as I handed him a mug of coffee. 'Thank you.' He took the hot mug gingerly turning it in his hands until he had hold of the handle. Resting it on his knee, he summarised the day's events. 'There's bound to be someone with a grudge against a bookie: an unpaid debt, an unpaid bet, even.' He took a sip of the coffee, blowing the steam from the top.

'And we know what links him to the others.' I said.

'Exactly. I need to speak to Lord Blackwood. I'm afraid he's in the firing line now so I'll have to speak to him Blake. You understand, of course.'

'I do.' I nodded.

'Maybe…no…' He had a look about him that I've only seen on Rob's face a couple of times.

'Spit it out!' I said.

'Well, Lord Blackwood is probably far more likely to admit his financial problems to a friend; correct?'

'It's been a long time since we were close…'

'You have a bounced cheque and therefore a reason to ask about his financial matters…'

'True.'

'So you visit him tomorrow, say, ten a.m. I'll turn up at about quarter past to speak to him myself. That way if he clams up, he's already told you and you get the chance to tell him about the cheque. If I confront him with it, he'll know you've told me and then he'll tell neither of us anything.'

'Again, true.' The strong smell as I sipped my coffee reached up into the back of my throat and the cream left a film on my lips that I rubbed away with the palm of my hand. 'It feels a little underhand.'

'You are going to have to talk to him about the cheque, anyway.' Rob said, offering a reassuring smile.

'I was.'

'Then that's settled. You go and see him first and I'll follow you up there. He needn't know we've spoken.'

I smiled. There was no getting out of it. This was the truth of our arrangement. I was informing the police, whether it was an old friend or not. The thing was, I hadn't felt uncomfortable about it yesterday, when the finger of blame was pointing in Dockerty's direction.

'So, tell me what you know about James Dockerty.' Rob said changing the subject.

'Not a lot. I've never been a betting man.' I got up to get a teaspoon and stir my coffee again, distributing the cream a little more fairly around the cup. 'He was a grumpy man, that's a fact. He'd never say hello to you in the street. Moved here from Ireland with his family about eight years ago. Well known in the village but still very much an outsider.'

'What about his wife?'

'I never met her. I heard about her. Delilah said she was an alcoholic. Drank wine from half-eight in the morning until three in the afternoon when the kids returned home from school. Dockerty spent his evenings drinking Stella in the pub to avoid his wife. Rumour, of course, but Dockerty was a regular in The Badger's Holt so it's within the realms of possibility.'

'What do you reckon then, either of them capable of murder?'

'By all accounts, Dockerty was an aggressive drunk. Perhaps you should speak to Braydon Deveraux. He's the landlord of The Badger's Holt. From what I heard, Dockerty was more verbally than physically violent. Landed himself in A & E a couple of times when he picked on the wrong person.'

'He had no record.'

'Oh, no one ever presses charges. Braydon won't have them back in the pub if they bring police to his door.'

Rob nodded. I stood up and took the empty cups across to the sink.

'So we've got Braydon Deveraux to add to the list of people to interview. I'd better get on with it. I could go down to The Badger's Holt now,' Rob said looking at his watch, 'plenty of time. I'll have dinner there. Care to join me?'

'Why not?' Suddenly a hearty meal and a pint, sounded very inviting.

The dogs sensed our intention to depart and dragged themselves up onto four legs, all eyes expectantly on the leads hung by the door.

The pub was a short distance from the allotments and as Rob and I chatted about the state of the world's politics, I was distracted and the dogs behaved atrociously, pulling the whole way.

Behind the big wooden door, the warmth of the pub was stifling; a blanket of humidity enveloped you as you entered. The wood fire was still going. Although the weather outside was beginning to warm up, Deveraux was often reluctant to let the fire go out. He was frequently heard saying, *'Stick another log on that, will you, it's a devil to start again,'*. Bertie knew all too well where the biscuit jar was on the bar and made a beeline for it.

'Hello, Bertie,' Deveraux acknowledged the impatient Jack Russell and, reaching for the biscuit jar, continued: 'How can I help you, gentlemen?' He looked at Rob with this question, clearly not expecting custom from him, but instead, inquisition.

'We'll have some dinner, I think.' He smiled. 'Any specials?'

Deveraux was on the back foot. Hand half out of the biscuit jar, his forehead softened and he half smiled. 'Of course. The menus are here and the specials are on the board over there. You can sit at the table in the window if you like. It's open to let a bit of air in. I daren't put that fire out, it's a devil to start again,' and threw two biscuits, one each, to the dogs.

Rob took the menus.

'Can I get you a drink while you're deciding?'

I'd noticed they had Jennings Bitter on today. The Badger's Holt kept their ales well. Brewed in Cumbria, this particular bitter was something that didn't often venture so far down the country. I'd discovered it on holiday, when the family was younger.

'Pint of bitter, please, Braydon.' I took my gloves off, pushing them into the pockets of my wax jacket.

'A half for me, thanks and can you put them on a tab?' Rob looked at me and I nodded agreement.

Biscuits finished, the dogs were edging towards a large table of diners. I called them back before they got too close and gave them a warning look. They knew they were not to beg, or at least Bertie did. Prince would learn by example if he didn't already know.

I watched Deveraux pulling the drinks. He pulled the pump first with his right hand, placing the pint on the bar and, as he did so, began pulling the second half pint with his left hand. A slick and adept method of pint-pulling, I wondered how long it had taken him to perfect it.

Taking our drinks, we moved towards our table to peruse the menus. We chose a table in the pub area, rather than in the restaurant. Unfortunately the only table left was next to Mr and Mrs Faba. Thankfully they were deep in conversation as we settled ourselves, so polite acknowledgment was not necessary.

The Badger's Holt offered basic pub grub, sausage and mash, gammon egg and chips, scampi, fish goujons, the sort of fare that warmed you up. Made to sate appetites rather than look pretty on a plate.

The special was belly of pork with dauphinois potatoes. It still said *'Rawlinson's'* next to the pork. The butcher had only re-opened yesterday after a period of five days closure in bereavement. It felt a little odd ordering meat from a dead butcher, but I had noticed his son had taken over the running of the business. After fifteen years as his understudy he must have learnt some of his father's skill.

The name chalked on the board and my subsequent order brought us back to the subject of murder.

'So, that makes five.' I said, 'I suppose this isn't looking very good for you, is it?'

'Bloody awful.' Rob said, wiping the foam from his beer off his top lip with his thumb and forefinger. 'I've got Gabbett and Knighton on my back and I have nothing to give them other than a killer with a penchant for nail varnish and middle aged, male shop-owners.'

'Hmmm,' I took a sip of my pint. The thick malty bitter was the perfect temperature in the warmth that was the pub.

'This is what I'm struggling with. I didn't really know any of the victims well: wrong age group. Jane might know Rawlinson but the others didn't go to school here so she won't know them. I could ask her if you'd like. I'd risk incurring her wrath. She's dead against my involvement in any more murders.' I said.

'Shouldn't you be out there catching whoever did this!?' The forthright voice of Mr Faba came from the next table. No doubt spurred on by his wife who was sitting opposite him, his question was directed at Rob.

'We are doing the best we can, Mr...?'

'Faba. It's not good enough though, is it? Five people in this village dead, and not one suspect.' The pub was silent. Even Deveraux had stopped pulling pints to watch the show. 'I'll tell you who I think did it...'

'Mr Faba.' Rob raised his voice to interrupt and the dogs raised their heads in unison. 'Speculation is not going to help matters. If you have information I would be more than happy to speak to you at a more appropriate time.'

Mr Faba was open-mouthed at the assertiveness of the interruption. Rob stood up and approached their table.

'Here's my card. Do not hesitate to contact me if you have anything you wish to discuss.'

'I...'

'And if anyone else has anything they'd like to tell me then you are very welcome to do so. I am at the police station on the London road most days and I'll leave my mobile number on the cork board here.' Rob walked over to a small board by the bar and pinned his card decisively on to it. 'I wouldn't mind a glass of water please.' He said to Deveraux, who obediently fetched it. A few moments of silence reigned. Faba sat with his mouth open, his wife smirking at him from the other side of the table.

'Eat your soup, John, before it gets cold. You heard the sergeant, he's doing his best.' She followed this with a sickly smile directed at Rob as he returned from the bar and sat back at our table.

The dogs settled again and the general hubbub of the pub resumed.

'Well, that was an interesting diversion.' Rob said, finally.

'We don't have to stay...' I ventured.

'Nope, we're staying. I'm used to this and I'm not having them hound me out of my local. No if a police presence is what they want, a police presence is what they'll get.' He smiled raising his half pint. 'Besides, I want to see what I can get out of Deveraux later.' Rob lowered his voice another notch; the party of six, two tables away, had resumed their conversation with the vigour that had previously camouflaged our conversation. 'I thought we were onto something with that racehorse business. Now Dockerty's dead, I'm not so sure.'

'Well, other than the obvious age of the victims and their occupations, the only things that link them are Tipingee and the crosses. It might not be Dockerty that held the grudge. I don't like to admit it but maybe you're right about my old friend. Maybe there is something he's trying to cover up.' I didn't dare say his name out loud and I felt disloyal even suggesting it, but if I was going to help the police, I needed to start thinking like them: unbiased and matter-of-fact.

Rob took another sip of his beer and the kitchen door swung open as desserts were delivered to the table of six. Another couple entered the pub, bringing a welcome draught of cold air with them.

'Could it be the trainer?' Rob offered, probably trying to make me feel better. 'He left rather unceremoniously.'

I nodded. 'There's something about that nail varnish that's bothering me too.' I said. 'I'm not so sure it's someone playing a prank. It's a bit elaborate to go to the effort of using a different colour polish and a different hand to draw the cross, to put us off the scent. Better to not leave a cross at all. Unless...' I stopped; I was overthinking things.

'Go on.' Rob said, overtly interested in my surmising.

'Well, perhaps the killer didn't realise they had used a different hand or a different colour. Scarlet and cerise must look similar on a moonless night and the painter could be ambidextrous, freely able to use either hand.' I shrugged and picked up my pint again.

'Interesting.'

'Then again, the crosses might be nothing to do with it. Perhaps I'm obsessing on the wrong thing when we should be looking at a betting syndicate, as you suggested in the first place.'

'It is a bit too much of a coincidence that five crosses appear and then....'

The main course arrived and Rob stopped talking abruptly. Condiments were ordered and the dogs shuffled under the table at the smell of the freshly cooked food.

Taking up his knife and fork, Rob muttered at his food. 'Five deaths! I need to catch this guy.' He stabbed at a sausage. 'I can't have six deaths on my patch within two months.'

22.

Carrefour

The crossroads between the mortal and spirit worlds.

We enjoyed the rest of our meal without mentioning the murders again. Everyone deserves a night off, although I was all too aware that Rob was never entirely off duty. Meals finished and the bill settled, I headed home, while Rob hung on to speak to Deveraux about the locals. As I am sure Rob had calculated, the landlord was a businessman and more than willing to provide a paying customer with gossip, as opposed to a nosey police officer.

It was a new moon; a tiny sliver of light, the very end of a fingernail glinting from in-between the clouds. Despite what I had said to Rob, I still found it hard to believe my old friend was possibly the epicentre of recent events. It was undeniable that the horse and the betting shop were the only solid leads that tied the victims fates.

There was a good chunk of our lives that Rufus and I had not spent together. In fact that accounted for most of it. My first memory of Rufus was when I was five. It's one of those idyllic rose-tinted glasses memories of climbing trees and grazed knees followed by ice creams, melted in the sun, running down your arm. The consistency of those heady summer days did not last long, as the whole family had to move with his father's job but, when you have experienced childhood memories like these, there is something that ties you together. Sentimentality is a weakness of mine.

I reached my front door and opened the dark cold house that had been empty all day. Closing the door behind me, I bent down to take the dogs' leads off. Leaving my coat and gloves on, I rubbed my hands together for warmth. I walked into the lounge and turned the light on. My eyes adjusted to the bright bulb in opposition to the darkness of the night and the hallway. I walked across the room and put the fire on. The dogs immediately placed themselves in front of it. Returning to the hall, I removed my coat and jacket, my mother's words singing in my ears: *'If you don't take your coat off you won't feel the benefit when you go outside.'* It's funny how our mothers' words stay with us throughout our lives. Oracles of our childhood and no matter how often you discover they were wrong, their words still have the capacity to make you feel guilty.

I took a tumbler from the kitchen cupboard and returned to my faithful Chesterfield. Pouring myself a glass of Talisker, I sat back and listened to the creaking of the house, the clicking of the fire, the ping of the hot water tank and the gentle roar of the boiler as the house kicked into life again.

I tried, once more, to put myself in Rob's shoes: become neutral, view Rufus from a detective's detached and analytical standpoint. When I was eleven years old I remember coming home from school and complaining that one of my peers had laughed at me when I'd commented on his eating habits. My mother had told me I didn't read people well. I hadn't understood at the time but as I grew older I started to people watch and I began to understand.

Now, as I struggled with the reality that Rufus Blackwood was our prime suspect, I was reminded of her words again. My friendship with Rufus distracted me from the truth. My own values had led me to assumptions that weren't true. The boy in the dining hall had been happy eating his dinner with his knife and fork in the wrong hands. My eleven-year-old self had assumed that he did not know there was a better way. When I replayed the scene in my head, I could see his embarrassment at my words, the awkwardness of his friends around him unsure whether to laugh or defend their friend. The truth was, I had imposed my values on him, I had not considered that he may have a different way.

Age kicks a lot of this out of you, but just occasionally it can creep up on you. I didn't want to suspect Rufus because he was from a good family, with money, land, a history in the village, he held his knife and fork correctly and most importantly I had shared childhood memories with him. My overriding assumption was that the Lord of the Manor and my childhood friend could not possibly be involved in nefarious dealings, and certainly not murder!

But what if he was the sociopath we were looking for. There are differing degrees of the condition and they don't announce themselves. They just are; potentially lurking in the mind of you friend.

If Rufus was struggling for money then I was pretty sure he wouldn't want people to know. He was a proud man. But would he go to the lengths of fraud or even murder to cover that up? It was just possible Rufus had sacked his trainer, not to cover up a dodgy deal but instead because they had genuinely had a disagreement. Maybe I was too willing to believe the worst. There I was again blundering around in a quagmire of assumption without a pair of Wellie boots. But convincing myself my assumptions were the antithesis of the truth was as bad as making the assumptions in the first place.

Perhaps I wasn't as good at reading people after all. I was beginning to wonder why Rob had asked for my help at all. What possible assistance could a sixty-two year old balding, slightly obsessive, hat making, people watcher be? Was I in fact a fraud, an impostor in a world I shouldn't be in? But I had made an agreement and as a gentleman it was my duty to keep it. I would have to go and see Rufus and ask him about the cheque. There had to be a simple explanation.

Self -doubt was clouding my thought process. It was not something I was used to. I'd always been able to solve problems easily. As a child, chess was a pleasure.

The last two murders in Tuesbury had virtually unravelled themselves for me. The clues were there if I paid attention. But my memory was failing me. I was missing Delilah's enthusiasm and encouragement; her indefatigable confidence that we would solve the case.

I must have drifted off on the sofa because the next thing I knew it was three a.m. Taking myself to bed, I slept for a further three hours and arose aching, feeling my age. I was not relishing the thought of today's task. Procrastinating further, I took the dogs for a long walk around the village and through Druid Wood. Returning them home, I ran out of excuses and headed for Blackwood Manor.

Rufus was positively ecstatic to see me again so soon. He herded me into the large drawing room, fetched coffee, and immediately started to tell me about Tipingee. I tried not to show any emotion with regard to the horse but my distance eventually led to the question, '…is everything all right, Blake, old chap?'

I could not hide my face as I was asked a direct question that required a direct answer. Not the vague nods, smiles and mmms that had preceded it.

'Well…' I tugged at the knees of my beige cords. I noticed the socks I had chosen this morning were ever so slightly different shades.

'Come on, Blake, it can't be that bad. What's bothering you?'

'It's a bit embarrassing.' I said.

'Women trouble?' Blackwood smirked into his coffee as he took a sip.

'Absolutely not!'

'Okay, okay, so you're a saint. What is it, then?'

'That cheque you gave me…it bounced.'

'Good grief.' Blackwood stood up as his cheeks burned red. 'I'm terribly sorry old chap, I can't think why that is. Here, I'll get you the money now, I should have it in the safe.' He ran his words together quickly and headed towards a desk in the corner of the room, still holding his coffee cup.

'It's not a problem, Rufus, I was just concerned about you.'

'Not a problem, not a problem, I must pay you for your work, Blake. It's outrageous, I shall get straight onto the bank as soon as we've finished catching up.' By this point he was talking into the safe, which was under a desk. I looked at my watch. Any minute now Rob would be appearing.

'What do you mean, concerned?' Rufus said, head reappearing from the safe. He closed the heavy door and walked back towards me with a roll of notes.

'Well….'

'Come on, spit it out.'

'There's a rumour about your horse, Rufus.' I knew I was stepping on the sergeant's toes, but I still had a loyalty to my friend.

'My horse?'

'Yes. Tipingee.'

'Tipingee? Well, what are people saying?'

'That she's not a winner.'

'But she is, everyone's seen her win.' Blackwood sat back down on the sofa; his face was the embodiment of confusion.

'Well…' how was I going to say this? I'd started and I had to finish, '… some people are saying you fixed it.'

'Fixed it! My horse! Fixed! Blake, you know me better than that!' He bellowed.

'I rather hoped I did,' I said before I could check myself. Blackwood's aggression had caught me off guard. In my experience, people were rarely so aggressive in their defence, unless they had something to hide.

I was saved as the doorbell rang.

We sat looking at each other for a couple of seconds at the most. Rufus stood up and straightened his shirt collar. 'I'd better get that. I'm not sure we should continue this conversation, Blake, we may end it as enemies and I wouldn't want that.'

It was difficult not to agree. Rufus left the room to answer the door.

'Well, this is a surprise,' I heard Rufus' voice. 'How very nice to see you again, Claringdon.' I envisaged him extending a hand towards the sergeant, who given the reply, extended his warrant card.

'I'm here in an official capacity I'm afraid Lord Blackwood. I need to ask you a few questions. Is now a good time?'

There was a pause and I heard the door creak as it was opened a little further, 'Of course, come in.' Blackwood's voice was light and jovial. Calm, given the recent outburst. I imagined his face, as inscrutable as only a Lord with plenty of experience in the diplomatic corps can manage.

Rob's shoes clicked on the parquet flooring of the hallway and I stood up from the chair as they both entered the drawing room.

'Ah, Blake, Sergeant Claringdon here wants to ask me a few questions, so I'm afraid I'm going to have to cut our chat short.' Rufus said as he entered.

'Not a problem.' I said, grateful to be able to extricate myself from what was turning into a very awkward situation. I took my coat and made towards the door, passing Rob on the way.

'Mr Hetherington.' Rob said.

'Sergeant Claringdon.' I said, not making any solid eye contact. I have never been very good at subterfuge and I felt like a complete cad.

I'd accused Rufus, one of my friends, of having no money and fixing a horse, in one clumsy fell swoop. I only hoped I hadn't blown the sergeant's element of surprise and tipped Blackwood off, putting him on the alert. He hadn't asked me who had started the rumours. Was this because he knew? Was he fully aware of the betting circle? Had he tipped them off as Kinney suggested?

It wasn't until I was well on my way back along the road to Tuesbury that I realised I'd left without the money. Now I was out of pocket and, very likely, minus a friend. Rufus had been incandescent. Was it bluster or did he truly have nothing to hide? Was Rob correct in persisting with the line of questioning in regard to the racehorse? With the sudden recognition that I could no longer trust people I had known for years, I was beginning to suspect everyone.

I felt sure we had reached a crucial moment in this investigation: a crossroads. One way would lead us to the answer, the other to a dead end. The question was, which way should we go?

23.

Regler:

Someone who has command over the Voodoun gods or loa and is able to quiet and restrain them.

'Blackwood has an alibi, for every murder,' Rob announced. Ten a.m. had been my usual coffee break, when I had the shop. It was a chance to read the paper and gather my thoughts before the lunchtime trade. I no longer had the predictable ebb and flow of the shop custom but I had recently taken up the habit once more and Rob hadn't taken long to learn that ten was coffee time again. It had been no surprise to me when he'd knocked on the door, a minute or so before ten. I even had a mug out ready for him. Rob was clutching a bag from the bakery, which had finally reopened.

I eyed the bag, hoping for almond croissants but knowing they'd never be the same again. 'I can't say I'm disappointed.' I said 'The idea of someone I've known all my life, being a murderer is disturbing.'

'I'm in the shit Blake.' I rarely heard Rob swear. He wasn't a dramatic man, always very matter-of-fact. 'Potentially we've got a serial killer here and the commissioner has given Gabbett a flea in his ear, who in turn has told Knighton we've got forty-eight hours to come up with something. This can only end one of two ways: I catch this guy, or I'm back in uniform.'

'I see.'

Rob opened the bakery bag onto a side plate I'd provided. Doughnuts: at least I wasn't going to be disappointed by lacklustre croissants. I resigned myself to the fact that this was not going to be simply a ten-minute coffee. Rob wanted a brainstorming session. He was sitting forward in his chair, elbows resting on knees, hands out in front of him holding his coffee. His lips were tight together and his forehead creased. His dark manicured eyebrows shadowed his eyes.

I looked out of the window across the allotment, patiently waiting for Rob's inevitable questions. It was a brilliantly sunny day and the rooks were making their usual racket in the far trees of Druid Wood. The wispy clouds that populated the blue sky were at a standstill. I could see Olea Faba tending to her borlotti beans in her greenhouse. There were a couple of other allotment regulars, digging over the soil and planting new crops. I felt a pang of guilt at neglecting my own allotment. If Rob hadn't been there I might well have taken advantage of the fine day. The Derby was two stitches from finished. I consoled myself that with the likelihood of a dry day I would get out there this afternoon after the dogs' walk.

Rob stood up; I half expected him to start talking but instead he paced the shed, coffee in one hand, the other on his chin.

I went back to watching the digging.

'I still think it's got something to do with this horse.' Rob said, finally stopping in the middle of the shed. 'Blackwood's denying everything. Says it's all above board, but he was shifty.'

I cringed inwardly. Thank goodness I was still looking out of the window or my face may have betrayed me. I knew I had essentially tipped off Blackwood.

'Kinney didn't do it, he was at the cash and carry, so two cashiers plus CCTV can vouch for him. His alibis for the other murders check out too. Blackwood though: he says he was having dinner at home with his lady friend, Darensky is it?'

'So she's still on the scene?'

'Yes, she's his alibi.'

'Well, I don't like to say this of a lady, but she is only in it for the money. Rufus admitted as much to me….'

'That makes his alibi fallible then! Maybe he's paying her.' Rob interrupted.

I balked at this. The idea of Rufus paying a lady of the night, which is what I assume Rob was implying, was outrageous.

'I only mention it, because if Rufus was so desperate for money that he had to fix a racehorse and possibly commit murder, she wouldn't still be around.' I said.

'Ah…yes.'

I went to the back of the shed to pour myself some more coffee. I raised the cafetière in Rob's direction and he held his mug out for more.

'So there has to be someone else involved in this.'

'The trainer? Have you caught up with him yet?'

'No. We've put out an APB and posters asking for information but nothing. It is very suspicious that he's gone missing but you'd think he'd have been seen somewhere. In this village someone should have seen him, or he should even have been on the CCTV that covers the High Street, something to put him in the vicinity of the murders over the last few weeks. The officers have gone over and over the tapes. There's nothing. No one behaving differently. No-one that fits the profile.'

'So you do have a profile?' The amateur psychologist within me was interested.

A shadow caught my eye and Mrs Dellaware rounded the corner of the shed. I frowned. It wasn't unusual for people to use the allotments as a cut through to Poets Avenue but I objected to people walking directly across my allotment in order to do so. Ever since the dispute over the ancient right of way last year, people seemed to care even less about the carefully constructed paths across the plots. A lot of them believed Nyeman was right, that this was public land and the public had a right to walk where they wanted.

She didn't look in the window as some do, so I did not get the opportunity to visually express my displeasure. She was preoccupied, muttering to herself. I couldn't hear what she was saying.

'Who's that?' Rob said, doughnut halfway towards his mouth. His voice caught Mrs Dellaware's ear and she looked up, startled. She folded her arms around a plastic bag and held it close, hurrying on across the allotment.

'Mrs Dellaware.' I replied when she was out of earshot.

'She seems familiar. Do people often walk across your allotment?'

'Unfortunately, yes. Mrs Dellaware's a long-standing member of the community and is therefore of the opinion that all land in Tuesbury is her land.'

'Wasn't it her nephew that was on the green at the same time as Pane was found?'

'Yes, it was.' I turned to look at Rob now who was watching Mrs Dellaware as she scurried across the allotments and disappeared down Poets Avenue.

'Santa Domingo he said he was from, didn't he? Profiler thinks it's likely to be a new person to the village. Someone with no loyalty.'

'Well he's new.' I replied, 'But how on earth would he be involved with Rufus Blackwood's horse? Rufus doesn't even know him.' I finished the rest of my coffee.

'Or does he? We never asked Mr Yveny him about his leisure habits. Sure, we know he's a Morris dancer but that doesn't mean he doesn't like to place a bet or two.'

Something in the way Rob said this jogged my memory. Donald Yveny *was* new here. He'd blended into the background up until now. 'Wait a minute, I saw him coming out of the bookie's a few weeks ago.' I said triumphantly setting my cup down in the tin sink with a clang that sent a blackbird, rooting around outside, caterwauling across the allotments.

'Worth checking out. It was him who suggested we speak to Elroy Tuvey, wasn't it?'

'Perhaps it was a smoke screen. All this Voodoo nonsense with the crosses is just a red herring.' Rob became animated. 'Maybe he was just trying to divert attention away from himself and onto Tuvey.'

'True. Elroy wasn't able to give me much more information, although our discussion was very informative. Voodoo's an interesting subject.' I said.

'Yes, but what if that was just to put us off. What if Tuvey's in on it too!? That would mean we're on the right track with the racehorse. Excuse the pun.' Rob was now standing in the middle of the room again, staring at his feet. 'Blackwood's clammed up, and the trainer's AWOL, so I'll have to find another way,' he said and waited for my addition to the conversation, but I was out of ideas.

'I don't think he's likely to want to speak to me again.'

Rob raised his eyebrows.

'I'm afraid I may have inferred Tipingee wasn't all that legitimate.'

'I see.' Rob said. He was looking out of one of the windows now, composing himself. I knew he was irritated with me but I couldn't right my blunders now. Rufus wasn't going to welcome me with open arms.

Even if he had forgiven me, he was bound to be more guarded.

'Well, that explains a lot.' Rob said looking back at me. I was uncomfortable under the scrutiny of Rob's gaze. He'd given me my first task and I'd failed him: let my friendship with Rufus get in the way. But I could tell Rob blamed himself. He'd let an untrained civilian become involved and one whose judgement was clouded with sentimentality. I only hoped he would be able to trust me again, as I had every desire to help in any way I could. If Rufus was at the middle of this then I would feel responsible if my blunders let him off scot-free.

'Never mind,' Rob continued, 'we'll just have to find another way. I can't help feeling Blackwood and that horse are at the bottom of this. Somehow the bookie's holds the key. I have several books of betting records to look through. I need to see who else bet on that horse.'

Thinking about Tuvey once more and Rob's assertion that he may somehow be involved, I made another suggestion, an attempt to recompense for my misdemeanour. 'What if this is a religious thing, not Voodoo?'

'What do you mean?'

'Well, Elroy tells me, Voodoo has some of its roots in the Roman Catholic Church.'

'Don't let them hear you say that.' Rob smirked.

'No, but what if it's someone who believes gamblers are sinners. It might be nothing to do with the horse they are betting on, just the simple act of betting that has brought them to the attention of the murderer. Could they feel that they are doing the Lord's work?'

We went on to discuss the pros and cons of the religious aspects of the case. Again the crosses came up and again they were consigned to the red herring pile. Rob was convinced a betting ring had formed, got greedy and now needed to be silenced. He left not long after he'd finished his coffee to look further into the bookie's records. He gave me no indication of when I would hear from him next or what I was to do to help, if anything. It could be that I was being over-sensitive. I was only helping in a consulting capacity after all. Until he had something else to consult me about, I wasn't much use.

He'd only been gone a few minutes when there was a tentative knock at the door. I got up, frustrated to be interrupted again. I still hadn't completed the final two stitches of the Derby, which were now tormenting me.

Getting up, I opened the door to find Mrs Dellaware standing on the slabs that led through the onion patch. At least she was on the path this time.

'Hello.' I said. The sun was bright and low in the sky and I squinted at her silhouette.

'Mr Hetherington, I need your help.' She said, her hands fidgeting with the buttons of her duffel coat.

'You'd better come in.' I didn't know Mrs Dellaware well, but she had an urgency in her voice which could not be ignored. 'Can I get you a cup of tea?'

'No it's fine, thank you.' She stood in the middle of the shed still plucking at the buttons. Then her hand went to her head and she frowned, as if she were in pain.

'Are you okay, Mrs Dellaware? Sit down, please.' I guided her to one of the armchairs.

'I'm fine, it's the light.' She said wincing at the little strip light I have above the kitchen sink. The sunshine outside meant that I hadn't noticed it was on, let alone that it was flickering.

I took a couple of steps across the room and turned it off.

'There.' I said, 'Now, are you sure you won't have a drink.'

'Some water, thank you.'

I filled a glass from the bottle on the workbench. Her face was no longer compressed in pain and instead was flushed and her eyes had a distant look about them; a sleepwalker in the afternoon.

'Thank you,' she said, taking the glass from me. Her voice was thick and groggy, and she took the glass in both hands, steadying it.

'Are you sure I shouldn't get your nephew?'

'NO!' She almost shouted this, but checked herself and looked up, giving me a weak smile.

I sat in the chair opposite her and waited for her to steady herself. I wasn't sure what all this was about but I sensed she should not be rushed. A picture formed in my mind: a memory. Mrs Dellaware sat with her head in her hands at the bus stop and Donald standing over her. This was obviously something that happened often.

It was about ten minutes before Constance spoke again. I had busied myself with tidying away the Derby. The stitches would have to wait. Karma clearly didn't want me to work today.

'Is Prince not here?' Mrs Dellaware finally said.

'No they're at home. I only intended to be here for an hour or two this morning. I was just finishing up and then I'll go and walk them.'

'They must keep you fit.' She smiled.

'They do. Especially when they run off after squirrels in the woods. It's all I can do to keep them in earshot.' I smiled back.

Mrs Dellaware took another sip of water and smoothed her mousy brown hair back into its ponytail.

'So how can I help you?' I ventured, hoping to bring us back to the reason for her visit. I was worried the dogs would be getting restless. I had been gone almost three hours now and it was midday: walk time.

'What?' She looked up, puzzled, and then as if the proverbial penny had dropped she said. 'Oh…yes. It's Donald. I'm worried he's in some kind of trouble.'

'Your nephew?'

'Donald… yes.'

'What sort of trouble would that be?'

'He's got in with the wrong crowd.' She tapped her fingers on the side of the glass; the light from the sun outside glinted off the convex shape.

'The wrong crowd?'

'Yes, those Morris Dancers,' she said, indignant but concerned.

'The Morris men?' I said. It was all I could do not to laugh. Okay they liked their beer and in some counties they even blacked their faces, but I never thought of them as the wrong crowd.

'They drink too much.' Her voice crescendoed, 'and he's always down that pub, gets back at all hours; I never know where he is.'

'I see.' I said. I couldn't help feeling that as a man, who I presumed was in his forties, Donald Yveny was perfectly entitled to make his own decisions and spend his time as he saw fit. From the brief encounters I'd had with Mrs Dellaware, a drink is precisely what I'd need if I spent long in her company.

'...and he's betting.' She finished leaning forward and placing the glass decisively on the bench.

'He's a grown man, Mrs Dellaware, I'm afraid I fail to see what I can do to help.' I smiled.

'I thought you might look out for him, you know.'

I did not know, and I remained silent. I was not about to become the village mentor.

'You took Miss Delibes under your wing when she had no one. Donald doesn't have anyone. His father's not interested.'

I processed this information. She must have read in the papers about Delilah's mother going missing, two years ago now. Donald hadn't mentioned his father when he'd told us of his trip here from Santa Domingo. He'd mentioned the death of his mother, but no father.

'I see.' I cleared my throat. I was trying to find a way to put this delicately but there was no other way. 'He's a grown man, Mrs Dellaware, and Delilah is a grown woman, a friend. I assure you I do not influence her behaviour.' This fact was to my chagrin, when it came to the hatinators Delilah insisted on wearing.

'So, you won't help?' She held me in a steely look. Her voice was clearer now; firm and determined.

'I fail to see how I can.' I replied.

'Fine.' She said, standing up with such force that she pushed the chair back a good foot.

Her sudden movement surprised me and I was still sitting in my chair as she reached the door and opened it, letting in a bright shaft of light. I stood up to see her out, but there was no need.

'I'm sorry to have troubled you, Mr Hetherington.' And she was gone.

A most peculiar visit, from a most peculiar woman. I searched my brain for an explanation. I didn't even know Mrs Dellaware that well. I remembered her father had travelled with his job. She'd spent most of her childhood away from the village, as many of us had. There was nothing peculiar about this. It did mean that there were chapters of village life you'd missed. Often there was an unexplainable bond and yet you didn't fully know each other. Like the bond Rufus and I had. Perhaps this is what had brought Constance to my door.

However, she must know that her nephew was his own man. The one thing that did resonate was her mention of his betting habit and his *'return at all hours of the night'*. I should pass this on to Rob. Was it indeed as he suspected? Was Yveny involved? There were plenty that placed a bet in the village, plenty put out by the closure of the betting shop while the family grieved and plenty that would see it as an omen. Every time I looked once more to the significance of the crosses in the model village, something else was pointing at the betting shop. I couldn't help but feel someone was manipulating us, controlling the direction of this investigation, but who was it?

24.

Wanga

A magic charm of malevolent intent.

It was Friday. Admin day. I hadn't spoken to Rob for three days now. I presumed he was interviewing punters who had bet on Tipingee, or who perhaps had just run up large debts. Either that or he was back in uniform as threatened.

Terry Kinney had taken his family to Ireland. It was hardly surprising. With five of the six models' counterparts dead, Kinney had more reason than ever to be worried. Returning to one's roots in times of need is a natural reaction to such a situation. Terry Kinney was just protecting his family the way he knew how. What was surprising is that the police had allowed it. The chip shops continued to run themselves with reliable staff, and, according to village gossip, a cross was yet to appear on the model fish and chip shop.

Today I was in need of some new needles. The dogs would enjoy the walk to the haberdashery on the London road, a little longer than their usual jaunt around the wood. Despite ominous grey clouds hovering that morning, I was confident it would not rain. The barometer in the hallway pointed stubbornly at 1050 isobars - very dry. The barometer never lied.

Even though we were now into March, the grey clouds meant I had to turn the lights on in the living room. I was reminded of the light I had to fix in the shed. The flickering strip light above the sink needed a new bulb, which could also be obtained on my visit to the London road. Huskin's Hardware would provide me with the correct bulb. I needed a whiter light than your usual strip lights and the daylight bulbs I used were both expensive and hard to come by. Huskin's seemed to have a reliable source for these bulbs and they often lasted over a year.

Once I had a cup of tea in my hand, I turned the computer on. I had some invoices to file and e-mails to respond to before going anywhere. I knew there were five non-urgent e-mails I'd been saving for today. Two from previous customers thanking me, one from a customer wanting a quote - I usually sent them out within five days - one from the County Show asking if I would be interested in a stall, and finally an e-mail from the electricity board, telling me my bill was ready to check online; an e-mail I hated. Why couldn't they just stick to good old paper?

One of the emails looked like spam. Then I realised it contained the words *'D Delibes'*. It was a direct link to a website. Both my daughter and Delilah had warned me about e-mails that wanted you to enter information, bank account details etc. As if I was likely to do that. This one didn't ask for anything, though. There was a link that you should click on. I carefully highlighted it, right clicked and copied the link. Opening the Internet browser I pasted the link into the address box at the top, rather pleased with myself that after a year of using the computer I was finally getting to grips with the whole thing.

The screen whirred and ticked and within a few seconds Delilah's face appeared under the heading *'Haiti Adventure'*. She was posing in a very muddy fleece beside a shallow trench that contained what looked like a skeleton. She had a huge grin on her face most unbefitting for such a macabre scene. Below the picture was the title *'Dig at En Bas Saline - could this be one of Columbus' crew?'*

There was no other message with the e-mail and I presumed Delilah had sent me the link to encourage me to read it. I had a feeling I may be questioned later and diligently read on. It was a very interesting article on what I now know is Delilah's Blog; an electronic log of her work in Haiti. In the article she explains the story of Christopher Columbus and his ship, the Santa Maria. The Santa Maria was his flagship and it met its fate on a reef near what is now En Bas Saline. The indigenous people of a nearby town helped him and his crew salvage what they could of the wreck. The chief of the town offered Columbus a large house as refuge. His fleet now one vessel short, Columbus had no choice but to leave a crew of thirty-nine men behind, with the promise of returning for them in a year. They were ordered to make a tower and a moat around the house and to search for gold. When Columbus finally returned he found his men dead and the fort burnt to the ground.

The frustration and guilt Columbus must have felt on returning to such a scene must have been overwhelming. Although a conquering colonial may not have these feelings. I was impressed by Delilah's article but, more than that, she'd tapped into a feeling I'd pushed deep down unwilling to analyse: good old guilt.

Eleanor had been taken into hospital at 5.47 a.m. on a Thursday. I had stayed by her side all day. Jane was travelling up from Devon later that day after work. They told me she was stable. *'Go home, Mr Hetherington,'* they'd said, *'get some rest.'* So I did. I believed them. They were medical staff. My daughter was a nurse and I'd heard her talk about distraught and worn out relatives becoming a hindrance when treating patients. I went home at eight that evening. I kissed her goodbye. She had smiled weakly. Her face lopsided, sad and as I remember it, lost. At 20:34 on the 12th December 2003, Eleanor died of a massive stroke. That's what they told me. Gone: my lasting memory to be always of a woman lost in her own body. I now know that several small strokes lead up to the *coup de grace*. But my guilt is not assuaged. It's still there: it still bubbles under the surface. In truth, deep down, this is what drives me to help Rob. I want to stop more people losing loved ones unnecessarily. I want to prevent it happening to them: the guilt of not knowing you were saying your final goodbye, the weighty feeling of unfinished business.

I turned off the computer. I needed some fresh air. A walk up the London road would clear the ghosts of the past that had lodged themselves in the cobwebs. The dogs lifted their heads as I got up from my seat, anticipating a walk. Attaching their leads once more, I turned off the lights, grabbed my coat and cane, and headed out.

On the allotments, the owners were conspicuous by their absence. It being a Friday, people often had other things to do in preparation for the weekend: tidying the house ready for weekend visitors or last minute shopping in town.

The dogs stayed on the lead for the walk along the High Street and to the top of the London road. Traffic rarely paid attention to pedestrians on the pavement, even less so dogs and I wasn't sure enough of Prince yet to let him off his lead. Bertie, I knew, would trot along the path sniffing at the hedgerow. Prince was becoming a very worthy companion and certainly listened to my commands when Bonios were on offer, but I wasn't yet confident of his obedience.

A familiar gold painted van whizzed by and beeped as we were rounding the corner for the walk down the London road. It was Derek Nyeman. I tried to avoid the man if I could but ever since he had been involved in the arrest of a murderer last year, he seemed to consider us allies. This was the last thing I considered. He was a bad penny; an unwelcome wasp at a picnic. I hoped he was not going to the industrial estate, or if he was, I hoped he would be gone by the time we got there.

The haberdashery is a little slice of heaven. The smell of the fabrics, the wide aisles full of familiar tools; it was like coming home. Of course it pales in comparison to the Paris shops. Their rainbows of felt and handcrafted hat pommels. You wouldn't find that here. I had to rely on old contacts and online ordering for the more specialised end of my trade. But the haberdashery on the London road kept the correct needles, a good supply of Gutermann threads and excellent quality ribbon, which I could use as hatbands.

The dogs remained outside, leads tied to the bicycle rack. I noticed Nyeman's van was parked at the far end of the complex. If I was lucky I could get in and out without bumping into him, I knew he'd have no reason to enter the haberdashery. I was woefully incorrect. I was alerted first by the dogs barking. Over the couple of weeks I'd had them, they hadn't worried about being left outside. They had each other for company and were often fussed by passers by. From where I was I could see through the double doors what was making them bark. They had the good sense to show affront at Derek Nyeman. Their little doggy brains were not fooled by his attempts to make friends on the way past. I ducked down the aisle of needles and embroidery frames. I studied the various packets and I waited. Two minutes passed: an age.

'Mr Hetherington,' announced a loud voice. The shop fell silent, or at least that's how it felt. The tills still beeped and conversations continued. The surrounding fabric deadened the background noise, all except for the voice of Nyeman, clear as a bell. There was no pretending you hadn't heard.

'How are you?' he enquired.

'Very well, thank you.' I did not ask in return. I do not like being rude. However, when faced with the possibility of an agonising conversation with such a man, one has no other choice.

'What do you reckon to these murders then?' he said.

I looked away from him and towards the needles once more. To any normal human being this would indicate my unwillingness to discuss this subject, but not Nyeman.

'Come on, Blake. I know you've got the inside info. Who do you reckon did it?'

I looked at him with the most neutral face I could muster. Nyeman was a gossip. He had his fingers in many pies. He had probably seen Rob coming in and out of the shed over the last week and put two and two together. It wouldn't have been difficult.

'I'm not sure what you mean.' I replied.

'Blake, Blake,' he said lowering his voice. 'Yes you do, so come on, tell an old comrade in arms eh?'

The presumption that he could use my first name coupled by its overuse raised my hackles. However, Nyeman was not an enemy that any sensible man would want. His ability to stir the proverbial was unrivalled. Nyeman's intent was never anything other than ill-willed.

'I'm sure that when the police have arrested their man, it will be all over the papers.' I said.

'So, it's a man, eh?' Nyeman replied. I could have kicked myself. The implication was out there and there was no backtracking. It hadn't occurred to me until just now that in my mind the murderer was a man.

'Look, Nyeman,' I said taking a step closer. 'I really can't help and I don't like gossip so perhaps….'

'All right, all right, you've made your point, you always were a bit stuffy.' Nyeman cut me short. He screwed up his nose and waved his hand dismissively with this last word. I resented it. We were almost the same age. He was only five years my junior. I remembered him in the first year of senior school barging through the doors, running and shouting in corridors, while I as a fifth year prefect tried hard to prevent the smaller children falling in his wake. I recalled something I told Jane when she was younger. *'If you've nothing nice to say, don't say anything'*. So, I did not reply. Instead I turned back to the needles and my eyes fell conveniently on the packet I had been looking for. I plucked it from the rack and headed towards the till. Unfortunately this meant I had to pass Nyeman. He was taking a breath in to restart the conversation when the unmistakable sound of *ribbiting* came from somewhere in the vicinity. A frown overtook Nyeman's face and I looked at him expectantly, thinking he must have the answer to this strange noise. It took me a second or two to connect it to the subtle vibration in my pocket. Putting my hand in my pocket I pulled out my phone. I stared at it. Why on earth was my phone making frog sounds? Then I remembered. Delilah had taken my phone to programme in the number of her lodgings in Haiti, in case of emergency. It was just the sort of thing she'd think was funny.

'Are you going to answer that, then?' Nyeman said and stropped off down the aisle back towards the main doors. Not so much saved by the bell as saved by the frogs.

I answered the phone, 'Hello, Blake Hetherington.'

It was Rob. His voice was exuberant and loud in my ear.

'Blake, we've got our man!' he said.

25.
Engagement

This is an alliance between a mortal person and a loa. The person rewards the loa for providing certain services.

I arranged to meet Rob back at the shed in as long as it would take me to walk back down the London road, onto the High Street and back to the allotment. Nyeman was left standing outside the haberdashery, mouth open, annoyed but thankfully easily ignored. Before I could go anywhere I had to untangle the dogs where they had wandered around and underneath the bicycle rack. What ensued was an awkward few minutes of Nyeman watching me deconstruct the *cat's cradle* of leads.

Twenty minutes later and the four of us were settled, once more, in the familiar surroundings of the shed. The chair with the tartan blanket across the back of it, facing the door, was fast becoming Rob's second office. He placed a large A4 diary on the small table beside it and his mobile squarely in the middle of it. His fingers steepled thoughtfully, he waited until I was seated and the dogs were settled under the bench before beginning.

'We got him...' He said leaning forward. All of a sudden he leapt out of the chair and crawled under the bench with the dogs. The case had finally got to him. Five murders were enough to tip the most seasoned professionals over the edge, I felt sure. It wasn't until there was a knock at the door and I peered through the spy hole, that I realised what was going on. But policemen don't normally hide from visitors; it is normally the other way around. Prince growled at the intrusion. I shushed him, got up and lifted the chair so that it didn't make too much noise as I placed it in front of the bench to shield the policeman's shiny shoes from the door as I opened it.

'Mr Hetherington, I'm glad you're here.' It was Mrs Dellaware again. 'Donald's in trouble and I need your help.' Her voice was shrill, her eyes focused and she held her gaze. There was no fiddling with buttons; her hands were thrust firmly in her pockets, shoulders hunched.

The door was not open fully and I held my stance; careful not to invite her in with any implication in my body language. Why was Rob hiding from Mrs Dellaware?

'I'm afraid now is not a convenient time Mrs Dellaware.'

'I see.' She said. She looked back along the path to the allotments and then back at me. 'I'm sorry if I was abrupt with you the other day, it's just I'm worried about Donald. They've arrested him.'

'I think you'd do better to get him a solicitor then, Mrs Dellaware.'

'I need your help, Mr Hetherington.' She was pleading this time, tears in her eyes and I felt awful when I replied.

'I don't think I can help you with this, but I can give you the name of a good solicitor if you'd like?'

'No!' She shouted. 'You're as bad as the rest of them.' She was talking loud enough for Olea Faba, who was digging up some new potatoes, five plots away, to hear. Although I could not see from where I was, the familiar chit and thunk of the soil being turned had stopped. Prince started to bark. Rob must have silenced him because he was quiet again before I could turn and admonish him.

'I'm sorry….' I started as I turned back.

'Forget it, forget it, I'll have to sort it out myself. My relatives will help, they'll know what to do.' Her voice lowered.

'I think that's a very good idea.'

'They'll tell me what to do about you!' She said; this time her eyes were slits and her finger jabbed the air, pointing in my direction. Taken aback by the venom in her voice I said nothing. 'As bad as the others.' She muttered.

She started to walk back down the path.

'I'm very sorry Mrs Dellaware. If you need a good solicitor, let me know.' It was all I could think of to say. I do so hate animosity and Mrs Dellaware was clearly very distressed. Quite how her relatives could have anything to say about me, I did not know. I didn't even know any of Mrs Dellaware's family, apart from her nephew and I'd been nothing but polite and courteous, I was sure.

I watched her disappear up the path again, muttering as she went. I was transfixed. She reached the little gate of the allotments and turned around. Raising her hands up to the sky she chanted, but it was so brief I couldn't tune into it properly; two lines of a poem, perhaps. Her arms fell back to her side and she hurried off through the gate and on down the High Street.

'You can come out now.' I said, closing the door.

Rob crawled out from under the bench and stood up, brushing himself down. He was covered in dog hair. The dogs looked at him, hurt by his departure. A new friend to join them was a real treat in their opinion even if he hadn't brought dog biscuits.

I looked at him with my best *'care to explain?'* look. One I had learnt from years of being a father.

'She's a nutter!' Rob said, brushing his jacket down with both hands.

'I'm not sure that's all that politically correct, Rob.' I said, handing him a lint roller I kept in the top drawer of my desk. Dog hair and hats didn't mix well and I was fastidious about removing every trace. 'You have arrested her nephew.'

'She's been in the police station all morning, driving the desk sergeant mad! Mr Yveny may well be her nephew but he doesn't want us to discuss anything with her. I have to respect that.'

'Even if it means hiding under a bench?'

'Okay, okay, you've made your point. It was unprofessional, but she'd never have left if she'd seen me. I saw her walking over the allotments and it was a split second decision. Hide or endure another hour of how innocent her nephew is.'

'And he isn't, I presume.' I said, taking a seat in the chair opposite where Rob had been sitting. I was getting used to sitting with my back to the door but it still unnerved me. My penance for being too polite to turf Rob out of what was usually my seat.

'Nope!' he resolutely tore off a strip of the lint roller and, with a fresh sheet, attacked his trousers. 'In fact, he's confessed.' He said at the floor.

'Confessed?' I was surprised. The last time we'd spoken there was only a possibility that Yveny was involved in all of this and now he was the perpetrator.

'Yes. I'd better start at the beginning. But this is between you and me, Blake, right?'

'Obviously.' I replied.

'Constable Alston checked through the Dockerty's books and found several people had run up debts. Not surprising.' He placed the lint roller on the bench and sat back down, picking up his coffee. So Constable Alston was back from honeymoon; that explained Rob's absence. He had his right-hand man back at last. 'Some of them had managed to clear a lot of their debt by betting on Tipingee; just a bit too much of a coincidence. There were five in total; that included Pane and Davies, whom we can't interview. So we started with the three remaining names: those betting on Tipingee and who weren't dead.'

'Live suspects is a good place to start, I imagine.' I said.

He nodded, choosing to ignore my sarcasm. 'They had the biggest motive. Two names I didn't recognise and one other I did. Donald Yveny. When we went to speak to Yveny he was distinctly unhelpful. His aunt was there, of course, so that could be the reason for his reticence. I suggested he might want to speak to us later, down at the station. With a lack of any real evidence other than betting debts, which there is no law against, there was little else we could do. I went on to interview the other two but they were all very open about their debts, said Tipingee had been a bit of luck.'

I nodded and walked across to the kettle. Rob continued.

'Then, yesterday Yveny came into the station. Strode right up to the desk sergeant, said he wanted to confess to the murders. The sergeant almost choked on his tea. That sort of thing doesn't happen very often in Tuesbury. In fact there's been talk of closing the station down, it's seen so little action, and of creating a satellite desk in the library. I doubt that will happen now all these murders have occurred. *'Crime central'* the chief's calling it.' Rob seemed to switch off for a moment, staring into his coffee cup, perhaps recollecting the horrors of the last few weeks, the relief visible now the search was finally over.

'So, Yveny's your man?' I ventured, handing him a cup of tea.

'Yup. Confessed all, told us how he'd taken the models and how he'd killed each corresponding vicitim. We even found all the models at the back of his sock drawer when we searched the property. He told us about Voodoo, how he'd learnt it from his mother as a child growing up in Santa Domingo.'

'I see.' I had a feeling there was a *'but'* coming up.

Rob looked up from his cup. 'It just seems a bit too convenient.' He said.

I said nothing.

'I mean, why confess now?'

'Maybe he thought you were too close to finding out the truth?' I said.

'Maybe. But we had nothing on him, save for a few betting debts and his only alibi being his aunt. A good solicitor would get him off. It's just a bit too convenient.'

Bertie came to join the conversation and settled on my feet, legs in the air, demanding his tummy be scratched. 'So it was nothing to do with Tipingee after all.' I said.

'Well, yes and no. Donald's motive isn't all that clear either. He says that all the victims had cheated him out of money but he wouldn't say how.'

'And it's not Rufus' horse at the epicentre.'

'No. That was coincidence.'

I was relieved to hear my friend cleared of any murderous intent, although this did not clear him of being a horse ringer. 'Or was it a red herring?' I thought, out loud.

'What? You think Kinney's involved?'

'Well, he has just rushed off to Ireland.'

'I know, I was not happy about that. We couldn't stop him.'

'A natural reaction, I suppose, had you ruled him out?'

'We should have put out a warrant for him, but what for? We had no evidence. He had a good alibi; mind you, we hadn't checked all of them for every murder. There were a few holes.'

'Do you know where he is?'

'Yes, but the Super won't act on it. As far as he's concerned we've got our man. He's chuffed to bits. Made some sarcastic comment about ineptitude and a good job some criminals have a conscience. I trust my instincts though, Blake, and this just doesn't feel right. That's why I wanted to speak to you. What do you think?'

I was quiet, recollecting the moments I had spoken to Donald. I could count the times on the fingers of one hand. Apart from the occasional polite smile, there was the incident at the bus stop, the Morris dancing on the green, the pub doorway with Tuvey and...

'Perhaps I should talk to Tuvey again.' I said. The sentence was thoughtful and not entirely confident. Rob was confused.

'Because...?'

'Well, you said Yveny told you he'd used Voodoo. That's why he'd stolen the dolls. Did he tell you how?'

'No. He knew how the victims died and that's enough for us to be sure it's not a false confession.'

'If it is Voodoo, then Elroy might shed some light on it, help you feel a bit better about it.'

'Maybe you're right. I'm probably just tired. I haven't slept in days. It just all seems so implausible. I mean, Voodoo in Tuesbury?'

'There's a lot of history in this village. You only have to walk down the High Street to see Pane's ancestral tradition of corn dollies and Elroy's juju cats.'

'Juju cats?'

'Yes, they're for good luck.'

'Ah.' Rob took a sip of his tea.

'Lots of people spent time abroad in their youth: Diplomatic Service, training like myself, travelling with their fathers' jobs. We had a lot of evacuees here during the wars too. I remember playing with children whom I never saw again; it leaves you with strange memories. Do you think there is something in Donald's past that he's not telling you?' I wasn't sure whom I was trying to convince.

'You're right, of course. It is what he's not telling us that's bothering me. He's holding something back.'

I straightened the cushion behind me to support my back better. Bertie had flopped onto my feet, pinning them to the floor. I wasn't getting up for a bit; I may as well be comfortable. 'Do you think he had an accomplice?' I proffered.

'Maybe, although he's insisting no one else is involved. Normally, once people are caught they are more than happy to share the blame with a comrade, but not on this occasion.'

'More tea?' I said.

'That'd be good, thanks. I've been interviewing all morning: dries you out.' Rob said.

'Do you mind?' I said, indicating the dog lolling on my feet.

Rob laughed. 'No, no problem, white, no sugar?'

'Yes, thank you.'

The convenience of Yveny's confession bothered me too, and I thought the conversations through once more in my head. I recalled the concern he had had for his aunt at the bus stop and yet there was a complete lack of physical contact. Standing there awkwardly, hands in pockets, slippers still on his feet. A complete contrast was the friendly disposition he had shown on the green, the keenness to ingratiate himself and then the matter-of-fact organisation he had shown by moving people off the green when we discovered Pane's body. Finally, there was the clandestine conversation he had with Tuvey, in a different language. I remember reading that this contrasting behaviour would certainly be characteristic of someone with a sociopathic tendency. But I hadn't seen him as sociopathic. There were other people in the village I would far more readily label with this psychological complaint, Nyeman being just one. Maybe Tuvey did hold the answers after all.

Rob handed me my refilled mug. 'We'd better go and see Tuvey,' he said.

26.

Mambo

A Mambo is a Voodoo priestess.

I was surprised by the use of the word *'we'* in reference to the meeting with Tuvey but I was more than happy to accompany Rob. My presence would explain why he was the second person to ask the only black man in the village about Voodoo, as opposed to the police blundering around as I had done.

Tuvey patiently repeated a lot of what he had told me. Voodoo dolls had not originally been created to harm, but instead, to protect. There were two sides to the Voodoun religion: Rada and Petro. Good and Bad; light and dark; as with all things in the world, there was a yin and a yang. In his childhood he'd been taught by his mother to make good juju dolls. Dolls to protect, bring love and good fortune. The slave trade and later, Hollywood, were in his opinion responsible for the deep suspicion that surrounds Voodoo and the overwhelming opinion that it is black magic, created to do harm. He did not mock the idea of sticking pins in dolls. On this subject he was deadly serious. If a person believes strongly enough in something then they can do another harm. When Rob asked him about the possibility of the dolls from Little Tuesbury being used for Petro Voodoo, he did laugh. In Tuvey's experience people created their own effigies and did not steal those that were made with good intentions. He did not believe that they would be effective vessels of ill will. He did add, however, that it was not impossible.

Rob was careful not to mention the name Yveny throughout the conversation and I had remained quiet, observing and listening. So when Tuvey announced 'I hear Donald has been arrested,' our combined surprise was visible.

'Where did you hear that?'

'A journalist. There's been a journalist in here most days now for the last week. They've been in here asking questions.'

'I see.' Rob looked at Tuvey's honest face. His dark eyes hid nothing and his soft accent lulled the listener into a false sense of security. 'And what did you tell them?'

'It wasn't him, you know.' Tuvey went on ignoring the question. 'I know he's confessed, but it wasn't him.'

'You reckon?' Rob was cautious, not keen, in his reply.

Tuvey's eyes wrinkled in a smile. 'You are suspicious of me sergeant. You think I make it up.' His hand waved at a non-existent fly. 'I assure you I do not.'

Rob said nothing. We'd spent the last half an hour talking about Voodoo, perhaps Rob didn't trust this man who had a knowledge of cultures and magic far beyond his own. With knowledge one can deceive.

'As you say, Mr Yveny has admitted to the murders.' Rob answered

'So, why are you here?'

'I'm afraid I don't know what you mean.'

'Why are you here asking me if it's all possible, if as you say, you believe the man?'

Rob stood up straight and pushed his hands into his pockets. Clearing his throat he said 'Thank you for your time Mr Tuvey, it's much appreciated.' He turned and started to head towards the door. I remained at the counter, lost for a moment in the scene before me. He'd hit the nail on the head.

'Don't you want to know how I know he didn't do it?'

Rob turned, hands still in his pockets he moved them, palm outward, so his jacket flapped open. 'Okay.'

'Mr Pane was murdered on the fifth, correct?'

'Yes.'

'Well, Don was in the pub with me.' My face gave away my frustration with my own memory. I'd seen them talking in the doorway. But I had only seen him for a few minutes. There were many more minutes when he may have been committing murder.

'Mr Hetherington here saw us talking in the doorway.'

I went to interrupt and profess the unreliability of this as an alibi but Tuvey raised his voice slightly, stopping me.

'We were in the pub all night; he was with the Morris dancers. There are plenty of witnesses.'

Rob approached the counter.

'I'll need you to make a statement.'

'Of course and he was in there on the twelfth too. That's when Mr Dockerty was killed, wasn't it?'

'If you…'

Tuvey interrupted Rob again. 'Of course, sergeant, I will make you a statement. I will come with you to the station immediately.' He smiled and disappeared out the back.

Rob and I were left in stunned silence, looking at each other. Rob rubbed his forehead with his thumb and forefinger. He looked dog-tired. His shirt was creased from more than twelve hours wear. The grey circles under his eyes were more apparent and the lines on his forehead, emphasised.

Tuvey reappeared with his coat and a bunch of keys and we left the antiques shop. Tuvey went in the direction of the station with Rob and I returned home to walk the dogs.

Three hours later, fed and watered, the dogs were sleeping in front of the electric fire. The telephone rang. It was Rob.

'We've had to let him go. Charged him with wasting police time of course, but his alibis are solid.'

'He must have been protecting someone.' I said.

'Who? He's only been here five minutes. No, I think he's just one of those cranks that come out of the woodwork in cases like these; his way of achieving fame.

Thankfully it didn't go too far, although why Tuvey didn't come forward yesterday when he was arrested...'

'Do you think he knows more than he's telling us?'

'Undoubtedly. I wouldn't trust Tuvey as far as I could throw him. All that guff about Voodoo and now effectively withholding evidence...' Rob's voice trailed off.

I didn't reply, I wasn't so sure Voodoo could be completely discounted.

'Well, I'd better head home and put my macaroni cheese in the microwave. This station's starting to feel a bit too familiar.' He said, and chuckled. 'We'll have to start the investigation again tomorrow.'

'I have some lasagne in the freezer.' I said, breaking my thoughts. 'There's enough for two and you'd be welcome to join me.' Eleanor's recipe for lasagne was still taped in the front of my *'101 Meals For One'*. The only recipe book I still owned. The trouble was, her recipe was for a family of three. It never tasted right when I scaled it down. So, I always made the full recipe and froze it in portions. It was handy for impromptu occasions. 'You could join me for the talk at the village hall later this evening on Family History, it might take your mind off things.'

'That's very kind, Blake, but I should go home. I need to change.'

'You'd be very welcome.' I said again, checking Rob wasn't just being polite.

'No, I should go, Delilah's calling later. I have an appointment with Skype...'

I laughed, 'Very well.'

'Thanks though.'

'You're very welcome, any time.'

The phone clicked and I was left once more with my own thoughts. I had an hour and a half before I had to head down to the village hall for the talk. I settled on the sofa with Colin Dexter and tried to take my mind off the unsatisfactory ending to the day.

By ten-to-seven I was sitting in the second row of chairs in the village hall ready for the talk. Genealogist, Dr Fraser, was presenting a talk on how to trace your family tree. Always willing to learn, I was intrigued and wondered if maybe it was time to start learning about my ancestors and Eleanor's, in order to pass down our traditions to the grandchildren. They loved to hear tales of my grandfather's hat shop and it occurred to me that perhaps I should start writing some of this down. I had started in a large leather bound notebook. It was black with reassuringly thick pages. A customer had brought it for me on my retirement with a card that said *'For your memoirs.'* So that's what I was doing. If I could add a family tree to it, then that would be all the better. I remember Eleanor saying her ancestors were saddlers and ironmongers and that a cousin had gone missing in the First World War. I knew she'd approve if I could find out what happened. Even if it was an inevitable name on a memorial somewhere. These people should not be forgotten.

The hall started to fill. Three teachers from the local school filed in, Miss Derby among them. They were all with who I assumed were their partners, wives or husbands. They sat down behind me and I heard them chattering about lesson plans and how this subject would work well with the children: engage them in learning about social history. They were behind me and so to turn would have been rude, but on the way in I had noticed the grave and solid face of Miss Derby's friend. A silent man with dark hair and dark eyes, he was strangely familiar. He'd said nothing during the conversation and the two female companions of the other teachers were gossiping. I have no idea what about. I was far more interested in the strong silent character accompanying Miss Derby.

'Of course Edward never knew his father, did you sweetheart.' Miss Derby was talking about her friend, to Mr Danver the geography teacher.

'No,' came the blunt reply, from whom I assume was Edward. She did not take this as a cue to stop.

'It's so hard these days, families are so dysfunctional, I wonder what on earth will happen about tracing family trees in the future. I'll be surprised if we are able to.' She sighed and I heard her unzip her handbag and start digging around. There was a brief silence.

'My family functioned perfectly without my father.' Edward's deep voice was only just audible to my old ears as the room started to fill up.

'I'm sorry, honey.' I heard Miss Derby reply. 'Besides, you've done very well for yourself with that lovely second-hand bookshop,' she compounded her previous patronising and thundered on, 'of course that's how Edward and I met.'

'Brilliant! I love a good second hand bookshop. Where is it?' Mr Danver deftly steered the subject towards safer ground.

'The Huckspeth Road' Edward replied.

'Oh, I haven't seen that one, how strange. Have you been there long?' Mr Danver had been in the village for several years, it was strange that a teacher would not have noticed the establishment of a bookshop in the village. I myself had not noticed, but I rarely walked further up the Huckspeth Road than the greengrocer's. I listened for the answer.

'I've just opened. I've spent the last month sorting…'

I didn't hear the rest because Olea Faba plonked herself down beside me, husband in tow, and began to talk at me.

'Mr Hetherington, I'm glad you're here. I've been meaning to talk to you about your shed.'

I braced myself for complaint. Olea Faba had been the leader of a small group of allotment owners who had objected to me moving my business to the allotment. When the council had been unable to prove I was running a business from the shed, she had not spoken to me for several months. A blessing. Unfortunately, being of a suspicious mind, when it came to Olea Faba, I was concerned that this may indicate the hatching of another plan; another onslaught of objection. How anyone could complain I did not know, in fact my sustained presence on the allotments deterred errant youths from vandalism. There had been a distinct fall in such activity since my business moved to the shed.

I must not have covered my frown well enough as Olea suddenly burst into a series of placating gestures, her hand on my arm, the other to her forehead, her eyes half shut and her cheek bones high in a false smile as she spoke, raising my suspicions further.

'Oh no, Mr Hetherington, I'm sure we can put that little misunderstanding behind us. No, no, I wanted to talk to you about a commission.'

'A commission?' I asked incredulously.

Her husband had settled into the seat beside her, cap pulled down over his eyes, he was already dozing. I'd rarely seen the man awake. I completely understood why. Feigning sleep was probably the best way to avoid talking to Olea. If only I'd been quick enough to do the same myself.

'Just a little piece; I have an idea for a hatinator for the summer show. I'd love you to make it.' She spoke with a strained attempt at refinement. An impression of what she thought was the correct way to speak, rolling her r's in certain words in a ridiculous manner that was most off-putting.

A tingling in my ear lobes, told me this was a surely a trap. Ask me to make a hatinator and then send the council round. I waited.

'I was thinking a cornucopia would be simply wonderful.'

'I'm sorry?' I was being purposefully obtuse but the idea of making this woman a hatinator was repellent on many levels.

'You know; with grapes, apples, blackberries, beans, all water-falling out of the hat. I understand you can use needle felting for it.'

'Oh, I see.' I folded my arms and looked towards the front of the room where the speaker was gathering her papers together. 'Well I'm afraid I can't help you there. You see hatinators are not my area of expertise.' I plumped for this answer. Not an out-and-out-lie, semi, if not in fact, true.

'Oh. Oh, well, right.' She gathered her handbag towards her and folded her arms across it. 'Did you hear that John?' she said, awakening her sleeping husband with a jab to the ribs. 'Mr Hetherington doesn't do hatinators. Whoever heard of a hat maker that doesn't make hats?' She'd dropped the accent and was talking far louder than needed.

I was saved from my irresistible urge to tell her exactly what I thought about hatinators, when Persephone

Lambert took to the stage and clapped her hands together for silence.

Once she had introduced Dr Fraser, Reverend Lambert took up her seat on the end of the front row, just in front of me. I was treated to a waft of Lily-of-the-valley perfume as she settled herself for the talk.

The speaker was very engaging and the hour went quickly. Talk of birth records, marriages, death certificates and how to trace them, kept the room's attention admirably. The talk came to an end and I was about to leave, to avoid any further conversation with Mrs Faba, when Reverend Lambert turned in her chair.

'It's a terrible business these murders, isn't it, Mr Hetherington?'

'It is.' I replied with a lack of anything better to say.

She eyed Mrs Faba nervously. Olea was not only a gossip but obsequious when it came to the Reverend and rarely missed an opportunity to tell her how devout she was despite her complete lack of attendance at church. Reverend Lambert needn't have worried as one of Olea's friends hailed her loudly from two rows back and now engaged her in conversation.

'I spoke to Mrs Dellaware earlier today.'

'Did you? I must confess, I think she's under a lot of stress at the moment.'

She raised her eyebrows. 'Why does everyone feel the need to confess when they're around me? You never know, Yveny might have been caught earlier if I'd got him in my steely gaze one Sunday morning.' She laughed at herself. A skein of her wavy auburn hair escaped her ponytail.

'He went to church?' I said unable to keep the surprise from my voice. A believer of Voodoo attending a Christian church just didn't seem plausible. I was choosing to ignore the fact that Donald had now been released. This was obviously not common knowledge yet.

'Oh yes, all sorts of heathens darken our doors, Mr Hetherington, the Lord speaks to them all.' She pushed the escaped hair back behind her ear.

'I suppose it's your job to shepherd them.' I ventured, continuing the analogy. I'd rarely spoken to Persephone Lambert until now. She had a small pug dog I'd seen her out walking, but we'd never actually had a conversation before. It was strange she should seek me out now, or was she just being friendly?

'Villages like this must have all sorts of history.' She said.

'Yes.'

'It's like Dr Fraser said, sometimes digging around in your family history unearths things you didn't expect.'

'Indeed.'

'Painful memories, secrets that should be left in the past.'

'You make it sound very sinister, reverend.' I attempted a smile.

'Secrets are normally the root of most sin. It's amazing what some people will do to keep a secret.' She looked across at the door to the hall. Not looking at anyone, choosing her words. 'Donald Yveny didn't seem to me to be the secretive type.' She said. 'He's barely been here five minutes, hardly long enough to bear the grudge required for man's most deadly sin.' She turned back to look at me.

'It's funny you should say that.' I said reluctant to say any more. Rob would have enough trouble when it was reported, never mind the gossip mill. But that was the crux of it. This had been what had bothered Rob and me about Yveny's confession: the speed at which this had all happened, the convenience of the betting debts. Was that enough reason for serial murder? That's what made his alibis all the more convincing. I searched Persephone's face for an answer. I felt sure she was trying to tell me something. She sensed the unspoken question.

'I've had to carry out a lot of funerals over the last two months. A sad time for the village. It brings out the community spirit in people; most people attend.'

I looked down at the floor, uncomfortable with the fact that I had not attended any myself. I started to make excuses in my head. None of the victims were firm friends of mine. I was well aware that in the past I'd attended the funerals of people I didn't know, but this was in a supporting capacity. Something I had not been asked to do this time. Funerals reminded me of my own losses and there was something distinctly morbid about hanging around at funerals on the off-chance a murderer may reveal themselves. Two of the funerals hadn't even been held in the village.

'It's not the people that don't attend that are conspicuous.' She said, laying a reassuring hand on my arm. 'It's the people that do. Grief brings out the strangest behaviour.' She said standing up. 'Jim Dockerty's funeral is on Friday, perhaps we'll see you there.' She finished, gave me a smile of such divine innocence that it could only be found on a vicar and walked towards the door.

It is rare that I am speechless but on this occasion I was, completely. She had definitely been trying to tell me something. Was it about a member of the congregation, something about the funerals? Rob, or one of his officers must have attended them. It was part of police procedure, wasn't it? To attend the funerals of murder victims. Rob would know who had attended and who had not and maybe this was the answer.

27.

Vever

Veve or vevers are symbols used in Voodoun ritual. They are often drawn in the ground at ceremonies to call upon the gods.

Thursday came and I was back in the shed, working on a new commission. It was a flouncy number for a customer from outside the village. The base was a cartwheel hat in cream and lemon and the client had drawn me pictures that I was attempting to emulate with lace and silk. Whatever I did, it reminded me of a lemon meringue pie. After the brief spell of sunny weather the clouds had returned, my hands had shrunk and the old carpal tunnel scars pulled again, making it awkward to manipulate the fabrics in the cold air.

I put the hat down and rubbed my wrists, frustrated at the depletion of my dexterity, age had brought with it. Turning on the oil heater earned me grateful looks from the dogs. They were huddled together beneath the bench and one of Prince's ears flopped over Bertie. It was almost a month since Delilah had gone to Haiti, I could safely say I was missing my chatty and sometimes annoying colleague.

She wouldn't have needed telling twice. She'd have been at the funerals from the off. I'd stopped us going though, considering it ghoulish voyeurism. To attend the funerals of murder victims in order to find clues as to the perpetrator just didn't feel right. I wasn't sure why, after all I was happy to go asking all and sundry about the case. But I was careful not to ask inappropriate questions, I told myself. But whom was I kidding? The real reason for my reticence was Eleanor; guilt looming large in my mind once more. Guilt, that I wasn't there, regret that I didn't tell her I loved her one more time, reproach at the possibility that there was something I could have done to help.

Ultimately I didn't want to attend funerals where that feeling was likely to be overwhelming. So many people ashamed at being glad it wasn't them, repenting the fact that they didn't know the person better, feeling responsible for not seeing something that would help solve the crime and, finally, perhaps even guilty of the crime themselves.

Old memories turned once more to Rufus and how I'd offended him. I had heard nothing from him. Not even a new cheque in the post. I supposed the move was mine. The money didn't matter. I worried for him in that big house with only a woman with a cash incentive for company. I remembered his words at the races that day. He'd been sorry that he had no son to pass the estate on to. It occurred to me that these were not the thoughts of a man who has nothing for a son to inherit. Surely if he had no money he'd be glad there was no one to pass the debt on to? So why use a ringer for Tipingee? It didn't make sense. It was neat enough in places all right, but there were holes.

Persephone's words had stayed with me: *'Villages like this must have all sorts of history.'* Indeed they did, some of it hidden deep in the souls of its inhabitants. She had been trying to tell me something. She wanted me to attend that funeral but I didn't want to. Cowardly, but there were some feelings I just wasn't willing to confront. There I was, dwelling on souls and funerals again.

Taking my mobile from my jacket pocket, I made a decision and rang Rob. He picked up after two rings.

'Detective Sergeant Claringdon,' came an officious answer.

'Rob, it's Blake.'

'Blake. Are you okay?' His voice was confused and slow. I looked at my watch. Eight thirty.

'Sorry did I wake you?'

'No problem, no problem.' I could almost see him pushing himself up in bed, rubbing the sleep from his eyes. I hadn't even considered he might not be awake. 'Just catching up on my sleep. I finally got a day off, now Alston's back.' He sounded almost apologetic.

'Ah…' Now I felt wretched, 'I can ring back later.'

'No, no, now's fine. How can I help you?'

I considered insisting on calling back but decided that the insult had already been caused so I may as well continue.

'Did you attend any of the funerals of the victims?' I said

'Yes, all of them.'

'Anyone acting strange there?'

'It's a funeral, Blake, it's hardly average behaviour. People generally follow certain social protocols. That in itself is strange.'

'Of course, but anything, you know, odd?'

'Where's this going?' Rob never was one to beat about the bush. It was one of the things I liked about him. You always knew where you stood.

'Persephone Lambert said something very interesting about the funerals.'

'The vicar…?'

'Yes.'

'What did she say?'

'That it wasn't the people who didn't attend that were conspicuous but the one's that did.'

'I see, and you want to know who she was talking about.'

'Yes.'

'Well, I couldn't tell you everyone's names but Kinney was there at most of them, which makes sense. Tuvey your antiques shop owner, the couple that own the model village, Tudbury isn't it? And there was Nyeman, oh and that nutty woman, Dellaware. The relatives of the victims were there, that goes without saying.'

'Did you notice anything odd about any of them?'

'No, although now you come to mention it…'

'Yes?'

'Well, Yveny wasn't there. Sometimes the perpetrator turns up, that's why we attend, a good way of gauging who to talk to, but he wasn't there.'

'Does that mean anything?'

'No, no, it actually makes sense. After all, his alibis say he didn't do it.' Rob said, changing the subject.

'So you think he did? I sensed the reticence in Rob's voice.

'It's possible, although it would mean Tuvey and all the Morris men lying for him. It's unusual but possible. I still think it's got to be something to do with that horse; they must all be in it together somehow. Twelve good men...' His voice drifted off thoughtfully.

'What?'

'Agatha Christie.' Now that did surprise me. Rob must have taken the silence as a lack of interest rather than surprise, because next he changed the subject dramatically. 'How was your talk last night?

'Very interesting.'

'I bet. I often thought about looking into my family history,' he said, 'but it worries me what I might find. I'm a third generation copper. My mother hated the idea. *'Dangerous job'*, she said,' He laughed.

Something jogged my memory and all of a sudden I could see Constance Dellaware's face in her plea for help.

'She came to see me, did I tell you?' I said, my thoughts leaping back to the original purpose of the conversation.

'Who, my mother?' Rob was suitably confused.

I was guilty of starting in the middle not the beginning. 'Sorry, Mrs Dellaware came to see me about Yveny.'

'I know, I was there, remember?'

'No. No, before that, she said he'd *'got in with the wrong crowd'*.'

'The wrong crowd?'

'Yes…'

'Why didn't you tell me this earlier?' Rob interrupted.

'Because the wrong crowd is hardly going to be Morris dancers! Look that's not what I just thought of. Something about the way she spoke about him, it wasn't, well…it wasn't like an aunt.'

'How does an aunt speak?' Rob was starting to sound impatient. To be fair, I had woken him from a well-deserved lie in and was now in his opinion rambling.

'It was maternal.'

'Well, aunts are, aren't they? Mine is.'

'No, it was more urgent. Aunts are more despairing, they see the faults, but want to protect. Mothers don't see the faults in their sons. *'The wrong company'* she said. To me that means she saw others at fault, not Yveny.'

'Okayyy.' Rob let the last consonant run on. I could tell I needed to get to the point fairly quickly.

'I think you should ask Yveny who he really is.'

'But we've checked him out, his passport says he's Donald Yveny, his used to live in Santa Domingo and his mother's dead. I have no reason to believe he's not who he says he is.'

'But what if he's not?'

'How? He checks out! Look, Blake, I don't know what you're driving at. I'm pretty sure Yveny did it but I don't want to get done for harassment. I've just got to find another way to prove it. Confessing and acquiring an alibi, so that you are then released and are no longer a suspect is the oldest trick in the book. I think you're looking for something that isn't there.'

'But you said yourself when they arrested Yveny that something wasn't right.'

'I meant, that it was all too easy. That doesn't mean he didn't do it! Look, Mr Hetherington, I appreciate your help, really I do, but we have our man, I've just got to get evidence and that's what Alston's doing. Yveny ran up betting debts, has a screw loose and he's finally tipped over the edge. Finished, finito, end of.'

The use of my full name took me off guard. Instead of being respectful it had the opposite effect. I did not want to fall out with someone else I had grown to quite like so I decided to retreat gracefully.

'Right. I agree Yveny's involved in this somewhere. Look, I'm sorry to have woken you. Perhaps I could buy you Sunday dinner at The Badger's Holt at the weekend?'

'Oh… Thank you… That would be good; I'm still on rest days.'

'Good. So twelve okay?'

'Perfect.' Rob said and the conversation was concluded.

Rob obviously had his reasons for now believing so vehemently in Yveny's guilt. There was a nagging thought in the back of my mind that didn't want to go away. It just seemed like an awful lot of bloodshed for betting debts. There had to be more to it. Rob was right; Yveny was mixed up in this somehow but I wasn't convinced of how, yet.

A clunk from the back of the shed startled me. I looked up and saw a figure of a person stand up from below the window at the back of the shed. I only saw the back of them. A full-length duffel coat and a bobble hat pulled down tight over their head. They were running towards Druid Wood, moving fast, and even as I dived for the door they were already an allotment away.

As I got round to the far end of the shed trying not to stamp on my onion plants and new potatoes, I shouted at them to stop, but they were long gone. The back shed wall had been to the left of me while I was on the phone and I had been looking out of the window above the bench. The person who had hidden under the back window had not come past. He or she had come across the allotment and not used the path. I tutted. This in itself was annoying but it was unsettling that someone had been crouched under the window. At least I assumed so, as when I'd heard the noise I'd turned to see the figure stand up, suggesting they were crouched. It was a still, quiet day and it would have been easy to hear my phone conversation from inside the shed. Soundproofing was not something I had invested in. I had not seen the need for it.

I thought about ringing Rob again to tell him. His last formal *'Mr Hetherington'* made me think better of it. It was probably just a teenager playing a prank. Ever since the events on the allotment last year we'd had various pranks, the most elaborate of which was a silhouette of a body painted on what had been the Devine's shed. I'd feel pretty stupid if I rang Rob again just to discover it was just a foolish prank.

Standing there, thinking things through, something caught the corner of my eye. A tiny carving about eight inches from the bottom of the shed. I bent down to get a closer look. It was intricate and very detailed. It must have taken some time to carve. About four inches by four inches it depicted a cross on a three level plinth. Either side were what looked like two tiny coffins and at the ends of the cross, stars. Goodness knows how long the person might have been crouched there in order to carve it. Why hadn't I heard at least some scratching as they etched it? The mud around the carving was disturbed and there was a clear footprint in soil.

I should report it, but I felt silly, wasting police time on a little bit of religious vandalism. It was probably one of the Goths I'd seen a few times on the High Street. Black duffel coats were right up their street and the figure had been slight and nimble on their feet. I did feel I should report vandalism on the allotments though. Surely they couldn't think me batty for doing that? In fact better still, I'd take the dogs for a walk and on the way there, drop in at the police station to report it personally. Back in the shed, I gathered the dogs and, laughing at my previous paranoia, I was consoled that I had a plan.

28.

Canzo

An ordeal, using fire, that is a vital step in the initiation of new subjects. If you have passed this ordeal, you are referred to as Canzo.

The desk sergeant was very polite, despite remembering me from an unfortunate incident that involved gerberas last Christmas. He took the details and said an officer would be over in the next few days to look at the scene. I mentioned the footprint, but he said something about it being public land and expensive forensics so I did not push the matter further. I was already becoming a familiar face in Tuesbury police station and I didn't want it to be for the wrong reasons. A public nuisance was not something I'd considered myself to be but I knew there was a fine line.

The dogs were happy now they were on their usual path towards the woods and they sniffed their way along the hedgerow lining the pavement. To their disgust I made a last minute detour to Blackwood Manor.

I decided to take the bit between the teeth and attempt to apologise to Rufus. This was against my better judgement. I still felt aggrieved at the bounced cheque. I couldn't help but feel the misunderstanding wasn't entirely my fault. However, I was prepared to be the bigger man.

I pulled the cord that rang the large old bell hanging on the wall beside the servants' door; a side entrance used more regularly than the grand front door. A magnolia was beginning to flower across the porch and it reached right up to the third floor attic room windows, framing them against the eaves. The big solid oak door was modern but sympathetic to its surroundings. I saw someone approach through the small square panels of swirled glass. They gave a goldfish bowl effect, blurring the outline and giving the viewer no clue as to the true shape, height or size of the person inside.

The dogs sat patiently at my feet. They were now used to my body language and knew we were there for a while. Coupled with the dog biscuits they knew I had in my pocket, this meant they would behave impeccably. That is, until the biscuits were gone.

Opening the door, I was surprised to be greeted by Mrs Darensky. I'm sure Mrs Darensky, as the future Lady Blackwood, had every right to be there. The fact was though, that until Cheltenham I had never heard of this woman, let alone seen her. It gave their engagement a clandestine feel. It was only a week before the races that I remember Rufus teasing me about Delilah and wondering where he might get a *'filly'* like that. The truth of the matter must surely have been that he already had himself a very fine thoroughbred.

'Mr Hetherington, how very nice to see you again.' Her body language denied it.

Matilda Darensky was dressed in a lilac linen suit and smart black court shoes. A light blue silk scarf with small turquoise flowers was tied neatly around her neck, perhaps to disguise the ageing process. Hands and necks never fail to give away a woman's true age. Gloves and scarves provide a welcome deception.

'And you too, Mrs Darensky, how are you?'

'Vell, thank you, and how can I help?' She did not move from the door. She was standing, with one hand grasping the solid oak door and the other resting on her hip.

'I wondered if Rufus was in?'

'No, he's out.'

This woman was a tough crowd. She was giving nothing away. Did she know I disapproved of her motives for marrying Rufus, despite his complicity? Or was she just naturally austere? Could she even be trying for mysterious and completely missing her mark? Who knew?

'Do you vant to come in?' She said, sensing my hesitation, but as she said it the door moved ever so slightly closed, giving away her subconscious desire to be rid of me. I touched the front of my cap and bowed slightly. I have rarely done this in my life but something about Mrs Darensky's manner demanded it.

'It's quite OK, thank you Mrs Darensky. Perhaps you would tell him I called?' I finished.

'Of course.' She said and started to close the door. I turned and made my way back up the drive. Druid Wood was behind the manor. You could get to it through the grounds and Rufus never minded people he knew taking the shortcut.

I didn't think much more of Mrs Darensky's feigned politeness. I assumed Rufus had told her we'd fallen out. It was a reasonable assumption, so I returned my thoughts to the case. Rob had been initially reticent over the arrest of Yveny, so why was he now so sure Yveny was double bluffing? Conversations ran through my brain. Mrs Dellaware's concern for her nephew, Reverend Lambert's intrigue at village secrets, hot on the heels of a lecture on family history; a lecture that had already inspired the conversation between the teachers and embarrassed poor Miss Derby's beau. I did not know him but I felt for him in the situation. Something about him had stayed with me. He was deeply sad and yet very matter-of-fact. This may be why he now found his solace in old books. Other people's tales allow you to escape from your own, for a while at least.

What it came down to was why would you kill a harmless, gay newsagent, a philandering grocer, a chain-smoking baker, a prize-winning butcher and a money-loving bookie. There were a few paradoxical matters. For example, Yveny joined the Morris dancing, drank in the local pub, made friends easily and yet his relationship with his aunt seemed strained. Harold Salter was a harmless, hardworking businessman in a stable and loving relationship and yet Steve wanted nothing to remember him by, including Prince.

Cogitation didn't seem to be getting me very far. I was going round in circles. I should just leave it to Rob.

Reaching the wood, I let the dogs off the lead. They immediately ran off into the trees and I could hear them scratching around, snuffling as they went. We'd approached the wood from a slightly different angle today and I noticed a charcoal kiln that was new. It hadn't been here last month. It looked very new. I had no idea who would have taken it upon themselves to make charcoal in the woods. It could have been one of Blackwood's staff; there were plenty of fallen trees after January's storms to keep someone's fire going for a long time.

Curious, I walked up to the kiln. The dogs were still busy investigating the woods. Peering in, I was surprised to find not just charred wood in the kiln. There were some scraps of paper too. I couldn't reach it and neither could I see what was written on it in the tiny cursive text. They looked as though they'd been burnt. I picked up a stick from beside the kiln and managed to stab one of the larger scraps of paper. The letters were even and purposeful. It was the corner of a page and from the placing of the letters I could see it was the top right hand corner. The letters spelt *uary* and then underneath *aturday*. It could have been the corner of a diary or a dated letter. I understood why someone would want to burn a diary. Secrets often written in moments of madness were best not recorded. But why on earth would someone bring a diary all the way out here to burn?

I leaned in and made another stab at another of the fragments, this time skewering the largest piece. Gently raising it up, I grasped it and was about to read it when the dogs started to bark. In my attempts to investigate the kiln I had nearly forgotten they were with me. Their barking was frantic. I assumed they had found a squirrel, which was now cowering in a tree. I called for them both; confident the lure of biscuits would bring them back. After the third call, I was resigned to the fact that they weren't coming back. It must have been something pretty interesting for them not to return, knowing I had a pocket full of biscuits. Pushing the paper into my pocket, I sighed. I was going to have to find them.

They didn't sound far away but as the sound rebounded off the trees I was finding it difficult to pinpoint their position. I knew roughly in which direction they had run off and a startled deer running east suggested they must be west of me. It could have been the deer they were barking at, but they weren't following. Their barks were not mobile.

I walked approximately three hundred yards into the wood in the opposite direction to the deer before I found them. As I walked though the wood I realised I was heading in the direction of the small stream that ran through it. I expected to arrive and find both dogs in the water playing havoc with the stream's wildlife. The barking did not let up. As soon as I arrived they worried around my feet whimpering and dancing like dressage horses. Both were bone dry. They had not been in the stream. Then I saw what they had been trying to tell me about.

In the small clearing amongst the pine was the most hideous sculpture I have ever seen. I have been walking in Druid Wood for many, many years. I played there as a child. Never in all my days have I seen something like this. I call it a sculpture but it was more of an accumulation of strange *objet d'art*.

The mainstay of the sculpture was a tree trunk that had been struck by lightning. The rest of the tree had been removed and the remaining trunk had a few branches still protruding from it. From these branches, hung small dolls, five of which I can only describe as corn dollies. The sixth sat on the very top. Its head, was that of a child's doll, like the ones I'd seen in Tuvey's book. The rest of the tree had bits of coloured wool and tinfoil hanging from it, a pocket mirror, a hairbrush and, nailed to the centre of the trunk, a gruesome sheep's skull. Around the bottom of the trunk were dried dead flowers and tea-lights. A very peculiar sight and I stepped forward to have a better look. Bertie came with me but Prince wouldn't. He stood glued to the spot, growling.

It was at that moment my phone rang. If it hadn't, I may have realised why Prince had not moved and what he was growling at.

'Blake Hetherington.' I said, answering the phone.

'Mr Hetherington?' came an urgent voice.

'Yes.' I replied.

'Oh thank goodness, I was ever so worried.' I tried to place the voice. It was definitely familiar but the caller was using a phone voice, which masked their usual accent. The reception was terrible which confused the matter further. My silence prompted explanation. 'It's Mrs Tudbury? From Little Tuesbury?'

'Oh, Mrs Tudbury, hello. Well, how can I help you.' Prince was still growling and I shushed him.

'Sorry?'

'Oh no, not you, I'm walking the dogs up in the woods and they are making an awful racket.' I explained.

'Oh I see, well I afraid I've got some un…news.' I could barely hear her voice. The phone crackled. I lifted it away from my face. One bar of signal.

'Have you?'

'…hope you don't mind me ringing, I got your n…from your website, see.'

'Ah…I can only just hear you, Mrs Tudbury, you'll have to speak up.' I fully suspected the next revelation would be that she had a mystery for me to solve; another innocent, spurred on by Delilah's subtitle for my site.

'There's…en another incid…in the m…village.'

I managed to decode the message. So this was Mrs Tudbury's mystery. 'Oh yes?'

'Yes…your shed.' Came another broken reply.

I laughed, imagining it had been blown over or something had fallen on it. There couldn't possibly be anything mysterious about my shed. Mrs Tudbury took the models very seriously and had consulted me on every aspect of the new shed, taking care to deck the inside out the same as the real thing and even keeping the curtains closed at all times from prying inspectors. Only we knew the truth. It had been rather fun.

'Yes,' she continued ignoring my laughter. 'I'm afraid…well…I'm afraid …red cross…door and…'

I didn't hear any more after that. A sharp pain encompassed my head and the forest spun. I felt the phone fall from my hand, the smell of the pine needles on the floor below reaching up to greet me, the cold damp of the rotting leaves against my face as I hit the ground, and the world went black. Just before I lost all consciousness I heard Prince barking and felt Bertie rush up to me pushing his nose against my face. The familiar smell of Lily-of-the-valley was intoxicating. So this is what heaven smelt like.

29.

The Astral Planes

Places that exist in other dimensions, that people may travel to, or project themselves into.

The sound of birds calling to one another in the canopy was the first thing I became aware of. A hazy glow of sunlight through the leaves of newly budding trees filtered through my eyelids. There was a rustling in the undergrowth and I could feel soft leaf mulch on my left cheek. I opened my eyes, still squinting from the light, aware of a searing pain in my head. Reaching up, I felt a warm sticky matt of hair, to the back of my head.

'Take it easy, old boy,' a familiar voice. 'You had a nasty knock.'

I focussed and a wave of relief enveloped me. Never before have I been so glad to see an old friend's face. Rufus Blackwood looked concerned and every one of his sixty-seven years.

'The dogs?' My dry voice croaked. The last thing I'd remembered was Prince's frantic barking.

'Mrs Tudbury's taken them. It was her that found you. Good job she's so quick on her feet, used to run marathons, she tells me. She ran all the way from the model village to find you and then ran to the Manor to call for an ambulance. No reception on her phone, she said.'

'Oh.' My voice was weak. I had a dim memory of talking to Mrs Tudbury before I was hit. 'But…'

'You're lucky your phone got some reception. Pure fluke. Saved your life, old boy.' Rufus replied, reading my thoughts. 'Mrs Tudbury heard the dogs barking and when you didn't reply she was worried. She said something about a cross, put two and two together and came up to the woods to find you. Thankfully the dogs were making so much noise it wasn't difficult.'

I heard a snuffle from behind me and a paw pushed at my back.

'Bertie!' Another voice; Mrs Tudbury's, and I felt the paw pulled away again.

'Hello?' New voices, I had my back to them. Rufus looked up.

'Over here.' He and Mrs Tudbury said in unison. My vision was filled with green uniforms and the friendly faces of health care professionals, well and truly in control. Rufus stepped back to let them do their job and in what seemed like minutes I was surrounded by bright lights in the back of an ambulance and on my way to hospital. Safe once more, all I could think was what would Jane say? I drifted off to sleep, lulled by the whirr of the blood pressure cuff inflating. The last thing I heard was the shout of the female paramedic to her colleague in the front.

I woke up two days later. The curtains were drawn around me and a nurse was leaning over me, pulling a tube from my mouth. I'd been unconscious. It was the best sleep I'd had in years. Unfortunately the crashing headache was the trade-off.

'Mr Hetherington.' Came a soft Scottish accent. 'Mr Hetherington, time to wake up.'

The light had a synthetic blue glow to it that formed a corona of light above the nurse's blond hair.

'You're all right, Mr Hetherington. You're in Intensive Care, you've been very poorly, but we're looking after you.'

My brain heard the words, but they didn't fully compute. I tried to speak but my mouth was so dry. I champed my jaw together as a mask was placed over my face. The dry air made me cough and I tried to pull it off again.

'You're going to need oxygen for a bit, Mr Hetherington. You need to keep that on.'

I wanted to push myself up on the bed to see what was going on, but I had no strength in my arms. I tried to speak again. I wanted some water.

'We'll sit you up, just a minute.' The nurse said in her lilting accent. I felt pillows behind me and arms pulling me upwards like a rag doll, but I was sitting up. I reached for the mask again, so I could speak.

'You need to leave that on, Mr Hetherington.' Came the soft yet firm reply. Why couldn't she see I was thirsty?

I managed to form the word '*water*' with my dry lips.

'Here you go', she said. Moving the mask to one side and offering me what I thought was a straw but turned out to be a sponge on a lollipop stick. The sponge felt awful against my chapped lips and I must have indicated this with my face.

'I'll get you some water to drink when you've woken up a bit Mr Hetherington. This will stop your mouth feeling so dry.' She smiled, a beatific smile. There was no way I could have argued with it, even if I had been physically able.

I don't know how long I was asleep for, that time. I gradually became aware of a beeping noise beside my ear, the gentle hum of voices and laughter and someone holding my hand. Jane was beside me.

'Hi, Dad.' She was trying not to cry.

'Hello.' I croaked. 'Have you got some water?'

'I'll ask the nurse,' she said standing up and placing a kiss on my forehead. She smelt of patchouli oil and shampoo. A memory shouted to be recalled and I frowned.

'Don't move, Dad, I'll get it for you,' Jane put a hand on my shoulder gently pushing me back into the lumpy pillows. As my weight fell back against them there was a hiss of air escaping. Plastic hospital pillows, I smiled. I remembered Eleanor complaining about them when she was on the maternity ward with Jane. They had made her neck hot. I reached to the back and my neck. It was damp with sweat. She was right, as always.

'Nice to see you awake, Mr Hetherington.' The nurse said as she approached with a jug of water, a plastic beaker and a straw. She had a neutral accent, not as soothing as the Scottish nurse, whom I felt sure I had dreamt now. 'Just take a little sip for now, you've been asleep a long time.' She leant over me, smiling. Jane hovered at the end of the bed waiting for the nurse to finish. 'Shall we sort these pillows out for you?' The nurse continued.

'Mmmm.' I managed, trying to push myself forward on the bed.

'Oh, we'd better change that one.' She said and pulled a sort of blue fabric cloth from the top of the pillowcase. Deftly, with one hand, she pulled another from the drawer and replaced it; the entire time holding me up with the other hand.

I rested back into the pillow.

'We'll get your dressing changed as well.' She said and hurried off to get the necessary equipment.

'She seems nice.' I said to Jane.

'Her and Gilly have been at the end of your bed for three days, Dad.'

'Who?' I had no recollection.

'The nurses: Laura during the day, Gilly at night. They sit at the board there and make sure you're safe. They're off tomorrow, so there'll be some new nurses for you to harass.' Jane seemed to perk up a bit, happy to talk about the things she knew. The workings of an Intensive Care Unit were not so mysterious to my daughter.

'Have I been here that long?' I asked.

Jane moved around the side of the bed again and sat down on the chair beside me, 'Yes, Dad. You're lucky to be here. You suffered a subdural haematoma.' She squeezed my hand.

'In English please, Jane, I neither have your training, nor a dictionary to hand.'

She laughed, properly this time. 'Well, it didn't take you long to get back to your old self. It's a bleed on the brain, Dad. They had to drain…'

'Okay, okay, I don't want to know.' I said raising my unclasped hand to confirm this fact.

'You should have listened to me. This wouldn't have happened if you'd just…' And she burst into tears.

A different nurse came over from the desk in the middle of the ward and offered her a tissue and a cup of tea. Tea always made things better and he even offered to make me one.

The nurse who I assumed to be Laura, although I had no way of telling if it was night or day, appeared again and propped me upright once more so she could change my dressing. Jane had regained her composure and they chatted about the wound and how it was healing.

'The dogs.' I suddenly remembered my old friends, without whom I may not have been found so easily. Laura sighed as I moved my head at a crucial moment in the re-dressing.

'They're fine, Dad. I'm staying at yours and they are with me. They miss you.'

'As soon as we've got you better, Mr Hetherington, you'll be home to see them.' Laura soothed.

'How long do you think that will be?' I said as Laura wrapped the bandage around the top of my head.

'We'll have to let the doctors look at you first. They'll be round this evening to talk to you. I've let Dr Carter know you're awake.'

'Thank you.' I said.

The tea arrived. Mine in a polystyrene cup with a straw. I was glad as I was still a little shaky and I wasn't sure I'd manage to grip the cup. 'You'll have to let it cool, Mr Hetherington, it'll be a bit too hot at the moment.' The second nurse said.

Tea: normality. So close, yet so far. Laura sat back at the desk at the end of my bed and made some notes on the sheets of paper in front of her. More bureaucracy no doubt, I knew how Jane complained about the paperwork. I doubted this nurse's lot was very different.

Jane sat drinking her tea and holding my hand. We didn't say anything and I was glad of the company. I started to try and piece together the events that had led to me taking up a precious bed in intensive care. The scarcity and demand for these beds was also something Jane talked about often and I knew she was right when she said I was lucky to make it. That's the only reason you ended up here. As soon as you were well enough you were moved, to a ward or home.

Home: how I wished I could be at home now, in my own bed; my own clean linen, rough, comforting cotton.

Not the smooth polyester sheets and depressing holey blankets that covered me now. I may as well get used to it. I had a feeling my daughter wasn't going to let me go home until I was better.

I wished I could remember something about the incident. I had been hit, that was for sure, and clearly from Jane's reaction she knew this too. I vaguely remembered Rufus and the shafts of light that struck through the treetops. I remembered voices shouting, a familiar smell but what it was I couldn't recall. Feeling sorry for myself and cursing a loss of memory wasn't going to get me anywhere. I had to concentrate on getting better and ultimately getting out of here. Hospitals made me feel old.

'Is Mr Hetherington awake yet?' I heard a voice I recognised coming from the other side of the curtain.

'Rob!' A reflex reaction to the voice and Jane's hand tensed where it had been holding mine.

'Blake! Good to see you awake.' Rob's beaming face appeared around the side of the curtain and Laura stood up from the desk. Rob had that effect on people. Even out of uniform, people sensed the authority.

'Am I okay to visit?' He said more to Laura than me.

'Yes. But don't wear him out.' Laura replied and smiled.

He walked up to the side of the bed and shook my hand firmly. Jane did not let go of my other hand and for a moment I felt as though I was in some surreal tug of war.

'How's the head?'

'Sore.'

'Delilah sends her love.'

'Oh. Does she know? I do hope she's not worrying.'

'She's fine, she just wants you to get better.'

I nodded.

'I'm afraid I'll need to ask you a few questions Blake, but they can wait.'

'I'm not sure I can remember anything, officer.' I said wryly.

'It might come back to you. I'm so glad you're okay.' He frowned, a look of concern falling over his previously elated face.

'So am *I*.' Jane said this in a way that was meant to project more meaning than the three words held. She was glaring at the sergeant with a look she'd inherited from her mother. It was a look she only ever used if you were in trouble.

'Jane, this is Sergeant Rob Claringdon.'

'I know who it is.' She said; sharp and brusque. I hadn't brought her up to be this rude to people she barely knew.

'Mrs Grosmont and I have met.' Rob gave a thin smile.

Jane nodded, her lips pursed together, her grip on my hand tighter than ever.

'Ow.' I said as she squeezed just a little too hard.

'Sorry, Dad.' She said and moved her hand away. She sat upright and clasped both hands in her lap, looking at

Rob, waiting for his next move. Rob shifted from foot to foot and scratched his nose.

'Well, I can see now's not a good time. Would it be more convenient for me to come and see you again tomorrow morning, when you've had a good night's sleep? I can take a statement from you. These things have to be done, unfortunately.'

'That'll be fine. I've had more rest than you can shake a stick at, but yes, perhaps tomorrow morning would be better,' I said, eyeing Jane. She still had that look about her: a Rottweiler measuring up its dinner.

'Well I'm pleased to see you awake.' Rob said, shaking my hand again.

'Nice to see you, Rob.' I replied.

He smiled at the nurse and left.

'I think I ought to be here tomorrow.' Jane said taking hold of my hand again.

'No! I'd like to talk to Rob on my own.' I said, as firmly as I could. I felt so weak.

'But….'

'No, Jane, I….' I was shouting but my voice was not much more than a whisper and I started coughing.

Laura got up and walked round the bed to help me sit up. 'Have a sip of water Mr Hetherington,' she said looking at the monitor next to my bed, 'and I think we ought to put the oxygen back on for a bit. I think you're getting tired'. She said looking at Jane pointedly.

Once I'd stopped coughing and settled back against the pillows, Jane spoke again.

'Don't upset yourself, Dad, it's okay. If you want to talk to the sergeant on your own, then that's fine. I just want to help.'

'You are, Jane. You're here and I really appreciate it…' Speaking into the mask was like talking underwater. I wasn't entirely sure anyone could hear me. But Jane understood. Her years of experience gave her the edge when it came to deciphering rambling old and tired men.

'I am very tired.' I finished.

'I know, Dad.' She said. She kissed my forehead and I drifted off into a wonderfully dark and dreamless sleep.

30.

Zins

Zins are cooking pots used in ceremonies. They are traditionally made out of clay but if they are to be used for the Nago loa, a loa of the Nigerian branch of Voodoo, then they are made out of iron.

A week later and, by the powers of the National Health Service, I was released into the care of my daughter, thankfully in my own home. There had been some murmurings about me joining her in Devon to recuperate but I'd quashed the idea with a mention of the dogs and the long journey wearing me out. Her husband had not been pleased as that meant more time off work for him to look after the children, but she had promised she would be back by the end of the week, something I hoped very much was a fact rather than a false promise; she was driving me nuts.

Do you need the toilet? Would you like a bottle? Can I get you some tea? Have you got a headache? Can I take your pulse? You're looking a bit pale.

No. No I don't, my legs still work. No, I'll need the loo again. Yes, but that would go if you left me in peace. There's nothing wrong with my heart and I've not been outside for two weeks, of course I look pale!

Naturally, these answers remained in my internal monologue and instead I took a deep breath and said *'Thank you'*, as politely as I could muster, and feigned sleep when it all got too much. The doorbell rang several times, casseroles arrived, macaroni cheese and even a bunch of flowers from Delilah but to my annoyance, none of my visitors were admitted entrance.

I did have some company. I had relented on my *'no dogs upstairs'* rule. Bertie and Prince had been sitting on the end of my bed since I returned home, only moving for mealtimes and walks. They are a great comfort and much better than hot water bottles. Even so, after two days of my daughter's interrogations, Sudoku and no sane conversation, save for the odd sniff or baleful look, I texted Rob an SOS, which he responded to with a policeman's efficiency.

A day and a half, two more casseroles and a box of Thorntons later, the doorbell rang. 'Sergeant Claringdon.' I heard my daughter's voice, trite in her announcement.

'Mrs Grosmont,' came the reply, 'I've come to see Blake.'

I heard the door creak on its hinges and I felt a draught creep along the corridor, up the stairs and into the bedroom. The dogs at the end of the bed lifted their heads in unison and whined.

'I'm afraid he's very tired…' She didn't get any further.

'He texted me yesterday, said he'd very much like to see me. I won't stay long.'

The door creaked again, in response to what I imagine was Rob stepping confidently over the threshold and into the house.

'I'll see myself up.' He said.

'Mind your shoes...' I heard Jane say as the door closed and she tutted. I had no idea where this lack of respect had come from. In my day if a police officer turned up on your doorstep you did as you were told. Just because you were friends didn't mean you no longer respected the law.

Rob's heavy footfall climbed the stairs two at a time, there was a brief knock at the door and he arrived in the bedroom, his shoes still firmly on his feet.

'Rob, come in, great to see you.' I pushed myself up the bed and indicated for him to close the door. The dogs were fussing around his feet and after an exchange of affection all three of them gathered on the end of the bed once more.

'How've you been?' Rob asked.

'Good, good. The headaches have stopped but that's boring. What about you?'

'I'm good. Delilah's home in a month. It's gone so quick. I'll be glad to see her.'

'I'm sure, and how about the case?'

There was a knock at the door and Jane entered. 'I thought you might like some tea. I brought you some of my sponge cake too.' She managed a smile for Rob. I was astonished but the ulterior motive wasn't far behind. 'I don't want you wearing him out or getting him involved in any nonsense.' She placed the tray on the chest of drawers and, turning to me, said, 'Do you hear that, Dad, you too. Murder's not a job for you, it's for the police.' She wagged her finger and left the room, leaving the door open. I leant to one side and pushed it closed again.

'It's worse than I thought.' Rob said in almost a whisper.

'Don't think I don't know what you're up to.' Jane's voice came from behind the door.

We burst into laughter. I laughed hard, tears rolling down my face. The bed shook as Rob held his stomach unable to control his laughter. I heard Jane's footsteps retreat back downstairs. I felt sure I would pay for that later, but this was the first time I'd laughed in weeks; a good hearty laugh, one that gets the blood pumping and the endorphins flowing. Life was good. Someone had tried to kill me and I'd survived. Jane had to be crazy to think I didn't want a part in finding out whom. Someone had to be held accountable for the paracetamol bill.

'So tell me,' I said regaining my breath and wiping the tears from my eyes, 'How's the case?'

Rob cleared his throat, 'Not great, I'm afraid Blake. We've hit an impasse. I'm sure it's Yveny but I can't prove it.'

'I wish I could remember more about that day. I just remember images occasionally. I remember a charcoal kiln, but I don't know why. I remember the dogs barking, that hideous effigy and this smell. A familiar smell, but the rest is fuzzy. Yveny's got an alibi, I suppose?'

'Yup; with Tuvey in The Badger's Holt. It's becoming a bit of a habit.'

'It does seem a little too convenient.'

'Hmmm.' Rob took a sip of his tea and got up to take a piece of sponge cake from the tray. 'Do you want some?'

I shook my head, hands holding my stomach, the thought made me feel ill. Food wasn't fun at the moment. The strong painkillers had affected my appetite.

'It's that bit of graffiti that's puzzling me.' I said

'What's that?'

'The graffiti, on my shed. It happened the morning before I had the accident.' Calling it an accident felt better than saying *'when an attempt was made on my life.'*

'I didn't know about that.'

'I reported it at the police station.'

'Which one?'

'Tuesbury.'

'Why didn't you tell me?'

I coughed, 'Well…I thought…I thought perhaps you were getting a little fed up with a troublesome old man after our last conversation.'

'I'm sorry if you thought that. You're nothing compared to some of the crackpots that crawl out the woodwork in most murder cases.'

I waved the apology away and the backhanded compliment.

'You should have told me.' He said.

'Well I reported it and…' a memory flashed back, 'oh…wait a minute.'

'What is it?'

'What happened about the shed?'

'The shed? Well, I didn't know about it, so I guess the community policing team took it up. I'll check when I get back to the station.'

'No the shed in Little Tuesbury.'

'*Little* Tuesbury?'

'Yes. I just remembered, that's what Mrs Tudbury was phoning me about. The cross on my shed.'

'Oh, that shed. Yes, there was a cross, I did say when I came to see you in hospital.'

'Sorry, I don't remember.'

'That's okay, it was one hell of a wack you got.'

'So was it just like the others?'

'The cross? Yes.'

'Have there been any more?'

'No.'

'I don't suppose he'll try anything again now.'

'It's unlikely, you're very lucky, Blake. You still need to be careful though. Your daughter is right. There's no reason why he wouldn't try again. He obviously thinks you know something.'

'Perhaps it isn't Yveny.' I tried this line of thought once more. 'After all, he has an alibi.'

'His alibis are either his aunt or Tuvey. I don't trust them but I have no way of disproving them. Other people in the pub saw him, but they can't have seen him for the whole time he was in there, which was sometimes three or four hours after a Morris dancing session.'

'They can sink their pints.' I agreed.

'Strange lot in my opinion. Not sure I trust a man that ties bells on his shins and waves hankies around for pleasure.'

'And you don't trust Yveny?'

'No! I definitely don't trust him!'

I could think of nothing to say in Yveny's defence. If Rob's theory was to be believed then it might be Yveny and Tuvey were in it together.

'Do you think the graffiti has anything to do with it?'

'I don't know, tell me what happened.'

'Well, I was on the phone to you, and when I hung up I heard a scuffle come from the back of the shed and I saw a figure stand up. I ran out of the shed to try and catch them but they were long gone. Towards the bottom of the shed, they'd graffited a little symbol.'

'What did they look like?'

'Short. Not as tall as Yveny, and slight. They were wearing a heavy duffel coat but they ran fast.'

'What was the symbol?'

'Here, I'll draw it.' I took my notebook from the side and drew it out handing it to Rob.

'Interesting.'

'Odd, isn't it? It looks religious, not your usual bog standard, *I woz 'ere.*'

'Can I keep this?'

'Yes. The desk sergeant did say an officer would be round to look at it, but I have no idea if they were.'

'Leave it with me.'

My eyes must have been drooping because Rob stood up and said 'I think you should rest now.'

He was right. I was tired. My whole body ached with the effort of laughing and the conversation. I had overestimated my recovery. 'I just wish I could remember more of what happened.' I said.

'Don't worry. Just get better. We'll catch him. At some point he'll slip up.'

'He won't get another chance at me.' I said.

'Not with Jane standing guard, no.' Rob replied and laughed.

'She's a good girl.'

'You have a very caring family, Blake, you're lucky.'

'I know.'

My eyes drifted shut and Rob left the room. I heard some hushed voices and the front door close. I hoped they'd made their peace. I knew Jane would like Rob if she gave him a chance. It wasn't his fault her father couldn't keep his nose out of a good mystery.

As I dozed, I heard Jane come in the room and remove the tray, stopping on the way back to pull the duvet cover up over me. My mind flicked through visions of the shed, graffiti, trees, birds, a charcoal burner, the barking, the river, and the phone-call; a nineteen-sixties View-Master of the day's events. In amongst these images somewhere was the answer, I felt sure. I just had to search hard enough to unlock the memory. Something I knew was valuable and the murderer knew it too.

31.

Invisibles

A term used to describe the spirits of the loa and the dead

The next visitor to gain entrance to the fortress that was now my house was the Reverend Lambert. She brought with her a large basket of fruit.

'It's the done thing.' She announced, standing by my bed proffering the cornucopia.

'That's very kind of you,' I said, eyeing up a rather tasty looking plum. 'Would you mind placing it on the dresser over there?'

She obliged. Next, in offering her a seat I suddenly realised I had nowhere for her to sit. Asking a lady of the cloth to sit on your bed didn't seem right. 'Ermm, if you wouldn't mind shifting those clothes off the chair, I'm sorry it's such a mess, I…'

'Oh no, no, no. Nonsense, you haven't been well, where would you like me to put them?'

'On the end of the bed, there, is fine.' I said.

The additional items, infiltrating their sleeping space did not amuse the dogs.

'Your daughter's looking after you well, I see.' Persephone continued.

'Yes, she's a good girl, but she has her own family. She'll need to go home soon. I'm going to have to get up, I can't lie around in bed forever.' I smiled.

'You must rest. It's a nasty injury you've had.'

'Hmm. I'm determined I will get up tomorrow, whether she likes it or not. I confess I'm worried about her neglecting her family.'

'There you go, confessing again.' Persephone smiled. She was sat upright in the chair, hands on her lap, looking distinctly uncomfortable.

'Are you all right?' I asked.

'Not really, no. I feel awful.'

'You must go if you're not well. Please don't stay out of a sense of duty.'

'No, no, I feel awful about what happened to you.'

'To me? Why?

'I can't help feeling someone was listening when I spoke to you at the family history talk.'

'Listening?'

'Yes. About my suspicions that Yveny wasn't guilty.'

'I see.'

'You see, what if the murderer was there and heard?'

'I see.'

Jane entered the room with a tray of tea, 'Oo isn't that nice, Dad? Just what you need, lots of vitamins.' She said swapping the tray with the fruit basket. 'That's awfully nice of you, reverend.' Jane's face was tired. Looking after me was taking its toll. Tomorrow I would get out of bed. 'Tea?' She asked the reverend.

'That would be lovely, thank you. I'm parched, I've been preparing my sermon all morning.'

'Well then you deserve a break.' Jane replied.

She poured the tea and left us to talk again. I think she hoped the reverend would talk some sense into her father's addled mind and persuade him to stay away from the influence of Sergeant Claringdon.

Jane had used the best bone china cups and saucers that were Eleanor's favourites. I rested my cup and saucer on the top of the duvet.

'But surely if they thought you had told me something useful they would have come after you too?' I said, picking up the conversation again.

'Well, that's just it.'

I took a sip of my tea and waited.

'While I was practicing my sermon this morning, the large cross that stands behind me fell forward. I was lucky to get out of the way in time.'

'Good grief!'

'Yes, and I heard footsteps, running. Miss Derby appeared when she heard the noise. I hadn't realised she was there.'

'Miss Derby?

'Well, she had every reason to be there; she helps with the flowers sometimes. Why, if it hadn't been for her the killer might have had another go while I was in a state of shock.'

'But you don't think…'

'No, no. Not Miss Derby. She said she saw someone running across the graveyard.'

'Oh?'

'There is a side entrance near the choir stalls. They must have left that way.'

'I see.'

'It sounds stupid, doesn't it, positively biblical when I say it out loud. It's an old church, it probably just fell. Ignore, me please.' She said and took a sip of her tea, blushing. Her hands were shaking slightly and I could see the experience had affected her much more than she cared to admit.

'Have you told the police?'

'But it sounds so ridiculous!'

'Still, I think you should report it, given the goings on in the village of late.'

'I suppose so. It took Miss Derby and me to stand the cross up again. It's heavy. Thinking about it, I can't see how someone could push it without me noticing.'

'Report it, reverend, just to be on the safe side. You don't want to end up like me. You might not be so lucky.'

She nodded and sipped some more tea. I was thinking about the plum again, all the way downstairs where Jane had taken it and how good it would taste, when another memory filtered back. This time it was of the family history talk. Persephone mentioning the talk had jolted some brain cells back into action.

'Funny.' I said.

'What's that?'

'Miss Derby being there.'

'Not really, she was doing the flowers, like I said…'

'No I meant at the talk. She was sitting behind us, do you remember?'

'Now you come to mention it, yes.'

'But you say it took the two of you to stand it up.'

'Yes.'

'I suppose that puts paid to her being able to push it over on her own then doesn't it.'

'It rather does, unless…well…she was just pretending…'

Bertie broke the conversation by getting up and turning around a couple of times, rearranging the warm patch of duvet he was occupying.

'Right, Mr Hetherington.' Persephone said decisively. 'It's time I let you get some rest. Please don't worry yourself any more with my silly imaginings.'

'I think they are far from silly.'

'No, think no more about it, you need your rest. I don't want to be responsible for any further illness. I'm so glad you're recovering so well.'

'Thank you, but please be assured I hold you in no way responsible for my predicament. In fact I think you may easily find yourself in the same waters. I think you should report the incident with the cross.'

'If it will stop you worrying I'll walk down to the police station now.'

'I'll get Jane to go with you; she can walk the dogs at the same time. Jane…!' I called out.

'It's not a problem I'll be fine. No, I insist,' I said as Jane came in.

'Jane, would you mind walking with the reverend down to the police station? You could take the dogs with you, they need a walk.'

'What have you been saying to her now, Dad?' Jane reprimanded me with a frown.

'Nothing, Mrs Grosmont.' Persephone interrupted. 'He's been a perfect patient.'

'Now that I find hard to believe.' Jane said.

'Something rather strange happened to me this morning; your Dad was worried and wants me to report it. He thinks an attempt may have been made on my life.'

'What?!' Jane was visibly shocked.

'I don't think so, but Mr Hetherington does and if it would make him feel better, I'm willing to report it.' Really, I thought inwardly, that's not what you said fifteen minutes ago, but I stayed quiet. The reverend clearly found it easier to blame me.

'I see.' Jane said, 'He does have quite an imagination, doesn't he? Besides, I'm not sure I should leave you for too long, Dad. The police station's a good two miles away.'

'You're going to have to leave me sometime, Jane,' I replied, 'and the dogs need more of a walk than five minutes around the block. Look at the poor things, they're obese.' I tugged at the weighted down duvet.

'All right, but I want you to keep your mobile on the side next to you so you can ring if you need me.'

'Okay.' I smiled. At last freedom was within my grasp.

As soon as they were all out the door, I flipped back the duvet. My pyjamas were getting far too comfortable. Why wait until tomorrow to get up? I was going to get up now. Jane had exaggerated; it was a one and a half mile walk to the police station from here. Jane would be gone about an hour and a half at the very least. When she got back she'd find me sat on the Chesterfield with that nice looking plum from the fruit basket. Then she'd feel happier about going home to her family.

I stood up; immediately the room spun. In my exuberance I had got up far too quickly. I sat back down, heavily. My head thumped but I was determined to do this. I reached for my trousers still lying on the end of the bed. The soft green cords felt homely and good. It had been weeks since I had worn a proper pair of trousers.

I dragged them up the bed towards me and something made a scrunching sound in the pocket. Reaching my hand in, I found a folded up piece of paper. It was old and burnt at the edges. It looked familiar, but I couldn't place it. There were a few words written on it in a calligraphy pen.

> butcher, baker,
> my son's right.
> the manor will,

It looked like a poem. The words butcher, baker reminded me of a nursery rhyme: butcher, baker, candlestick maker. But there was no candlestick maker on the paper. It was clear that the paper was part of a larger piece and that these words were fragments of sentences. But what could they mean and why had they been burnt? The smell of the paper reminded me of barbecues. That was it. That was why I'd been looking in the charcoal burner. This must have been in it. I was relieved. Things were starting to come back to me.

A wave of tiredness overtook me. I abandoned the idea of getting up and swung my legs back into bed. I should ring Rob. After all, a butcher and a baker had been murdered. But what about the candlestick maker? Maybe, as Jane said, it was just my imagination. Who knows what the blow to the head did to me. There wasn't even a candlestick maker in the village. Or was there? Elroy Tuvey made candles. His model hadn't gone missing but then again the models could be a decoy after all. But Elroy Tuvey was Yveny's alibi. Tuvey just kept cropping up.

> *Rub-a-dub-dub,*
> *Three men in a tub*
> *And how do you think they got there?*

The butcher, the baker.
The candlestick-maker,
They all jumped out of a rotten potato,
'Twas enough to make a man stare.'

Well, I had been staring. The image of the grotesque tree stump with all is paraphernalia reappeared. This was more than a crazed nursery rhyme killer. The village had also lost a greengrocer, a bookie and a newsagent. They now joined the butcher and the baker in the proverbial rotten potato. The question was: whom did the potato belong to? The candlestick-maker?

I rested my head back on the pillow and pulled the duvet back over me. Tomorrow was another day. I'd get up tomorrow; after a good night's sleep. The sun was starting to set outside and the bedroom window let in the hazy light of the dusk. I closed my eyes once more to dream of the forest and the birds. My mind did not relent, even when my body did. It was determined to remember what I knew.

I fell into a fitful sleep. I must only have been asleep for twenty minutes or half an hour when I awoke with a start. The curtains were still open and the sky was now black. The house was dark and silent. It was a smell that had woken me: the same smell that had invaded my senses in Druid Wood. Lily-of-the-valley. A perfume Eleanor used to wear. Had I been dreaming?

Then I saw what had woken me. A figure standing over the bed silhouetted against the white walls of the bedroom. It reached out towards me and I pulled away. Squeezing my eyes shut, I opened them again, hoping the darkness would become clearer and the spectre would vanish. It was still there and a deep heavy perfume filled the room.

32.

Maman

Mother.

Light flooded the room as the bedside lamp clicked on.

'I'm sorry, I didn't mean to frighten you Mr Hetherington. It's just, I knocked and there was no reply, so I was worried.'

I sat there in stunned silence.

'You see, I knew you were ill, the reverend told me you hadn't been out and were missing the company.'

Mrs Dellaware stood there, smiling, as if there was nothing at all unusual about walking into someone's house, uninvited, creeping up the stairs in the dark, wandering into their bedroom and standing over them while they slept. She definitely had birds in her attic.

'How did you get in?' Was all I could muster. I felt like a bumblebee awakened too early from my hibernation by a marauding cat.

'The door was open.'

'What? Wide open?' Now *I* was worried.

'No. I tried the handle when there was no answer; it was unlocked. Like I say, I was worried.' She continued to smile. 'Can I get you anything?'

'No, no, in fact I think I'd like you to leave.' I said.

'Are you sure? I don't mind staying and keeping you company.'

'No, no I'm fine, thank you. I'd like you to leave.' I repeated.

She didn't. Instead she sat on the end of the bed. Right on top of my suit jacket.

'I wanted to talk to you.' She said. She was wearing a duffel coat and a dark black fluffy beret. I didn't think it was that cold outside but then again, I hadn't been out for weeks save for the brief journey in the wheelchair from ward to car and then car to house. She pulled the beret off and started twisting it between her hands.

Dragging my hand down my face, I tried to wake up. I pushed myself up in the bed and I noticed my trousers were on the floor. Thankfully I still had my pyjama bottoms on, I hadn't got that far in my bid for freedom.

'This isn't a good moment.' I said, trying a different tack.

'I'm worried about Donald.' She said.

'Mrs Dellaware…'

'I'm worried about Donald. He needs a father figure in his life. He needs guidance. He doesn't have anyone else. He only has me and I've got to make sure he's provided for.'

She sounded like she was talking about a four year old, not a forty year old. She wasn't looking at me. Her face creased, deep in concentration, determined.

'Rufus doesn't care. I know he doesn't, he never has. It's up to me to sort it out. I've got to make it right, you see. Donald needs me. I'm sure you understand, that's why I want you to talk to him.'

'Who?'

'Rufus.'

'Rufus?'

'Yes! You're his friend, you'll make him see sense.'

'About what.'

'You know what.' Her voice was hard, her eyes icy, accusing and unrelenting.

'I assure you I don't.' I said.

'Of course you do. You're just like the rest of them! Denying it!'

'Mrs Dellaware, I would like you to leave now.' I was getting a headache, the room was spinning and I thought I might throw up.

'I bet you would. That would be very convenient, wouldn't it.' She had got up and was now standing very close to my face, her finger jabbing at the air. Cold dark eyes pierced the haze that surrounded my head. I took a deep breath in.

'I WANT YOU TO....' My shouting was cut short by the slam of the front door.

'Dad? Is that you? Are you all right?' I heard the dogs thunder up the stairs closely followed by Jane. Prince stood in the doorway, blocking Jane's entry. Standing firm, he growled, baring his teeth and snarling at the figure that stood over my bed.

Mrs Dellaware turned and smiled. She looked down at the fierce little spaniel. 'There's a good boy, protecting your master.' Smoothing down the front of her coat she drew herself up and looked my daughter in the eye.

'Who are you?' Jane said.

'I'm Mrs Dellaware. Pleased to meet you.' She said extending a hand.

Jane did not take it. She looked at my face, squinting in the light, a hand shading my eyes. I must have been whiter than whiter and I felt wretched.

'Dad, are you okay?'

'Not really.' I said.

'I'd like you to leave.' Jane said, to Mrs Dellaware, pointing back down the stairs. Prince started growling again. 'You're upsetting my father and the dogs.' She finished.

'I only….' She stopped and scrunched her eyes shut and raised her hands to her temples to massage them. I could feel the bile rising in my stomach. I needed to get to the bathroom. I began to get out of bed.

'Dad, stay where you are a moment.' My daughter's voice was urgent.

'But I think I'm…'

'Stay where you are.' She said again. 'Mrs Dellaware, are you all right?' Jane's voice had changed. It was official, professional, what you might call a nursing voice.

'Oh, fine dear,' Mrs Dellaware opened her eyes, 'just another one of my heads. Well, I'll leave you to it.'

Pushing her way past Jane and down the stairs, she was out of the door before Prince had a chance to express further his dislike of her presence.

The exit was clear and all I could think of was the bathroom. Holding my hand to my mouth I moved as quickly as I could before I was violently sick.

Jane had followed Mrs Dellaware back down the stairs, presumably to check she'd left. I could hear the dogs outside the bathroom door waiting for me. Then I heard a soft knock.

'Are you okay, Dad?' nursing voice, still.

'I'm fine; I'll be fine in a minute. Could I have some fresh water?'

'Shout if you need me.' I heard her footsteps go back down the stairs and the tap running in the kitchen.

The cold bathroom floor was a comfort through my old cotton pyjamas. There was an overwhelming sense of relief. I wasn't sure if it was because my unwanted visitor had gone or because I'd finally been able to relieve the feeling of nausea. I stood up slowly and pulled the flush. I rinsed my mouth out and returned to the bedroom.

Jane met me at the top of the stairs and tucked me up in bed the way I did for her when she was younger. The cycle of life amused me.

'That's better,' I said 'I have a tremendous headache.'

'Would you like some paracetamol?'

'Yes, thank you.'

Jane went to the bathroom, returning with painkillers and a cold compress for my head.

'You should be taking it easy, Dad, you've had far too many visitors today.'

'Well I didn't exactly invite the last one.'

'What?' She took her hand away from the compress and although I had my eyes closed I could feel her look of confusion. 'What was she doing here?'

'She said the door was open and she was worried about me.'

'What, *wide* open?'

'No.' I was getting tired but I needed to tell Jane. 'No. Unlocked. She came in when she got no answer.'

'Do people normally do that?'

'No.'

'I'm not altogether sure she's all that well.'

'You think?' My sarcasm was missed.

'Just instinct. She has an aura about her. I thought she was going to do something strange when she clutched her forehead like that.'

'Strange?'

'Yes. I suppose I shouldn't say strange. She looked like she might be having an absence.'

I laughed. 'Oh no! She was definitely here!' My head pounded with the laughter.

'No. It's like a mini epileptic fit. I've seen lots of patients have them. That's what it looked like.'

'Her nephew said she suffered from migraine.'

'Ah, that explains it.' Jane massaged the compress on my forehead. 'Wasn't he arrested for the murders?'

'Yes. Rob's now convinced himself Yveny did it, but I'm not so sure.'

'I don't know why you can't leave the police to it, Dad,' she handed me the water and the paracetamol and I took them obediently.

'Rob's a friend.' I said between gulps of water. 'Besides, he asked for my help.'

'Well he shouldn't have. That's what got you into this mess. I hold that man fully responsible.'

'Funny. I hold whoever murdered all those people responsible.' I said smiling.

An owl hooted outside and another returned its call. Jane stood up to close the curtains.

'Dad?'

'Yes.'

'The door was locked.'

I opened my eyes.

'I swear I locked it.' Jane said, pulling shut the curtains.

'Well I do keep a key under the plant pot out the front, maybe she found it.'

'I think I'll go and move it, *now*.' Jane said walking back around the bed towards the door. She pulled the duvet up around me again and I heard something drop on the floor.

'Oh, I didn't see this come. You've got a postcard from Haiti. Delilah, I shouldn't wonder, it's a bit tatty. You must have snuck downstairs to collect the post when I wasn't looking.' She said, tutting.

'Have I, I don't remember that.'

'Yes, it's here, it fell off the bed.' She handed me the card and went downstairs to move the key.

The colours on the card were washed out and old. A proud native woman was pictured on the front holding a huge basket above her head. In the background a thatched roof and some crops which were not familiar. I turned it over. It was not addressed to me. It was addressed to Lord Rufus Blackwood, somewhere in France and stamped across the top was RETURN TO SENDER. If the postcard wasn't mine and it wasn't my daughter's it could only have been Rob's or Mrs Dellaware's; the only two other people that had sat on the end of the bed over the last few days. Jane had changed the sheets this morning, so she would surely have found it then. It can only have been one of today's visitors that dropped it. The tiny cursive handwriting looked feminine. My curiosity would not let me simply discard the postcard. Persephone Lambert had sat in the chair so my conclusion was that this must have fallen out of Constance Dellaware's pocket as she was sitting on the bed. What I read next confirmed this.

The handwriting was cursive and elaborate but I managed to decipher the following:

My love, you must write to me. I have not heard from you in weeks. I have such wonderful news. Please write soon.
All my love

E

It smelt of Lily-of-the-valley, the same smell that had invaded the room earlier and brought on my bout of nausea. I also felt sure I'd seen that handwriting somewhere before.

I did not have my glasses and the smell as I held the postcard close was overpowering. I felt my stomach turn again, so I held the card away from me. Who was *E*? Without my glasses perhaps I had misread it. Could the swirling *E*, in fact be a *C*? Rufus and Constance? I couldn't believe it at first and then I started to analyse it. Rufus had been a womaniser in his day. The postcard was from Haiti. I remembered Rufus talking to Delilah at the races, about Haiti and his experiences there. It was entirely possible Constance and Rufus had been there at the same time.

I could hear Jane downstairs talking to the dogs, scraping food out of tins and into bowls. The rattle of dog biscuits as they joined the meat and gravy, the whimper of Bertie impatiently waiting for his dinner, then the click of the fire as she turned it on and the gentle rumble of the kettle boiling.

Resting my head back against the pillows I closed my eyes: more thoughts.

I remembered Rufus telling Delilah about how his family had been welcomed in Haiti and what strong family units they had there. I wouldn't have put it past Rufus at all to have had an affair. I knew he loved his wife, but he was easily bored, a trait I had tried to counsel him about, on occasion. Did this mean Constance had been the other woman? The smell wafted up from the postcard again and an image flashed through my brain.

I was back in the forest, the mulch of cold leaves soft against my face; the dogs barking, the light fading and that aroma. That's why it had turned my stomach. It was the last smell that had graced my senses as I slipped into unconsciousness. I reached for the scrap of paper on my bedside table and held it against the postcard. The *m's* had the same little flick at the start, the *i's* all joined with the next letter and *w's* had the same curved undersides. This was the same handwriting. I suddenly felt very lucky to be alive. There was a knock at the door and I jumped instinctively.

'Sorry, I didn't mean to make you jump, I brought you a cup of tea.'

I was a picture of utter shock, at my near escape rather than the knock, but my daughter wasn't to know that. 'You don't have to drink it if you don't want to, I just thought, as I was boiling the kettle….'

'Yes, yes, that's lovely, thank you.' I replied impatiently. It was unfair; she didn't know what I had been thinking.

'Are you sure you're okay, Dad? I should call the doctor, see if she'll pop out and see you.' Dr Caudwell was a lovely woman and a blessing of a GP in the village. Overworked and conscientious, no doubt she would have come and seen me had Jane called her. But it wasn't the doctor I needed.

'No, no. I'm fine but I think you should call Rob.'

'Rob? Dad, can't you just rest.'

'No. This is important.' I said, handing her the postcard. 'I think Mrs Dellaware killed all those people.'

My daughter's face was now as white as mine. Not even looking at the card, she didn't argue. Perhaps it was women's intuition but for once she had no trouble believing me.

'Christ!' she said, 'I'll call Rob.'

33.

Baton-legba

The baton-legba is the gnarled old stick of Papa Legba, loa of the crossroads.

Rob was there within half an hour. My headache was a distant memory, my brain running riot with the possibilities. What if Jane hadn't returned when she did? How could I not have seen it earlier? Of course Yveny was protecting someone. He was protecting his mother!

I showed Rob the postcard and the scrap of paper, and told him about the perfume, the conversations and the visit; it was undeniable, but as Rob stated:

'It makes sense of course, but it's not definite evidence. I need something more concrete, something that puts her at the scene of the crime.'

'Well, how about breaking and entering' I proffered. My pride was still smarting at the memory of an old woman, able to frighten the living daylights out of me, even if she was potentially a serial killer.

'I can arrest her for that. Did you want to press charges?'

'*YES!*' was my immediate reaction and then I thought about it. 'But I'd rather see her arrested for murder. If she's convicted of breaking and entering then it's detracting from the more serious crime of murder.'

'Still...'

'She didn't actually do anything. She told me she was worried. She would have no trouble convincing a jury that her intentions were not malicious, I'm sure.'

'That is an unfortunate side effect of trying to prosecute older women. The general public doesn't think they could possibly have done it. A jury rarely convicts. Personally, I think they're the ones to watch out for!' Rob sighed and sat down on the end of the bed, still holding the postcard, his outdoor coat still buttoned.

'I watched the CCTV footage again the other day.'

'Oh yes.'

'I was looking for Yveny, trying to place him there.'

'And?'

'Well guess what I did see.'

'Go on.'

'The figure in the model village was slight in build, about five two, with a dark black duffel coat and a dark black bobble hat. A scarf was pulled up round their face so we couldn't see them but...'

'...That's what Mrs Dellaware was wearing when she came to see me. It was a beret, but easily mistaken for a bobble hat from a distance or on fuzzy CCTV footage.' I said, finishing Rob's sentence.

'I still can't prove it!'

I heard a creak on the landing and the dogs lifted their heads from the bed.

'You can come in, Jane, you may as well hear all of this.'

Jane pushed the door open and entered the bedroom.

'How are you feeling, Dad?' She said almost ignoring Rob.

'Better. Headache's gone.' I'd discarded the compress on the bedside table and it now sat in a little pool of moisture. 'Rob agrees with me.'

'Well I hope you're going to prosecute her for breaking in.'

'Well….'

'Come on Dad, if she is the murderer, she could have killed you.' Jane ran a hand through her bobbed hair. 'God, that sounds so dramatic,' she said.

'But she didn't and you said yourself she's an ill woman.'

'She's a murderer!' Jane replied.

I had no idea why I was defending Constance. I suppose part of me felt sorry for her but regardless of any misguided loyalty I may have, she had potentially killed five people!

'We can't prove it…yet.' Said Rob.

'Well I hope you don't expect Dad to do anything about it. He's a victim!' Her voice was tight and fierce and in that moment she reminded me so much of her mother, it brought a lump to my throat.

'Jane,' I stammered. 'Calm down!' I pushed myself up against the pillow and pulled the duvet straight. 'Do you think you could make us some tea?'

'Tea? Really, Dad? I don't think the sergeant should be drinking tea! He should be out there arresting Mrs Dellaware.'

'Jane!'

'Okay, tea.'

Rob and I listened to her footsteps descending. The dogs rested their heads back down, resigned that Jane's appearance had not signified extra food or walks.

'We looked into the graffiti in your shed.' Rob said breaking the silence.

My eyes widened in enquiry. I'd forgotten about the incident in amongst everything else.

'I took it to Tuvey.' Rob continued.

'Did you?' The surprise was clear in my voice.

'I'm willing to swallow my pride when it's for the good of the investigation. I had an idea that that little bit of graffiti was some kind of Voodoo. Even if I don't believe in it there's no reason why someone else doesn't.'

'True,' I nodded, 'and your conclusion?'

'Tuvey had seen it before. He said it was a Vever.'

I frowned.

'A vever's a symbol in Voodoun rituals,' Rob answered. 'They are used to call upon the gods.'

'Ah.'

'So your graffiti artist could have been our suspect. Can you remember anything about them?'

'Nothing other than what I already reported. I can't remember rightly now but wasn't it….'

'...A black coat and a black bobble hat, yes.' Rob completed my sentence.

Jane entered with the tea, silent and sullen, she placed a mug beside me, and one on the dresser for Rob. As she did so, Rob's phone rang.

'Sergeant Claringdon...Yes...Yes. I'm not far from there. On my way. Are you sending a car?.........good.'

He hung up.

Jane was still standing beside the dresser as curious as I was about this one-sided conversation. Rob stood up from the bed, zipping up his jacket.

'I've got to go, Blake. There's been a report of a disturbance.'

'Where?'

'I've got to go, I'll speak to you later.'

'*Where*, Rob?' I wasn't letting him get away with this. He'd said to the voice on the other end that he was close. But close to where?

Rob sighed 'Blackwood Manor.' He looked at me a *'don't you dare try anything'* look.

'I'll come with you.'

'Don't be ridiculous.' It was the first time Rob had been so overtly dismissive of me. He'd always been quietly respectful. Perhaps it was the pressure of the situation; could I have finally got on his nerves; or was I being ridiculous? Jane was about to put her two-penn'orth in, when I interrupted them both.

'Rufus is my friend, I might be able to help.'

'In your state, Dad?' Jane mustered.

'Absolutely not, Blake! Now I have to go. Stay here!' Rob didn't wait for a reply. He was down the stairs and out of the door before I could protest again.

'He's right, Dad.' To Jane's credit, she said it without an ounce of triumph.

I said nothing. This was not a time to argue.

As soon as Jane was back downstairs I was out of bed again and trying to get my cords on. It was a struggle and my head spun but the adrenalin helped. I didn't even bother to remove my pyjamas first. This was an emergency. I had a bad feeling. What if I was right? What if Dellaware had gone to confront Rufus and now he was in danger. I'd let him down once and I was damned if that was going to happen again. Sick or not, I was going up to that manor.

I finally got my trouser legs over my feet and pulled them up over my pyjamas. Pulling a jumper off the back of the chair I put it on over my pyjama top. I caught sight of myself in the mirror on the dresser on the way past. In normal circumstances I'd have been shocked to find myself even thinking about going out like this, but these were not normal circumstances. I left my slippers off and I made a beeline for my shoes, which were by the front door.

I hobbled down the stairs as the legs of my pyjamas had gathered inside my trouser legs at the knees and made it difficult to bend them. By the time I got to the bottom Jane was waiting, arms folded, pursed lips and a frown.

'Exactly what are you doing, Dad?'

'Going to see Rufus.' I was breathing heavily from the effort. The paracetamol had staved off the headache to a point but a dull ache had returned from the exertion. Jane was barring my way. 'Please move so I can put my shoes on, I'd like to leave my house.'

She looked at my feet, 'You haven't got any socks on.' I got the feeling she'd encountered this situation before, possibly with a three year old.

'I'd like to put my shoes on now.' I said stepping down off the last step.

'You heard what Rob said, Dad.' She was only about two feet away from me but it was a narrow corridor. She moved as I drew up in front of her. I'd never touch my daughter but she'd crossed a line.

'No-one tells me when I can and can't leave my house. Now, I've had just about enough of this.' I bent down to pick up my shoes. I stood up too quickly, deflating my argument as I wobbled violently.

'*Dad*....'

'I'm going.' I said pinching the bridge of my nose and squeezing my eyes shut to regain my balance. 'That's the end of it.' I opened my eyes again and moved back to the stairs to sit on the bottom step. The dogs had followed me down and were making a nuisance of themselves as I tried to tie my shoelaces.

Jane went into the lounge returning with her handbag. Lifting her coat off the newel post, she helped me up from the stairs. I looked at her.

'Well, if you're going to insist on going then I'm coming with you.' She took my stick from beside the door and handed it to me. 'You can't very well go without this.' She picked up her car keys, shooed the dogs into the kitchen and helped me on with my jacket. The hall mirror showed a pale-faced man with wild grey hair and dark circles under his eyes. I was struggling but I was determined.

'Come on, then.'

I think Jane was secretly hoping that the reverse psychology she was clearly employing, would have the desired effect, but I had known her for all of her forty-two years and she wasn't pulling the wool over my eyes. She must know I meant what I said.

I made it down the front path and into the car. Jane held the passenger door open as I got in and we were on our way. I stayed silent, determined not to let the waves of nausea beat me. My friend needed me; I didn't care what he'd done, he needed my help.

34.

Débâtement

A débâtement is identified by intense and forceful movement. The movement is thought to symbolise inner conflict as a god or loa enters a physical body. Once the loa has possessed the body then the movement subsides.

We said nothing on the way over to the manor. The two miles felt like twenty. The ensuing ten minutes, a wait at the dentist. Jane disapproved of my stubborn determination and I resented being driven to the manor. There was, of course, no other way. She could not stop me going and I would not have managed the walk there.

Scenarios played out in my mind; a rattle from the glove box knocked in time with the juddering of the engine. Spraying the windscreen with washer fluid, it became apparent that the windscreen wipers were in need of replacement. The clear moonlit evening outside was obscured by a smear of insects and dust. I'd always been very particular about car maintenance, when I'd had one that was. *'Oil, water, washer fluid, windscreen wipers and tyres - all lifesavers',* I'd told Jane this on numerous occasions. I said nothing as she sprayed more fluid onto the screen. Jane described the old Ford Escort as a classic. I described it as a heap of junk and a pit to pour money into. As with many things, today's journey included, we agreed to disagree.

The manor's driveway was magnificent in the moon's spotlight. The eagles adorning the gateposts were sinister against the navy blue velvet sky of the night. It was one of those long, winding, gravel covered, conifer-lined affairs. You don't come in this way if you walk. This way is for visiting dignitaries: a chance for your estate to make an impression before your guest even entered the main hall.

Approaching the front of the house, we could see two police cars positioned at wayward angles. Jane had barely slowed down before I opened the door. She stamped on the brakes as I and we lurched to a halt.

'Wait…' She said struggling with the handbrake and the seatbelt at the same time. But I wasn't waiting.

The night air was invigorating, instantly curing the nausea induced by the car journey. A cold wind pushed through the zip of my jacket, through my jumper and pyjamas, reminding me of my insufficient attire.

The large, oak, front door, framed by a stone porch and pillars, was not the door normally used by the Blackwoods. It was closed but I could hear raised voices from the back of the house. I noticed a figure leaning against the side of the manor, about ten yards away. Dressed in black, they were clutching a portable radio, their jacket clearly identified them as POLICE.

I knew that this door, effectively the back door, was kept locked. I had to get round to the front but I had to get past that police officer. I thought about going along the side of the house to the old servants' entrance, but I assumed the officer would have a counterpart. I heard the door of the Ford Escort bang as Jane got out. The officer turned and I pushed myself against the wall.

'*Dad.*' Jane shouted.

'Stay back, please.' The officer was now approaching Jane with his hand outstretched and was talking into the radio. He crossed the ten yards and was two feet past me when I saw my chance. I dashed behind him and along the side of the house. Jane, of course, saw me and shouted again.

'Dad, come back…'

The officer did not turn. He was more concerned with trying to stop the oncoming missile that was my daughter running to catch me up.

'…but my Dad's…'

I didn't hear any more. I could only imagine the incandescence of Jane's rage, imparting her opinion on the state of today's heavy-handed policing, as she was manhandled into the back of one of the police cars and questioned.

The raised voices got louder as I reached the corner of the west side of the house. I looked down the back to see if there were any police officers guarding the doorway: none.

The magnolia floated gently in the cold breeze and the old servant's door stood wide open. I could hear three distinct voices.

'You stand there and tell me you don't know who I am?'

'Mother....'

'He should know! Was I that insignificant? Was I that worthless? Does he mean that little to you?'

'I am sorry, Mrs Dellaware, I can see you're very upset and I want to help but....'

'He's your son, Rufus!'

Silence reigned. The old brass bell made a slight ting as the wind caught it and the door creaked open a bit more. I heard the crackle of a radio behind me and, fearing I may be discovered, I took the invitation the night had given me to enter the manor.

The hallway was dark and I could see a figure standing at the bottom of the stairs. Light from the first doorway on the left shone in a triangle across the parquet flooring of the entrance hall.

'*Blake...*' came a violent whisper from the figure on the stairs. 'What are you doing here?' It was Rob.

A voice began again in the lit room.

'My *son*?' said Rufus.

Rob moved towards me as I continued to listen, waiting for my moment.

'Look, I'm sorry about this. Motter, this isn't 'elping anyone. You need to come 'ome.' I could hear the Spanish accent and finally the jigsaw was complete. This was Donald's voice. I had been right. Rob had almost reached me when I decided it was now or never and entered the room. My friend stood, two against one.

'Blake?' Rufus looked shocked, confused, tiny in his own home.

I took in the scene. Rufus stood by the fireplace, wrapped in a tartan dressing gown, barefoot, his hands outstretched, beseeching. I hadn't noticed her at first but sitting silently on the Chesterfield, also in a dressing gown, this time made of silk, was Mrs Darensky. Between them and the door stood Mrs Dellaware and Donald Yveny, her son. Donald stood a foot to the right of his mother, eyes focused on her, his back to the door. Constance Dellaware was sideways on to the door, still in her black duffel coat and beret; she was clutching a terracotta pot. It was about ten inches tall; glazed and plain in colour, it had a small lid.

They all turned to look at me as I entered.

'I came to see if you were all right. There's police outside, you know.' I said, looking at Mrs Dellaware.

'You're all as bad as each other. Think you're better than everyone else. *Think you know better, think you do better, think you are better!*' Dellaware shrieked. 'Well, my son will have what is rightfully his. My ancestors will avenge me.'

A concerned Yveny was trying to pull his mother away from Rufus whom she now lunged at. There was a glint of metal in the lamplight as she reached out with her left arm. If it hadn't been for the coffee table she may well have made contact.

Her foot caught on the leg of the table and she pitched forward. Her free arm stretched out to break her fall as she hit her head on the solid wooden tabletop and fell at Rufus' feet. We all watched the fall in slow motion, all powerless to help. There was a crash as Constance landed heavily, missing the rug and smashing the terracotta pot, breaking it on the exposed tiled floor between the sofa and the hearthrug. Rufus leapt back, an instinctive reaction and Mrs Darensky stood up from the sofa.

'Motter....' Donald shouted and moved forward to where his mother lay. He pushed the pieces of the pot away from her and knelt down beside her.

'She's not a well woman!' He said, looking up at Rufus. Rufus was too stunned to respond.

A strained deep growling voice emerged from Mrs Dellaware. *'The spirits of my ancestors will avenge us, son.'*

Her eyes rolled, her body stiffened and she started to shake violently. Her legs banged against the table and her head struck the cold tiled floor, over and over. Mrs Darensky moved quickly and efficiently, pulling a cushion from the sofa and placing it under Mrs Dellaware's head.

'Move the table, Rufus.' She said. He obeyed silently.

Rob finally appeared in the doorway shouting, 'Police!'

'Actually, Rob, I think we might need an ambulance.' I replied.

Rob took control of the situation and knowing that Jane was a nurse he sent an officer to retrieve her from the back of the police car outside. She was magnificent in her management of the situation. I'd never seen her at work before, but never was I more proud of her. Making her patient comfortable, reassuring the others in the room and, once the ambulance arrived, carrying out a handover of information that was both professional and concise.

I, I'm afraid to say, collapsed into the nearby armchair. Exhausted from the exertion of the last hour and, once again, feeling nauseous. The adrenaline was gone and I was left with the aftermath. The danger to my friend had passed and our murderer was at last apprehended.

35.

Dossu:

Dossu is used to refer to the first male child born after twins. This child is believed to have supernatural powers.

Rufus had requested we go out for lunch, away from the village. I couldn't blame him. A month on and the village was still rife with theory and rumour. All eyes were on Rufus, judging, shaking heads, pitiful looks. He had been incredibly British about it. An aristocrat through and through, he held his head up high and did not engage in conversation concerning his personal life. Mrs Darensky, to my complete surprise, stood by him throughout the whole affair, even suggesting they move the wedding forward to the autumn in order to show a front of solidarity. For once I was very pleased to be wrong. My friend had found a loyal woman. Even if I suspected the loyalty was to his money rather than Blackwood himself, one cannot help but feel there must be some affection there.

We were sitting in a small pub in the middle of London. Here, they didn't care what the papers said. They didn't even know Blackwood was a Lord. The walls were lined with beer pump clips and the food was wholesome and rustic. Nothing fancy. We'd been there for most of the afternoon now.

It was an old haunt of Rufus' from his student days. My student days had been spent studying millinery in Paris: another part of each other's lives we'd missed out on. So this is where the conversation had started, with a comparison of those heady days of youth. The first time we'd been apart in our education. We hadn't recognised it at the time but we'd missed each other's company. After that, life had just got in the way. Despite the fact that Rufus was my oldest friend, I had long come to the realisation that I did not know him at all. That afternoon with the sun streaming through the tiny sash window of the pub, nestled in a nook, overlooked by none, we'd had the most honest conversation that had passed between us in almost fifty years.

'Of course, I had no idea.' Rufus said as the subject changed to the events of last month.

'You don't have to explain yourself to me.' I said. My friend had been judged enough. Just because you didn't agree with someone's actions didn't mean they weren't your friend.

'I want to.' He said and took a sip of his fourth pint. The alcohol had liberated his thoughts. I stayed quiet. If he wanted to tell me something then he could. I would allow him to do so in his own time.

I looked out the window at a small group of youngsters, probably students, gathered around a picnic table in the courtyard of the pub. None of them were seated at the table in a conventional manner. One sat on the top with their feet on the bench, another was standing with a foot resting on the bench and a girl in jeans was sitting astride the bench opposite them. They all smoked, held pints of lager and were laughing and joking. Summer was finally here.

'It was when I was in Haiti.' Rufus started.

I turned back and gave him my full attention.

'I was there on diplomatic service, as you know; followed in my father's footsteps.' He smiled, remembering his father. Turning the beer glass in front of him, the beer sloshed around the pint and glistened in the sunshine. 'I was married. Jennifer was her name, I don't think you ever met her.'

I shook my head and took a sip of my pint. I knew of her, but I hadn't ever met her.

'She was a good woman. Didn't complain about the travelling. Didn't worry about the situations I put us in. Just got on with it. Supported me. The best wife a man could have.' He took a gulp of the beer. 'We were very happy.'

I nodded.

'You can imagine our delight when we found out she was pregnant.'

I raised my eyebrows. He'd never told me he had children, but I didn't speak. I let him continue.

'She was almost eight months. The heat in Haiti was getting to her. That's what we thought it was. The heat.' He stared at his beer. 'It wasn't. It was malaria.'

He wasn't looking at me. His face was filled with constrained emotion. The tears in his eyes were barely visible but it didn't make them less real.

'She lost them both. Twins, they would have been. I….I almost lost her too….' His voice started to crack.

'I'm so sorry Rufus, I didn't know.'

'How could you know?!' He shouted. He took a sip of the beer, collected his thoughts and continued in a more moderate voice. 'Sorry, I didn't mean to snap.'

I shrugged off his apology and reached out a hand, patting him on the shoulder.

'She was my life, Blake, and I'd almost lost her. I'd lost my children. It was my fault. If I'd taken the job in London rather than dragging her half way around the world…well…maybe...'

'You can't beat yourself up about it….'

'I can. What I did next was unforgivable.' He finished his pint. 'Oh you can blame it on grief, my own or Jennifer's, the distance that fell between us in our loss. You can find plenty of excuses if you look for them, believe me, I have.'

I smiled. I knew about guilt, I knew about excuses and I knew about *shoulds*. Life was full of *shoulds*.

'A young girl named Eliza Carlson, paid me the attention that appealed to my ego. I couldn't resist. Her father was a colleague, it was a risky business, but I told myself she was seventeen: she knew what she was doing.'

I said nothing. There was nothing I could say. I had a daughter. I knew what I would have done to any man who'd taken advantage of her naivety. I sat back on the worn bench seat and waited.

'I didn't know about the child, I promise.'

I nodded. He needed reassurance, I knew, but a nod was all I could give.

'She was sent back to England by her parents. I had no idea she was pregnant. I assumed she'd gone to university.' He put his head in his hands, pushing his thumbs into the corners of his eyes.

'Shall I get us another drink?' I said. I didn't wait for a reply. The time it would take me to go to the bar would be enough for him to compose himself.

I returned ten minutes later with a couple of double Taliskers. Something every confessional should not be without. He thanked me.

'I moved on quick enough….'

'You don't have to tell me this, you know, Rufus.' I said interrupting him.

He took a sip of the whisky, dragging his mouth into a grimace as he swallowed. 'I think I need to tell someone.'

I nodded.

'Jenny was lost in herself. I had one other affair after Eliza. They had a son, who I did know about. Jennifer knew nothing.'

I took a sip of my whisky.

'He came looking for me last year. I'm a good man, Blake, I wanted to make things right, so I set him up in business. His name's Edward.'

'Edward?' It couldn't be. It was too much of a coincidence.

'Yes.'

'With the bookshop on the Huckspeth Road?'

'Yes, do you know him?'

'Not exactly, he was at the family history talk and now you've said it the resemblance is uncanny.'

We drank more whisky.

'So, you have two sons?' I ventured.

'Yes.'

'So Constance Dellaware is Eliza I assume?'

He nodded, 'Constance Dellaware was Eliza Constance Carlson. Her son, Donald, was adopted by a Haitian couple. Her father had insisted. I never knew her middle name so when I moved back to the manor, forty years later, I couldn't possibly recognise Constance Dellaware as the same girl. She must have married.'

I nodded.

Rufus continued, 'When Donald lost his mother in the earthquake, he discovered he was adopted and came looking for his biological mother. That's when all this started. Now I have more deaths on my shoulders.'

'Rufus, you can't blame yourself for those deaths.'

'I think I can. When Constance heard the rumour that I had another son that I had welcomed and that he was a business owner, that I'd invested money in, well…I hate to say it of the lady, after the wrong I've done her…but she went a bit nuts.

'I'll say.'

'Constance just wanted the best for her son. She thought Edward was usurping Donald. She wanted Donald to have what he deserved....'

'...Only she had a bit of a finite way of going about it.' I completed his sentence.

'And I have you to thank for stopping her!' he said, taking a large sip of whisky followed by a further grimace.

'She almost succeeded in finishing me off.' I said, touching the lump of scar tissue on the back of my head.

'Yes, and for that I'm truly sorry.'

I waved Rufus' apology away. 'If I will go snooping around...at least that's what Jane says. Don't worry; the blame's truly in my court on that one as far as my daughter's concerned. It doesn't make sense though. Why didn't she go after Edward?'

'Donald's in his forties, she thought the second son must be about the same age as Donald. She had no idea he was ten years younger.'

'And Edward is, of course, younger. When I was trying to find a similarity in the victims I did see they were all of a certain age. It was a postcard that tipped me off in the end.'

'A postcard?'

'Yes. She came to visit me and dropped a postcard of all things. A postcard to you that had been *returned to sender.*'

Rufus blushed, 'I didn't know, I had to stop her sending me letters. Jenny would have found out. It would have broken her heart. I had no idea…'

'I know. I know.' I interrupted. 'The handwriting matched a scrap of paper I found in the woods just before I was hit on the head. It looked like it was from a diary. Turns out, it was.'

'Yes. Donald told me how he'd tried to burn the diary and cover up for his mother. I'll get him the best lawyer there is, of course. He had tried to make her see sense. It was him who took the models from the village. He was trying to protect people. He told me he'd learnt a good form of Voodoo from his adopted mother. Voodoo that protected people, he was using it on the models.'

'Ah, Rada.'

'What?'

'Rada and Petro, the two types of Voodoo. Good and bad. I've learnt a lot during this case, I have to say.' I said.

'You're good at this type of thing, Blake.'

'Not good enough to work it out before she killed five people and threatened my friend in his own home!'

'You worked it out before Claringdon though and I'm sure he couldn't have done it without your help.'

I shrugged.

'You should start your own private investigations agency.'

Now I laughed, 'Delilah would love that, she's already doctored my website to read…'

'*Hetherington's Mystery Millinery.*' Rufus joined me in the last three words.

'You've seen it then.'

He nodded. 'I think it's a jolly fine idea,' he smiled; the first time he had in the last hour.

'Perhaps you're right, I can't say it keeps me out of trouble but it exercises the old brain. I'm not sure what my daughter would think.'

'Sergeant Claringdon obviously has a lot of respect for you.'

'He does. I can't help feeling it's more to do with Delilah though.'

'Ah Delilah, your trusty assistant. She's been absent for the best part of this case though and Rob still needed your help. Who'd have thought the answer to all of this lay in Haiti, right where Delilah is.'

'So true; she's back next week. She'll be furious she missed all of this.'

We laughed, together this time.

'Seriously Rufus, it doesn't matter what's happened, I'm glad you're all right.'

'Thank you.' He smiled again and took another sip of his whisky. 'And I've got you to thank for that too. I thought the police were never coming.'

'They do seem to take their time with these things.'

'Oh no, they were there. I heard the cars arrive very quickly, but then nothing. No-one came in. Apparently they thought she had a weapon.'

'A weapon? What, a terracotta pot? Well, by that reckoning most things are a weapon.'

'No, no. I'd made the mistake of telling them I heard a scratching at the door. Matilda and I were having a nightcap in the study. I'd looked out the window and there she was scratching something into the front door with a knife. I could see it was a knife because the moonlight caught it.'

So, she had been armed. I didn't let myself think about the potential consequences of my actions. I don't know if I'd have been so brave had I known. Rufus continued.

'Unfortunately she saw me at the window and started banging on the door, woke the dogs up. Thinking I'd just tell her to go away, I made the further mistake of opening the door. By the time the police arrived she'd herded us into the living room.'

'So when the police got there, didn't they try to arrest her?'

'Well, Sergeant Claringdon did try talking to Constance from the doorway but she'd threatened Matilda with the knife. She was waving it around all over the place, ranting and raving. She had this strange little pot in her hand too. She was saying something about her ancestors. So Claringdon backed right off. I had no idea he was in the hallway, I assumed he was waiting for back up.'

'And Donald?'

'I'm not sure when he arrived. I think it was about the same time as the police. He said he saw the cars pass The Badger's Holt and he remembered something Constance had said to him earlier that evening; something about sorting things out once and for all. He put two and two together.'

'Sounds like a lucky escape.'

'I've had to have the door replaced of course; she made an awful mess of it, no idea what she was carving on it. It looked nothing like the crosses she'd been putting on the doors of the model village properties that's for sure.'

'It was probably a Vever.'

'A what?'

'A Vever.'

'And what's that, when it's at home?'

'Symbols in Voodoo ritual that call upon the gods.'

'Of course, Voodoo. That explains what Claringdon said about the pot.'

'The pot?'

'Yes the terracotta pot. It's called a Canari. Followers of the Voodoun religion keep the spirits of their most treasured ancestors in it. It's believed they can be called upon in times of need and can even possess the living. Constance believed the ancestors in her Canari could help her. She even believed she could invite them to possess her in order to do so.'

We both took another drink from our glasses as we contemplated Voodoo in Tuesbury.

'Why didn't she just come and talk to me?' Rufus said, finally.

'She's not a well woman, Rufus.' I finished my whisky.

'I could have helped. Epilepsy's not unmanageable. I could have got her better medical care.'

'She needs more than that. There's nothing stronger that the power of belief and you weren't going to change her belief in the gods with all the epilepsy medicine in the world. Epilepsy's a condition, madness is a state of mind.'

Rufus smiled, 'I suppose so.'

'And now you have two sons.' I said.

'I do.' He sat back in the seat, arms stretched out, hands resting on the table, he looked out the window and sighed. 'She won't inherit the estate, you know, not now.' He said.

'It's really none....'

'But I know what you're thinking.' He looked me straight in the eye. 'Matilda's a good woman, Blake. She wants to be with me and I love her. I'm not delusional; I know she likes the good life. She's got a small settlement, when I'm gone, to keep her, but the estate will go to Donald and Edward. It's more than I deserve in many ways, I don't want to be lonely.'

'I'm sorry Rufus. I shouldn't judge you, it's not my place.' I said.

'While I'm on the subject of your judgements.' Rufus smirked, his voice was light and jovial, not admonishing, and I blushed. 'Tipingee is not a ringer!'

I laughed. 'I see. Well then, she's a damn good horse.'

'She is. She even won weighted last week!' He beamed proudly. 'Tipingee was a gift for Matilda.'

'She's a lucky woman. Shame you had to lose your trainer.'

'Not at all, he was trying to fix the races.'

Realisation and embarrassment flooded my face and we both laughed together once more. Not even friends trusted each other all of the time.

'And about that cheque…here', to my embarrassment, Rufus produced a role of notes. I'd completely forgotten about the unpaid-for fedora. 'Sorry about the duff cheque, mix up with the bank accounts, you know how it is.'

'Don't be silly.' I said, 'After all we've just been through…'

'No. I insist.' Rufus interrupted. 'I always pay my debts, Blake.'

I took the money, knowing that to refuse would be imprudent and ungentlemanly in the circumstances. I looked at my watch, the sun was low in the sky and the dogs had missed their afternoon walk. Bertie had been anxious all week, perhaps sensing Delilah's impending return. I'd left them with Rob who'd kindly offered to look after them, despite it being a rare day off for him. If I left now, I could take them out for a walk around the woods before it got dark. I looked at my watch, 'I'd better be going,' I said.

'Me too.' Rufus stood up. 'Before we head back to the train though, I have one more thing to ask.'

'Oh?' I said standing and pulling my jacket on.

Rufus cleared his throat and tugged on the bottom of his jacket. 'Will you be my best man, Blake Hetherington?'

I stopped halfway through pulling the Barbour over my shoulders. I looked at my old friend's face, anxiously awaiting a reply; teeth chewing his bottom lip. This was my oldest friend in the world. A boy I'd grown up with, and now a man I stood beside.

'Of course I'll be your best man, Rufus Blackwood, I'd be delighted.' I reached across the table and we shook hands on the deal.

The unspoken words: we would never again grow so far apart.

Acknowledgements:

Much of the research for this book comes from Maya Deren's, Divine Horsemen: The Living Gods of Haiti, and Denise Alvarado's: Voodoo Dolls in Magick and Ritual.

My thanks are due to my friends and family for their support. Beta readers and proofreaders, thank you for your time and help with this project. Finally a huge thank you to my ever loving and supportive husband. You put up with my creative temperament valiantly and for that I am eternally grateful.

Thank you for reading 'MODEL FOR MURDER.' If you've enjoyed reading, then further information, on existing and future publications by D S Nelson, is available via: **www.dsnelson.co.uk**

You can follow D S Nelson via:

Twitter:

@WriterDSNelson

Facebook:

www.facebook.com/WriterDSNelson